Praise for

'A brilliant noir thriller set [...] World War'

STEPHEN LEATHER

'Ronson delivers a cracking yarn, convincingly told. John Cook is the Jack Reacher of 1940s Britain'

DAMIEN LEWIS

'A vivid sense of place with tension on every level, The Last Line dripped with historical detail and authenticity. I absolutely loved it'

MARION TODD

'A tough, taut wartime thriller that reads like a cross between Alastair MacLean and Lee Child and atmospherically conjures up the spectre of war, the threat of Nazi invasion and other evils uncomfortably close to home. Dad's Army, it ain't!'

ROBBIE MORRISON

'Thrilling and intriguing in equal measure. Like Jack Reacher on the Home Front in WWII'

MASON CROSS

'Addictively readable'

Irish Independent

Stephen Ronson grew up in Sussex, and spent a large part of his childhood exploring the woods and fields around Uckfield, many of which were still dotted with reminders of WW2 – pill boxes, tank traps, nissen huts, and graffiti left by soldiers awaiting D-Day. He is a passionate student of local history, and when he learnt about Auxiliary Units – groups of men who were instructed to lay low during the predicted Nazi invasion and lead the fight back – he knew he had to write about a Sussex farmer, one with a love of the land, and a natural desire and ability to get the job done. Many of the locations and characters in the John Cook series are inspired by real places and real people. In particular, Stephen was inspired by his grandparents, Eric, Bessie, Peter and Vera, each of whom did their bit on the home front.

Nowadays, Stephen divides his time between Vermont, USA, and Uckfield, East Sussex. When he's not writing, he can be found renovating his house, or walking the woods and the fields.

Also by Stephen Ronson

The Last Line
The Berlin Agent

THE
BLITZ
SECRET

STEPHEN RONSON

HODDER &
STOUGHTON

First published in Great Britain in 2025 by Hodder & Stoughton Limited
An Hachette UK company

The authorised representative in the EEA is Hachette Ireland,
8 Castlecourt Centre, Dublin 15, D15 XTP3, Ireland (email: info@hbgi.ie)

1

A CIP catalogue record for this title is available from the British Library

Paperback ISBN 9781399745734
ebook ISBN 9781399745741

Typeset in Plantin Light by Manipal Technologies Limited

Printed and bound in Great Britain by Clays Ltd, Elcograf S.p.A.

Hodder & Stoughton policy is to use papers that are natural, renewable
and recyclable products and made from wood grown in sustainable forests.
The logging and manufacturing processes are expected to conform
to the environmental regulations of the country of origin.

Hodder & Stoughton Limited
Carmelite House
50 Victoria Embankment
London EC4Y 0DZ

For Bessie, and the great many other ARP wardens who selflessly gave their all at Britain's darkest hour.

Never in the field of human conflict was so much owed by so many to so few.

Winston Churchill, 20 August 1940

Sunday, 1 September 1940
Hillingdon House
No. 11 Group, RAF Headquarters

Bunny didn't like Sundays. What he liked even less than Sundays was being summoned from his flat and dragged out to the middle of nowhere. But when Churchill sent a driver to pick you up, you didn't ask questions. Which was how he found himself in Uxbridge, descending sixty feet into the bowels of the earth, wishing he'd brought his hip-flask.

Churchill and Clemmie were already in situ, front-row seats in the dress circle – a balcony above the Group Operations Room. Below them, in a circular space, twenty highly trained men and women worked silently, pushing markers across a large map of south-east England. At the edge of the room, assistants stood with telephone receivers to their ears, gathering intelligence from secret stations across the region. Bunny had been inside some of those secret stations. People had died in those secret stations.

Bunny took his seat diagonally behind Churchill. The right hand of the father. The Prime Minister gave Bunny a disapproving scowl before turning his attention back to the action below.

'You're late,' Churchill said.

Bunny didn't reply. He'd learnt not to when the old man was in one of his moods. He settled in to watch the performance. Would there be lunch? Tea, surely, at the very least.

Covering the opposite wall, where the theatre curtain would have been, a gigantic blackboard was divided into six columns, one for each of the fighter groups tasked with defending the country. Within each column were sets of lights for each squadron. The lowest row of lights, when lit, showed the squadron was 'Standing By'. Above that, the next light indicated 'Ready'. Above that – 'Available'. Above that were two more rows – 'Enemy Sighted', and finally, red lights that signified 'Engaged With Enemy'.

To the left of all this, a glassed-in theatre box held five air-force officers, monitoring additional information from the many thousands of volunteer observers out in the field – men and women watching the skies with binoculars and calling in their observations.

'Expecting much of a show today?' Bunny murmured to the man sitting next to him. Air Vice-Marshal Park shook his head.

'We're hoping for a quiet one,' Park said. 'Not sure we can take another big push.'

Yesterday had been a disaster, Hitler throwing everything he had at the Royal Air Force, focusing his attention on air-fields and landing strips across the country. If he wanted to invade, he had to break the RAF. The Germans knew it. The British knew it. Every man on the street knew it, watching anxiously as the battle played out in vapour trails high in the blue summer sky. And everyone knew how it would end. Not a matter of if, but when.

Hitler had more fighters, more bombers, and more pilots.

It was only a matter of time.

Bunny sat quietly for half an hour that felt like a week, checking his pocket watch every twenty seconds. It looked like Park might get his wish. Perhaps the Germans had awarded themselves a lazy Sunday.

The first sign of activity came from a young woman directly below. Her telephone operator approached her, whispered calmly in her ear, and retreated. The young woman, a plotter, marked up a wooden sign and placed it on the vast map. Her sign read 'Forty-plus', and she placed it on the other side of the Channel – over Calais. Forty enemy aircraft, identified by the top-secret new technology they were calling radar.

In quick succession, more markers were placed on the board, and the bottom row of lights on the far wall started to glow, as squadron after squadron was brought to readiness. All of this proceeded in the hushed tones of a reading room at a library. None of the plotters or telephone operators exhibited any emotion, but Bunny wasn't born yesterday – he could feel the tension rising.

Still, the young men and women in the pit moved quietly, whispering commands to each other, pushing their markers across the table.

Soon, markers littered the map. 'Forty-plus', 'Sixty-plus', and in one instance, somewhere above Sussex, 'Eighty-plus'. Every minute the plotters pushed their markers further inland, the paths of the invading aircraft becoming clear – they were coming for the airfields. Those airfields had been hit every day and were on their last legs.

Now, glowing red bulbs topped every column of lights – every squadron in action. Bunny had his eye on a man walking calmly around the edge of the room. One of Bunny's recruits – picked him up from Oxford only a few months earlier. Lord Willoughby de Broke, solid chap, steward at the Jockey Club. Lord Willoughby looked up and made eye contact with Bunny. He was a fine poker player, Bunny knew from first-hand experience, but today his poker face was cracking. As they locked eyes, Willoughby gave the minutest shake of his head.

Bunny felt a cold chill shoot through his body.

Next to Bunny, Air Vice-Marshal Park made his apologies and rose to make a call. When he returned, he explained his absence.

'I've asked Dowding at Stanmore to lend us a hand. He's sending three more squadrons from reserve.'

Churchill nodded approvingly.

About time, too, Bunny thought.

Three new columns of lights were illuminated in swift succession – the reinforcements joining the fray. Now, every column was headed by a red light – every squadron engaged.

'Do you think he'll launch tonight?' Bunny asked, under his breath. Hitler had a fleet of ships standing by across the Channel. The thin strip of sea the only thing standing between Britain and the largest, most mechanised army the world had ever seen.

'Would you?' Churchill asked, turning to Bunny.

'Whether I would, or not, is the wrong question,' Bunny replied. 'The question is – what will Hitler do? Which I'm finding increasingly difficult to answer, because I'm not a raving lunatic. What would *you* do?' Bunny asked Churchill.

Churchill examined his cigar and found it had gone out. He patted his pockets for his lighter, until his wife reached over – lighter in hand.

He lit the cigar, puffing on it to build up a good head of steam.

'I'd be crossing the Channel already,' Churchill said. 'Synchronised landings while we're distracted by all of this.'

Bunny noticed more and more of the young men and women below were stealing glances up at the audience in the circle.

'How many more reserves do we have?' Churchill asked.

Park paused before answering. He shook his head. A slight movement. Involuntary.

'None.'

Churchill took another puff from his cigar.

'None?'

Park shook his head again.

'None.'

Churchill grimaced. Bunny detected a note of satisfaction. A grim welcoming – they'd been waiting for the worst. Now the worst was upon them.

'So this is it,' Churchill said.

Churchill turned to Bunny. Bunny knew what was coming and he was tempted to turn away. To remove himself from the process. To give himself a chance that in the future he'd be able to tell himself he wasn't part of it. It wasn't his fault.

'It's time,' Churchill said.

I

One week later
Saturday, 7 September 1940

Ruby checked her wristwatch for the hundredth time as the air-raid siren wailed to life. Her arm was sticky from where she'd let it rest on the polished marble. Only half five and the bar was packed solid. Seemed like every day more people arrived in London, coming from all corners of the globe, all of them headed straight here, eager to find out who else had got away. A boisterous crowd of Scandinavians had taken up residence at the end of the bar. One of them looked familiar – one of those European royals you read about in the papers, arriving in a small plane with a suitcase of jewels, getting out ten minutes ahead of the German invaders.

She had to go. She'd had to go at four thirty, and then quarter to five, then five, but each time she'd gathered her things, the bartender had delivered another drink, each with the compliments of one of the seemingly endless number of airmen crowded into the bar, mixed in with the aristocrats and the refugees. Invariably, each had come over to try their luck. Some had been nice, wanting to talk, others assuming they'd get something in return for the cheap G and T she'd never asked for. Still, better than buying your own drinks.

She saw him, at the far end of the room. Her pulse quickened with fear. She'd heard he'd moved on to another hotel, trying his luck with a different crowd, but here he was, his distinctive copper hair like a warning flag.

Now she really had to go. She should have been getting off the number nine bus at the end of her street by now, hurrying over the narrow bridge onto the docks, to the dark row of houses anchored by their pub on the corner. Still, no use crying over spilt milk. And she did want to see Frankie again, of course she did, after he'd been sent away to the country. Ruby couldn't think of anything worse. How miserable, biding your time in a godforsaken farm in the middle of nowhere, missing out on everything. There'd been a suggestion that Ruby should accompany Frankie, keep an eye on him, but she'd put her foot down. Besides, she wasn't a child, she had a job to do here in town.

The lights flicked off, then back on. Off again, then on again. A visual warning – a workaround for times like this when even an air-raid siren wouldn't penetrate the hubbub of the crowded bar.

Last September, the siren would have emptied the place. The first Ruby ever heard, she'd been sure it was the end of the world. Straight after Chamberlain had been on the wireless, telling them war had been declared. Mum had bundled them into the dank cellar and they'd sat there, gas masks fogging up, waiting to die. Two hundred thousand people would be killed in the first raid, the papers said. But the planes hadn't come. Frankie had been the first to take his mask off, earning him a clip round the ear from Mum, but half an hour later they'd all been back upstairs, talking excitedly about their first air raid. Had they heard a plane? Annie from round the corner had said a thousand parachutists had landed on the Kent coast but got rounded up by the police. Ruby heard stories of a landing craft going down in the Channel, and hundreds of bodies washing up

on the beaches, all in their German uniforms, rifles clenched
in their hands, bayonets fixed. None of the stories true, of
course. Even at the time Ruby hadn't believed them. Hitler
was busy razing Poland to the ground, all you had to do
was watch the newsreels. He wouldn't have thought about
England if Chamberlain hadn't declared war. He certainly
wouldn't have been able to mount an attack with the whole
of the French army lined up against him, their Maginot Line
the eighth wonder of the world, the most heavily defended
strip of land in history.

But that was a year ago. A lot had changed since then.

Ruby flashed a smile to the bartender as she climbed down
from the stool, smoothed her dress and went through the
familiar panicky grabbing for her gas mask. She'd left it on
the bar but it wasn't there. With a flash of relief she felt it
hanging from the coat-hook under the bar, the grey leather
box she'd bought with her first pay packet from Lyons. If you
had to carry the blasted thing around, might as well have it
look half decent, as she'd told Mum in response to the raised
eyebrow. In Mum's day, young women didn't go out to work,
apparently. Certainly not Up West. If they had, they *certainly*
wouldn't have spent half their pay on a replacement for something the government had already given you for free.

He was pushing through the crowd towards her. Last time
they'd met he'd made it very clear she wasn't to cross his
path again. Last time, he'd hurt her, and said it would be
worse if it had to happen again. Said the powers that be had
made it very clear – he was to disappear her if necessary. Or
even if not necessary. Perhaps he'd do it just for the fun of it.

2

Ruby hurried across the lobby, to the side door out onto Arlington Street. They didn't like the girls to use the front door.

It was hot outside. It had been in the nineties earlier, and it hadn't dropped off yet. It was jarring, emerging into the light. She'd usually be inside until the early hours, until the party moved to the downstairs bar, the one buried under twenty feet of concrete and steel. The safest place to get a drink in London. Safe, until she'd crossed paths with him, of course.

A bus was lumbering its way up Piccadilly from Green Park. Ruby squinted. Number nine. Perfect timing for once. It was on the far side of the road, and the stop was a hundred yards further down. If she hurried, she'd make it.

Something was wrong, though. People were standing on the pavement in groups, looking at the sky, pointing down the road towards Piccadilly Circus. Pointing east, the way her bus was heading. The way home.

The door opened behind her and he stepped out. He was distracted at first, looking up into the sky. But then he looked down and saw her. He started towards her with purpose. She had to get away.

The bus was pulling up at the stop, still fifty yards away and on the far side of the road. From experience, Ruby knew it wouldn't linger. If she could thread her way through the traffic she'd make it. She hurried into the road, anticipating the forward movement of the car in front of her, but the car slammed its brakes on and she smacked her hip against the boot. The driver's door opened and Ruby turned, ready to argue, to defend herself, stupid motorists thought they owned the road, but the driver wasn't looking at her. He was looking past her, into the sky.

Ruby skirted around the stopped car and ran into the road, but turned back when she heard a cry next to her. An old lady with her heel caught in a drain. Some people shouldn't be allowed out on their own, Ruby thought, as she bent to pull the woman's heel clear of the grate. The ironwork scraped off a long peel of paint, leaving the elegant heel disfigured.

'Are you all right?' Ruby asked. The woman looked at her with such undisguised distaste, Ruby took a step back.

'Take your hands off me this instant,' the woman said, clutching her purse to her chest.

Ruby smiled, a fixed grin. Don't let them see they've got to you. She glanced up. He was gaining on her. Her Good Samaritan act was going to get her into trouble.

The air-raid siren wailed again. Different this time – instead of the rising and falling tone it was a repeating note meaning danger was imminent. The woman heard it, fear flashed across her face.

Ruby felt a rumble that went right through her. A bomber. Not a speck in the sky, but a very real plane, above the rooftops, much lower than it should be. It was turning, almost on its side, like it was doing acrobatics at an air show. Smaller planes were on its tail. She heard a distant rattle, like a sewing machine. Fighters, trying to bring it down.

The woman with the scraped heel was the only person on the street not watching the sky. She bustled her way across the road, oblivious to the traffic, a black cab making a point of passing by with only inches to spare.

Ruby looked for her pursuer. He, too, was watching the dogfight in the sky. Her chance to evade him. She doubled back. Instead of crossing the road, she ran for the entrance to the bookshop, took shelter inside the recessed doorway.

She'd have to steer clear of the Empire for a few weeks. Try her luck elsewhere. She'd heard the Savoy was worth trying.

The bus collected its passengers, ready to move off. A young woman in a Lyons uniform ran to catch it, jumping onto the platform at the back as the bus pulled out into traffic, gathering speed. Ruby recognised her, and raised her hand to wave.

'Irene!' she shouted, before she remembered she was meant to be lying low, but it came out muted against the roar from the planes.

The woman she'd shouted to turned, hanging on to the pole at the back of the bus. It *was* Irene, the only one at the Green Park Lyons who'd been remotely nice to Ruby. Not exactly a friend, but an ally. The bus was already moving off into the traffic, heading past Simpsons, about to be swallowed up by the swirl of cars and buses threading their way through Piccadilly Circus.

Ruby watched as Irene disappeared from view. She imagined her pushing her way into the crowded bus, perhaps finding somewhere to sit, a gallant soldier standing up to make room for the pretty young waitress who'd need to get off her feet after a day serving tea.

What Ruby remembered most, when she thought about it later, was the swish. Like someone had drawn a pair of curtains. There'd been a flash, like lightning; a feeling of being pushed, like a giant hand had reached down and swatted her off the pavement, against the front door of the bookshop.

There never was a bang, like when a bomb went off in the flicks. There must have been, of course, but she never heard it. Just the swish, then the feeling, then staggering along the road, down towards Pall Mall, holding her hand to the back of her head, sticky and warm, not wanting to look.

The bus had caught it. Irene's bus. A bus that was suddenly not a bus at all, but a cage of twisted metal. A raging inferno.

3

Ruby staggered away from the main road. She couldn't quite remember why, but it felt important. She'd been about to cross, to catch a bus, but she'd changed her mind.

It would take another ten minutes for another number nine. There weren't enough of them on the route at the best of times, everyone said so, now they'd be down one. Would they bring in a replacement? They could take one from a lighter-used route? She should write in, suggest the idea.

She fumbled in her bag for a notepad. Suddenly it seemed very important to write. They'd thank her for it.

'Ruby?'

She looked up. A face in the crowd.

'My God, you've been hurt.'

He pulled a hankie from his pocket as he moved towards her. She stepped back, confused. It didn't fit, seeing him here, with the screaming behind her from Piccadilly, and the ringing of the bell from the fire engine, already making its way to the scene, and above all of it the siren – redundant surely now the attack had arrived.

'Let's get you home,' he said, taking her arm, a firm grip. Ruby recoiled but the grip didn't yield.

The car door closed with a clunk. A heavy car. Expensive. The inside smelt of leather and petrol and something else, talcum powder perhaps. Ruby felt for the door handle as he bustled round to the driver's door, but it didn't work, just pulled towards her without any click.

'Let's get you somewhere safe,' he said, as he started the engine. 'Get you cleaned up. What luck I was here.'

The world was spinning. There was a tartan rug, folded neatly on the back seat. Ruby laid her head on the scratchy wool. There was a distant explosion, and the car rocked, but it carried on. Soon it was threading its way through rights and lefts, and Ruby let herself give way to sleep, or at least a version of sleep, in which she dreamt she was a doll being shaken by an angry child.

She'd be late for Frankie's party, but at least she'd get there. Her mum would take care of her, make it better.

A tear slipped down her cheek as she thought of Frankie. She'd let him down on his birthday. Not the first time she'd let him down, not by a long shot.

4

John Cook wasn't a London man. He'd grown up in the countryside, working on his father's farm as soon as he could shoulder a bale of hay, learning what it was to be part of the land. To know the smell of the soil, the feel of it in your hands. To know your neighbours, for better or worse. When he'd gone away to war – The Great War – it had been to defend his own version of England, a rural country with more horses than cars, where people minded their own business, where a man could make his own luck if he was willing to put in the work. London was something else entirely. The biggest city the world had ever seen. Black stone buildings and smoke further than a man could see.

Cook was familiar with the aphorism – 'When a man is tired of London, he is tired of life.' But a clever sentence wasn't enough to turn the tide. Give him a quiet pub and the company of men who'd spent their days in the fields. You could keep the city and have done with it. It was too big. Too many buses and cars, and too many people.

But Cook had been out-manoeuvred. A train of events leading to him sitting on a double-decker bus crossing Tower Bridge, the dirty brown waters of the Thames drifting slowly out to sea.

It had started with taking in the evacuee. At first, back in '39, he'd put his foot down and told Mum he couldn't have a young child running around the place. A lot of dangerous machinery on a farm. A lot of ways a child could get themselves into trouble, unless you were watching out for them, and a farmer didn't have time to be continually looking after a child. Certainly not a farmer who'd lost most of his labourers to the war effort, one who'd put his life into the land, who felt a responsibility.

But he'd weakened. A winter of reproachful looks from Mum. Long nights of silent criticism from Uncle Nob, who'd returned from Flanders a broken man and hadn't spoken a word since they'd dumped him at the end of the lane, dressed in an oversized de-mob suit, carrying an empty cardboard suitcase. Funny how a man who didn't speak could make you feel his disappointment. So Cook had relented and said they could take an evacuee – if, and only if, the government saw fit to send another wave out from the cities.

May had come, and Hitler had turned his attention west, his armies rolling unchecked across Holland, Belgium, and then France, until the only thing that gave the blitzkrieg pause was the thin strip of the English Channel, and suddenly it had once again seemed prudent to send England's future out of London, into the countryside – away from the bombers and the parachutists and the poison gas that was surely on its way. Cook hadn't understood why the brains in Whitehall had thought sending a child out of London to the Sussex countryside – *towards* the predicted invasion route – had been a good idea, but he'd done his bit nonetheless. He'd escorted Mum to the dusty church hall, where the newly arrived children had been fought over like so many jars of chutney at a jumble sale – the pretty girls going first, the strong boys next, the weakest boys last. Cook and Mum had taken the last boy standing – a grey-faced lad who wouldn't look Cook in the eye, who gave every impression of being distinctly unimpressed at being sent out of London, out of harm's way.

'Wait 'til you see the island,' Frankie said. 'Have you ever been on an island?'

'Britain's an island,' Cook said.

'Doesn't count,' the boy said, not looking back. Cook had never seen him so animated. Mum had been right, he realised, it *was* good for the boy to come home for a day. See his family.

'It's only an island when they raise the bridges, of course,' Frankie said, now turning to Cook to lecture him. Cook nodded. He couldn't picture it. When Frankie said island, Cook imagined something out of a *Boys' Own* story – white sand, palm trees, skull and crossbones, that kind of thing. 'But they raise them all the time. If you're out late you have to be careful you don't get stuck, or when the tide's high and they need to get the big ships in and out of the basin.'

Still, it was good to see the boy so enthusiastic. It was a side to Frankie he hadn't seen. He listened to a continued litany of facts about the island as he sat on the bus, a shopping bag held between his knees. Food from the farm. A chicken. A couple of rabbits. A string bag filled with late tomatoes, and a punnet of blackberries Frankie had picked himself, from the patch down by the sewage works at the bottom edge of Cook's land.

Frankie stood up and pulled the cord, sounding a bell. He was in his element.

Cook followed Frankie down the narrow spiral staircase. The bus pulled over and Frankie leapt off before it stopped, Cook juggling the shopping bag and a wrapped birthday present in the shape of a cricket bat – fooling nobody. The bus sped away as soon as he stepped off.

This was a mistake, Cook thought, not for the first time. Bringing the boy into the heart of the city. Second-guessing the intent of the evacuation. Back into the lion's den. But what did he know? There'd been letters. To and fro. A birthday party. An excuse to bring the boy back for a day. See his family.

Cook had heard talk. A lot of the evacuees had gone back. Transplanting half a million of the country's poorest children from city slums to country farms with little or no oversight had been an admirable idea, executed badly. Frankie had wanted to leave at first, but things had settled down eventually. A truce, of sorts. Cook understood that this day trip was, in fact, some kind of admission it was going to work, that it didn't have to be all or nothing.

Frankie led the way down stone stairs from the bridge. They threaded their way through St Katharine's Dock, past a giant brewery, filling the air with the smell of malt. Cook looked longingly into the pub set into the corner of the brewery – the Red Lion – but he couldn't see past the crisscrosses of brown paper and tape across the windows, and the heavy blackout curtains hanging ready on the inside.

'Who's going to be there?' Cook asked. He was seeing a different side to the boy, who usually communicated in single words, mostly of one syllable. Yes. No. Fine.

'Mum,' Frankie said.

Cook waited to see if there'd be any more details forthcoming. He should have known better.

'Who else? Your dad?'

Frankie shook his head.

'Doubt it,' he said, his face clouding over.

'He'll be at work I assume,' Cook said.

The boy shook his head again. 'He doesn't come around much.'

'Cook didn't push it.

'Who else?'

'Ruby. My sister. She was going to get married, but her chap got called up. She was upset but we all reckoned it was for the best. She could have done better.'

Cook smiled, listening to the boy parroting what were presumably opinions he'd picked up from his mum.

'That it?'

'All the regulars.'

'I'm sure they'll all be excited to see you,' Cook said.

Frankie shrugged.

'They won't be there to see me,' he said. 'They'll be there to get drunk and talk about the good old days.'

5

The driver tried to calm himself, but his breath came out ragged, like he'd been running. He'd have to be careful. It wouldn't do to have an accident now.

His gloved hands rested on the steering-wheel in their customary three o'clock and nine o'clock position. He concentrated on smooth gear changes and soft braking. A kind of self-hypnosis. Imagine a pint of beer on the dashboard, his instructor had always said. Drive like you don't want to spill a drop. It was harder, of course, with all the fuss about the raids. Cars and buses stopped without notice. People hurried across the roads, aiming for the nearest shelter. But none of it seemed real.

He'd done it again. The thing that had been dominating his waking hours for months. How long had it been since the last time? It had been just after war had broken out. The blackout and all that.

He always worried, and this time was no different. He'd have left a clue. All the detective novels were clear on that point. There's always a mistake. Always a clue. The dogged investigator will pull that thread until the whole enterprise unravels. But so far he'd been lucky. Got away with it.

This time, though, there'd be no detective. No unravelling thread. It was too good to be true. A delicious gift. Everyone would think she'd been on the bus. A tragedy, of course. But a gift to him, nonetheless. The bomber had given him a way of taking the girl he never could have dreamt of. A girl who was undoubtedly dead. Killed by Hitler. There'd be a mass burial for all the victims. Paperwork rushed through for those who couldn't be identified. Sorrowful headlines in the papers. A public inquiry into the safety of buses in wartime.

But no investigations.

She was all his.

Free to do with as he wished. No one to slap his hand and tell him to keep his dirty thoughts to himself.

He calmed his breathing. Not out of the woods yet. Get her to the shelter – safely underground. Out of sight, out of mind.

As he waited at a traffic light, he allowed himself a quick look. She was asleep. As beautiful as ever. If anything, she'd grown more beautiful as the years went by, growing into womanhood, as he'd always known she would.

A shaft of late-afternoon sunlight rested on her face. A shame, he thought.

The last time she'd feel the sun on her face.

6

'Get out of it!' the bridge keeper shouted at Frankie, who was waiting halfway across the drawbridge, but the boy knew what was he was doing. The keeper couldn't raise the bridge while he stood there. Cook hurried after him, hopping over the gap between the two sides of the bridge as the keeper started the diesel engine that worked the mechanism.

'There's only two bridges,' Frankie explained as they stepped off the metal roadway. 'The bridge keepers have to keep the ships moving, in and out all day. If they decide they don't want you to cross, you can wait all day.' Cook turned and watched as the section of roadway clanked into its upright position. There was a finality in the sound, like a prison door slamming shut.

'This is the island,' Frankie said, grinning.

It was an illusion, of course, but now they were on the island, Cook really could smell the sea more strongly. There wasn't any white sand. No palm trees. But Cook could see how the place had got its name. A bend in the river half a mile long, cut off from the city proper by an interlinked series of docks and canals, wide and deep enough to take ocean-going cargo ships from all corners of the world.

'This is the high street,' Frankie said. A narrow canyon-like street led away from them, high walls on either side. It was unlike any high street Cook had ever seen. Rather than the usual collection of shops, the right-hand side was towering warehouses. The other side was tenement buildings, reaching up five storeys, and yet more warehouses. Metal gangways crossed the road at great height, presumably to ease the transport of goods from one side to the other. The road itself was choked with horse-drawn traffic and children playing. A group of young boys had tied a rope to the top of a streetlight and were swinging around it. Further down, girls were chasing after a pedlar, pushing a cart of ice chips. He turned back on them and they screamed, running away in mock terror.

To Cook's left, a large metal gate guarded the entrance to a dock – Hermitage Basin according to a weathered sign. Through the gate, a vast rectangle of water about the size of Cook's largest field. All around the edge of the water, freighters were docked next to huge warehouses. Some of the ships were being unloaded manually – men streaming from ship to shore, carrying tea chests. A larger ship was being unloaded by a crane on a massive shelf on the outside of the warehouse, sticking out over the water. The busiest port in the world, Frankie had told him, raw materials and finished goods from every part of the empire. Part of the torrent of information the boy had produced on the train journey up from Uckfield.

A strange place to live, Cook thought, as Frankie did his disappearing act yet again, this time down a narrow passage between two warehouses. Cook followed. After twenty yards the passage opened up somewhat to become an alley – low houses on either side and, at the far end, a pub nestled alongside a larger building belching black smoke. A painted sign on the brickwork answered the question before

Cook asked it – the source of the smell – Empire Fast-Stick Glues, Established 1892.

Cook recognised the name of the pub from the correspondence he'd had with Frankie's mum. The King's Stairs. A reference to an ancient right of access to the nearby shorefront, Frankie had said, dating all the way back to when all this had been marshes. The pub was narrow, not much more than a low door and a grimy window. Cook had pictured a thriving tavern, Frankie's mum a wizened landlady leading rounds of 'Roll Out the Barrel' around the piano. If this place was thriving, it was doing a good job of hiding that fact. If Cook hadn't known better, he would have assumed the place was derelict.

The door opened before Cook reached for the handle. A woman pushed her way through the heavy blackout curtains and threw a bucket of grey water into the alley, only acknowledging Cook once she'd done so.

She had a look of Frankie. Undoubtedly his mother. She looked like she'd lived a hard life. Her arms and cheeks were red, contrasting with her black and grey clothes. From the way she'd manhandled the heavy bucket, Cook got an impression of strength – she looked like someone who meant business, not someone you'd want to get on the wrong side of.

'We're open at six,' she said. 'Don't want any trouble.'

Cook looked back at Frankie, but the boy had disappeared. He realised she'd mistaken him for someone in authority. He held out his hand.

'John Cook,' he said. 'From Sussex. Frankie's staying with us.'

The woman straightened up, taking a proper look at Cook. 'What're you doing here?' she asked.

'We're here for the party,' Cook said.

'Party?' she replied.

Cook held up the present as evidence.

'You wanted him home for the day,' he said.

The woman shook her head, looking at Cook as if he were speaking a foreign language.

'Frankie,' Cook shouted. 'You've got some explaining to do.'

But when Cook looked back at the woman, she was smiling.

'Should have seen your face!' she said.

7

The pub was long and narrow. A small window next to the front door, looking out onto the alley, and another small window at the far end, clouded with condensation and darkened by the obligatory precautions – the ubiquitous blackout curtains covering a window that Cook knew would have been liberally applied with sticking tape to guard against blast damage. The first section after the front door was full width, like the parlour in a house. Small oak tables crammed in close, a fireplace, an ugly clock on the mantel. As they pushed their way through the crowd, the space narrowed, a bar running the rest of the length on the left side, a narrow staircase with a chain across it on the right. The low ceiling was bare wooden boards, blackened by centuries of tobacco smoke, held up by thick oak beams. In Cook's local, every beam was decorated with polished horse brasses. Here were row on row of curved hooks with wooden handles.

Frankie's mum (call me Gracie, she'd told Cook on the way in) slipped behind the bar, earning a grateful smile from the young barmaid – a pretty girl with a pale face, her hair up in a silk turban, busy serving from a shelf of bottles better stocked than Cook had seen in a long time. Gracie pulled a pint and set it on the bar in front of Cook. He took it gratefully, sipped it. That first taste.

'IPA,' Gracie said. 'Made to last the journey out to India.'

Cook nodded. He'd drunk more than his fair share out in India. A longer story for another time. Cook hadn't been ready to come home after the armistice. Couldn't imagine slotting back into real life. He'd re-enlisted to serve King and Country and had ended up serving the ghosts of the East India Company, protecting the furthest outreaches of the empire.

'You can put your money away and all,' Gracie said, as Cook felt in his pocket for half a crown. 'Least I can do, after all you've been doing, looking after our Frankie.'

Cook put his money in the collection box for the Spitfire fund.

The barmaid brushed past Gracie on her way to serve another customer. She muttered something in Gracie's ear, and Gracie's face coloured an even deeper red. They both laughed, looking at Cook.

'You're not what Dottie was expecting,' Gracie explained.

'I bet you went into the countryside when you were a girl,' Cook said, to the barmaid. 'Took a picnic. Hopped over a gate to sit in a field. Got chased off by an angry farmer. It's most people's first and only encounter with one of us, so they think we're all like that all the time.'

'And you're not,' Dottie asked, with a smile.

'Not all the time, although I do have a particular enthusiasm for chasing day-trippers off my land.'

'I know the feeling,' Gracie said. 'Barring people from my pub's one of the highlights of my day. Of course, I have to let them back in the next night otherwise I'd be out of customers in a week.'

'You should come down and visit,' Cook said. 'Frankie can show you around.'

'I'd like that,' Gracie said. Cook had the feeling he was being flirted with. Not such a bad thing, ordinarily, but it felt like there might be some kind of taboo – the woman being the mother of his evacuee. Some kind of family relationship, not by blood but there nonetheless.

Cook finished the pint, and Dottie pulled him another while he looked around. Cook liked a nice pub, and this felt like it might fit the bill. It was busy, but not too crowded. A buzz of conversation, but nobody having to shout to be heard, and nobody fighting, although it was early for all that. All in all, not the worst place to spend a couple of hours. A few nice pints. Let the boy see his people, then back home.

Not such a bad idea after all.

8

Margaret awoke with a start. An insistent knock, repeated. Polite. Precise.

She'd been reading. Dozed off. Now she was disorientated. She looked around for clues. She was in a farmhouse. Ancient timbers criss-crossed the rough plaster ceiling. A cavernous fireplace reeked of smoke even now in late summer, dried herbs hung in bunches from the mantel. She waited for a hand on her shoulder, a kiss on her cheek. He'd smell of the fields. The earth and the rain. She'd only been with the farmer for a couple of months, but it had felt like coming home. For the briefest period of her life she'd allowed herself to enjoy the small things. Sitting in the kitchen eating a simple meal with their makeshift family. The children, Frankie and Elizabeth, and Cook.

The door opened with a creak. A heavy oak door held on iron hinges, uncared-for. The knocks had been a courtesy but nothing more. Her captor stepped in cautiously, his SS insignia gleaming in the candlelight. Probably polished them before he came to collect her.

She'd been in France two weeks, and they still didn't know what to make of her. She'd come voluntarily, and she'd brought valuable intelligence they'd since corroborated, but they couldn't bring themselves to trust her. Quite right. Once a traitor, always a traitor. So they were keeping her away from the front line.

'Lady Miriam,' he said. 'My apologies. Frau Wassenberg requests all guests arrive by five.'

Margaret had arrived in France under false pretences. The U-boat captain who'd brought her had been told to expect an Englishwoman with expertise in radio-waves who'd thrown her lot in with the Nazi party back in '38. The captain had been given a dated photograph of Miriam at a rally in Munich, to guard against deception. Margaret had known Miriam since birth. They were not related, their physical resemblance was merely a coincidence, but one that was often remarked upon. A coincidence that the brains in military intelligence had taken full advantage of. When Margaret had been offered the mission, she'd been told the ruse might be expected to go undiscovered for a week or so. Long enough for her to make herself useful. But sooner or later she'd be discovered, and at that point she'd be advised to do everything she could to try to escape. Thin odds at best. The most likely outcome was a dark cell. That, or a firing squad. But the mission was vital. Calculated by the men with slide rules to delay the invasion by enough time to potentially make a difference. Margaret hadn't believed the men with their calculations. She knew how much more complicated the world got once you left the realm of numbers and predictions behind. But she'd said yes. Ours not to reason why, and all that.

The SS guard was waiting for Margaret's response. She ignored him. *Hauptsturmführer* Werner Schmidt. A grand title for a young man – thirty if he was a day. Younger than her, at the very least. He was intimidated by her, as ridiculous as that sounded, him with his pistol on his hip in its polished leather holster, with his immaculately pressed *feldgrau* uniform, with his commission in the elite corps of the most powerful army the world had ever seen.

'I need a minute,' Margaret said, eventually. It was already five o'clock. She could have gone as she was but it was an opportunity to needle the SS man. She'd spent a lot of time with the German side of her family and she knew starting times at social functions were not mere suggestions. The later they were, the more anxious he'd get.

Margaret took ten minutes. They'd given her a wardrobe of cast-offs. Most of the generals and their wives were aristocrats. They still kept the old ways, more so now the Nazis had come into power, a reaction against the brashness of Hitler and his deputies. Dressing correctly for dinner was a subtle defiance. Taking Margaret under their wing had been another. She's one of us, they'd said, without needing to say it.

She waited at the bedroom door and counted out another minute, Schmidt's impatient footsteps echoing on the stone floor downstairs, wearing out the leather heels on his ceremonial boots. When she finally emerged, clattering down the wooden staircase, he took one look at her and turned his eyes away. Schmidt was blushing, she realised, with a stab of triumph. She wasn't so naïve she didn't know the effect she could have on a man, an effect she was happy to use to her advantage.

'We'll be late,' Margaret snapped, giving every sign she'd have been on time if not for the ineptitude of her escort.

'Shall we?' she said, as she held the door open for Schmidt. Pushing her luck, as always. One day it would catch up with her, but not today. Not if she had anything to do with it.

It was a short walk from the farmhouse they'd given her as temporary lodgings to the chateau. SS staff cars lined the side of the gravel driveway, like limousines at a film premiere. The chateau was a fairy-tale creation in creamy-white stone like so many of the showpiece estates dotted along the Loire Valley. Two ornamental gardens flanked the building. To Margaret's right, an intricate rose garden, geometric shapes interspersed with neat grass paths. To the left, a wilder parkland. The chateau's history, she'd been told, was the story of two great women, both queens, their legacies respected and preserved in their respective gardens.

The chateau itself spanned a broad river, eight stone arches supporting a long gallery and rooms above. Margaret scanned the opposite bank of the river as Schmidt led her across the gravel driveway. The riverbank on the far side was a different country – the river itself a newly established border between Nazi-occupied territory and what they were calling Vichy France. Nominally free from Hitler's oversight, the southern half of France was to be self-governing, an experiment Margaret feared would end in failure.

Dinner was in the great hall. The conversation was thin. The army wives were tired of each other's company, tired of being kept away from their homes in Bavaria while also being kept away from the front, away from their husbands. It was like they were all being held hostage, even those whose husbands were unimpeachable and trusted deputies of the Führer. None of the wives were trusted with news of how the war was progressing, having to rely on snippets getting through, excitable stories told by delivery drivers, or passed person to person across the country at near-instant speed.

Margaret was seated next to the host – Maria Wassenberg. An old friend of the family. Margaret's family. Wassenberg was the only one present who knew her real identity, putting herself at considerable risk. It was Maria who'd vouched for Margaret when she'd arrived in France, claiming her and keeping her from an interrogation room in the cellars beneath Niederkirchnerstraße in Berlin, where enemies of the state with far less evidence against them than Margaret spent their last hours. Margaret tried not to think of what would happen to her old friend when the deception was discovered.

Dinners like this had been a regular part of Margaret's childhood, whether in England, Switzerland, or India. The same people, the same conversation, even the menu seldom changed. Margaret chewed on the overdone salmon.

'Have you heard?' Frau Wassenberg asked, softly. She kept her eyes forward as she spoke, scanning the room. The wives were interspersed with junior officers – men who were dispensable enough not to be needed at the front, men whose loyalty to their bosses was unquestioned. Prison guards dressed up as gentlemen, ostensibly keeping the women safe from the chance a disgruntled French peasant might storm the chateau. Their presence ensured conversation was kept to banalities.

'Yesterday was the deadline for the invasion, and it's passed,' she said quietly to Margaret. 'Politics, as usual. *Generaloberst* Halder says he can absolutely conquer the British Isles if he can land thirteen divisions along the south and east coasts. Admiral Raeder says certainly, Herr Hitler, we can transport your victorious Panzer divisions across the Dover Straits as long as the Luftwaffe can guarantee our safety. The Luftwaffe? Well, we all know about *Reichsmarschall* Goering. Leave it to me, he says, give me three days.'

Frau Wassenberg held up her empty wine glass and a serving girl stepped forward. The girl shook as she poured the wine, then crept back to her place, against the stone wall. A banner covered the white stone. Red background, with a black swastika. The serving girl flinched as a breeze rippled the material, pushing it against the back of her neck. Typical of the Nazis, covering a beautiful room with their garish icon, like a dog pissing on every corner of its territory.

'Have you met Goering?' Frau Wassenberg asked.

'A long time ago,' Margaret replied. 'He wanted me in his Christmas show. *Hansel and Gretel* I think.' She kept her eyes on the men. Schmidt had been called away as the main course was being set down, hurrying off urgently. Now he was returning, his heels clicking, a distinct sound above the hubbub of dinner. He was hurrying. Something was up. She'd got to know his sounds, she realised, after two weeks of forced proximity.

Schmidt appeared at the grand entrance to the dining room, his face white with anger. He headed for his place next to Margaret, fixing her with a glare that made her recoil. Something was different. His usual insecurity in her presence had evaporated. Instead of blushing as he looked at her, he allowed his eyes to rove. Margaret felt underdressed, suddenly, and pulled her shawl over her shoulders.

He knows, she thought.

'Forgive me, ladies,' he said, as he took his seat. He shovelled a forkload of rubbery salmon into his mouth and washed it down with a glass of wine. Without finishing his mouthful he took his fork and tapped it against the glass – ting ting ting.

Schmidt pushed his chair back with a scrape of oak on the ancient stone floor, planting his right hand on Margaret's thigh. He squeezed, hard, and Margaret gasped as he levered himself up. She blinked away an unwanted tear, as adrenaline flooded her body, as much fury as pain.

'Ladies and gentlemen,' the SS man said, surveying his audience. 'I have news. Our enemy has crossed the rubicon. For the past year, the Führer has imposed on our Luftwaffe the strictest instructions not to attack civilian targets. This is a war to be fought with honour, as our forefathers have taught us.'

He took a long drink of wine. His hand was shaking.

'Today, Churchill sent a squadron of bombers to lay waste to Berlin. Children massacred as they played in the Tiergarten. Homes destroyed as if they were military targets. Wanton destruction from a cowardly act. An act of desperation from a country that knows its days are numbered.'

There was a ripple of voices around the table. Anger. Fear. Many of the people here had family in Berlin. All had property there. Margaret kept her eyes down, aware many were looking at her. Looking at her in a different light. Easy to welcome a refugee from a country about to be invaded. Not so easy when that country fights back.

'You will be pleased to know,' Schmidt continued, 'the Führer has ordered swift retaliation. This act of cowardly aggression will not go unanswered. Churchill has unleashed a vengeance to echo through history.'

9

Margaret splashed cold water on her face, looking up as Frau Wassenberg opened the door to the tiny bathroom. The older woman frowned.

'It can't be all true,' she said. 'It's . . . what's the word . . . hyperbole.'

Margaret dried her face with a threadbare towel.

'You heard what he said. Annihilated.'

Frau Wassenberg shook her head.

'It's smoke and mirrors. All this talk about bombing Berlin – your Churchill's too clever. It's cover for Goering. He can't provide air superiority in time for the Führer's deadline, so he pretends he has a better plan. A big gesture. The Führer likes big gestures and Goering's the master of them. He'll dress it up in heroic language, a quest, like something Wagner would write an opera about.'

'They did it to Warsaw,' Margaret said.

'Warsaw's on the road to Moscow. London's a distraction. Hitler knows that. He doesn't even want to invade.'

Wassenberg put her hand to the side of her mouth.

'They say he's never been on a boat. We have a Führer who can't swim and who's terrified of water,' she whispered.

Margaret appreciated her friend's attempt to lighten the mood, but nothing could take the place of what Schmidt had said, his voice triumphant in the crowded dining room.

London was to be destroyed. Wiped off the map – joining the ranks of other ancient cities like Carthage and Babylon. More than a thousand fighters and bombers had already set off from airfields across northern France. The most significant assault against Britain since the Spanish Armada. The full fury of the Reich, more than eight hundred square miles of sky filled with planes, all heading for one target. The people of London were about to learn what it meant to pick a fight with the most powerful man in the world.

'I have to go,' Margaret said.

'There's nothing you can do,' the older woman said.

'They're not ready,' Margaret said. 'I've got to warn them.'

'He said the bombers took off at four,' Frau Wassenberg said, looking at the gathering dusk outside. 'I think by now they know.'

Margaret looked to the window, as if she could see hundreds of miles north, imagining London in flames. Churchill wouldn't take it lying down. Then what? Mutual destruction, city by city, until all of Europe lay in ruins? She thought of Cook, her farmer. Her lover. People come and go but the land remains, he'd said to her, as they'd celebrated the harvest, their arms still stinging from scratches won honestly from a day gathering corn. Cook would be all right. The whole world could get bombed, and when the smoke cleared, Cook would be there, the winter wheat already sown, watching over his fields. Watching over the children.

IO

The air-raid siren cut through the voices in the pub, and Cook felt a stab of disappointment. At the war, for not letting a young lad have a couple of hours for his birthday party, but most of all at himself, for bringing Frankie here, into harm's way. No good blaming the boy for asking, it had been Cook's responsibility to say no, and he'd failed.

'It'll be a false alarm,' Gracie said, knocking back a shot of whisky.

Cook felt foolish at being spooked by the siren. Nobody else seemed the least bit interested.

'What did you get him?' Gracie asked.

Cook put the present on the bar. A cricket bat, wrapped in yesterday's paper.

'Snap,' a man said, from next to Cook.

The man put his gift on the bar, next to Cook's. Same approach to wrapping – yesterday's paper, tied with string. A smaller gift, but a complement to Cook's. The noise it made on the polished counter was distinctive. A heavy knock that could only have been made by a cricket ball.

'Or should it be pair,' the man said, with a smile. He nodded to Cook. 'Great minds and all that,' he said.

Cook nodded.

'Beaumont,' the man said, holding out his hand. 'ARP warden.'

'And a bit more than that,' Gracie said.

Beaumont took the compliment with a good-natured smile. 'Just doing my bit,' he said.

Beaumont stood out, different from the rest of the crowd. His clothes spoke of a certain level of wealth. A tweed suit, well fitted. He looked at home in the pub, the way Cook imagined he'd look to a stranger who came into his local.

'What do you think of the IPA?'

'Had worse,' Cook said. 'Tastes better here than it does out there.'

'You were in India?' Beaumont asked.

'Royal Sussex,' Cook said. 'North-West Frontier.'

Beaumont grimaced.

'Heard it was a tough show.'

'This is Frankie's farmer, Mr Cook,' Dottie, the barmaid, said.

'How's he doing?' Beaumont asked.

'He's doing well,' Cook answered. 'We'll make a farmer out of him yet.'

'Where's Ruby?' Beaumont asked the barmaid, who looked over the crowd, checking to make sure.

'Must have kept her late again,' she replied.

There was a ripple in the crowd. People stepping back in a hurry. Hushed comments. In the centre of the disturbance, the eye of the storm, a man took off his cap and looked around, challenging someone to look at him.

He wore a heavy black coat, and he had a solidity to him, radiating a quiet anger. He stepped up to the bar, next to Cook, and nodded to Dottie, who jumped to it and pulled him a pint.

Cook held out his hand.

'Cook,' he said.

The man took his hand, squeezed. A powerful grip.

'Reynolds,' he said. 'Frankie's my boy.'

Cook met the pressure but didn't push it. Didn't seem right to pick a fight with Frankie's father.

Reynolds released his grip, satisfied he'd asserted his dominance. A smile flicked across his face. He'd had his suspicions about farmers, and he'd proved himself right.

Gracie passed Reynolds a pint.

'That's your allowance,' she said. 'On account of the boy. Drink that up and be on your way.'

Reynolds drank thirstily. 'Poor state of the world when a man can't toast his own son,' he said, an edge in his voice.

'Frankie's been telling us all about life in the country. You've been letting him drive the tractor!' Dottie said.

'He's doing a fine job,' Cook said.

'Sounds like we should all get evacuated,' Beaumont said.

'About your style, isn't it? Running away from the fight?' This from Reynolds.

'Didn't see you at the recruiting office?' Beaumont replied.

'Got to keep the country fed,' Reynolds said.

'So pilfering's a noble occupation now, is it?' Beaumont said.

There was a quiet sound, almost inaudible. A snick of a well-oiled mechanism. A flick knife appeared in Reynolds's hand.

'You want to be careful,' Reynolds said.

'Oi,' Grace snapped, from behind the bar. 'None of that.'

Cook stepped in front of Beaumont, putting himself in harm's way, keeping his eye on the knife that seemed to dance in front of his face.

Suddenly the pub was quiet. Cook realised he'd broken some kind of delicate social code. No matter. He'd never been much for following the rules.

Reynolds assessed Cook, as if seeing him for the first time. He took his time.

Cook knew the moment, he'd felt it often enough, in the trenches, and behind enemy lines. The moment enemy contact is made, each side assessing the other. A breath, before the fight.

There was a movement in the crowd and Frankie appeared in the space between the two men.

'Dad, this is Mr Cook. He's been looking after me. Doing a good job of it.'

Reynolds gave it a moment, deciding which way it would go. He smiled, closed the knife, handed it to the boy.

'Brought you this,' Reynolds said.

Frankie took the knife, eyes wide.

'What do you say?' Reynolds snapped.

'Thanks,' Frankie mumbled, flicking a glance up at Cook.

Reynolds winked at Cook.

There was a distant sound. A roll of thunder, muffled by the thick walls of the pub. If Cook had been out in the fields he'd have been able to judge the distance. The smell of the earth would have told him when to expect the downpour.

The threat of a fight gone, talking returned. Almost loud enough to cover the distant noise, but not quite.

More thunder. Cook felt it this time. Thunder, but not thunder. A tremor in the ground.

II

Cook hurried outside, followed by Reynolds – the two men with the same goal, to make sure the thunder wasn't anything worse than a summer storm. In the canyon formed by the surrounding tenements, Cook could only see a thin sliver of sky. Reynolds hurried away, disappearing into a narrow alley. Cook followed, and found himself in an open space – a churchyard, and an adjoining park. More sky.

Thick cloud gathered on the eastern horizon. The source of the storm. But this cloud was unlike any Cook had seen before. It was rising quickly, like steam from a kettle left too long to boil. Flashes of light lit the cloud from inside.

Cook smelt the air. There was an acrid smell, oddly familiar.

'Coffee,' Reynolds said. 'They're hitting the royal docks. There was a shipment in from Brazil last night.'

Now he'd said it, the smell was unmistakable. And the sound. Not thunder. Bombs. As many bombs as Cook had ever heard. Took him back to the Somme. But that was impossible. It would take hundreds of bombers. Thousands. It would take the entire Luftwaffe.

'Any military targets over there?' Cook asked.

'Woolwich Arsenal,' Reynolds said. 'But that's miles past the royals. Even the krauts wouldn't miss by that much.'

The thunder was louder, and Cook saw glints of light in the sky, like a shoal of silvery fish in a dark pool.

'Your idea to bring up the boy?' Reynolds asked Cook.

Cook didn't respond.

Reynolds winked. 'Welcome to the island,' he said, then slipped into the darkness of another alley.

Cook watched the sky. Hard not to. Hypnotic, in its own way. Thousands of bombers, coming from the east.

Churchill had called the city a giant sow, tethered and vulnerable. Impossible to defend. No amount of fighters or anti-aircraft guns could make a mark. The bomber will always get through, was the mantra of the newspaper headline and the military strategist alike.

The only response had been to prepare the defences. Gas masks. Sandbags. Public shelters. Tape on every window.

As Cook stood in the churchyard and watched the sky turn red, suddenly the defences seemed all too thin.

Were they ever intended to protect the population of the biggest city in the world? Or were they just to keep the people quiet? Keep them going about their work without complaint, while the great and the good built deep shelters for themselves, and laid out escape plans.

The bombers were above Cook now, and he had to crane his neck, looking directly up into the late-afternoon sky.

And all the time, the sirens wailed, and the searchlights panned.

So this is it, Cook thought. The end of the world.

12

Margaret tapped out her message amidst the dust of the farmhouse attic. Mice, in their hundreds, scurried in the deep recesses of the eaves, disturbed by her presence. A thin copper wire had been threaded up and down the rafters. The work had been done hurriedly, the wireless set parachuted into the woods across the river and ferried across.

The transmitter was Morse code only. No voice. Communicating this way was second nature from endless childhood games, the sets her father had strung around the house, delighting the young girl and infuriating the servants she'd forced to commune with her across the wires. Her finger moved quickly, not waiting for confirmation from the other end, wherever that was, her message going out into the ether. There'd be a calm young woman sitting in a government office somewhere, typing out the message, ripping the paper from the typewriter and handing it to a runner.

BOMBING RAIDS TO CONTINUE TIL LONDON
DESTROYED STOP
INVASION DELAYED STOP
G RUNNING SHOW WITH H FULL SUPPORT
STOP

They'd know who she meant without needing to spell out the names, and they'd know what it meant. Goering was a maniac. Fighting against the army and navy, normal tactics had prevailed, men on both sides having studied the same books, pored over the same maps, gone to the same schools in many cases. But Goering was different. Not from the same school. And air war was new, the ability to strike deep into the enemy's home, to wage total war against a population. It had driven the tacticians mad, trying to predict the worst, because the worst turned out to be unthinkable. Bunny had briefed Margaret during one of her first days of training, back in '39 when war was still on the horizon. A million coffins ordered. Vast asylums made ready for the hundreds of thousands who'd go crazy under constant bombardment. Iron gates quietly installed at all tube station entrances, to keep the people out, to stop the population turning into a race of subterranean savages, refusing to come to the surface. And evacuation, of course, which Margaret had already seen in action. A noble idea turned to chaos in the hands of a nation that made a god of bureaucratic process without a care about reality.

The front door clicked, two storeys below. Margaret was moving instantly. She pulled the wires from the transmitter and pushed it into its hiding place in the chimney stack. Was there time to replace the bricks that concealed the Bakelite machine? Don't think, just do, she commanded herself, jamming the crumbling bricks into place, hardly feeling the pain as a nail tore off.

Margaret peered out from the door to the attic, watching the SS man climb the stairs. He was different. A new-found confidence.

There was a time when she'd have been scared. A vulnerable woman alone with a determined man. Even now, Margaret wasn't a fool. She knew she was in trouble. But Margaret wasn't the woman this young soldier thought she was. He saw an aristocrat, someone raised to a life of ease, defenceless against a predator, relying on the rules of civilisation. He didn't know her at all. He hadn't seen her growing up in India, watching Father playing his role in what they'd called the great game – facing off against enemies known and unknown from rival European empires, coming home late at night, cleaning off his gun, sitting by the fire while the trembling left his body. When Margaret had been recruited by Bunny she'd lacked the hands-on knowledge of what to do with a weapon, or how to defend herself against an attacker, but her mind and spirit were already prepared, so when they'd put a knife in her hand and thrown her into the ring against a padded instructor, it had felt like something she'd been waiting for. And when the instructor had looked like he'd get the better of her, when she'd been forced to look deep inside her soul to find out what she was made of, she'd found a survivor. Bunny had taken that survivor, and turned her into a predator. Part of her hated him for that. But part of her rejoiced.

So when her SS captor reached the top of the steps, Margaret knew with a cold certainty what was next. More than that, she welcomed it.

13

Cook stood in the doorway, a slow crocodile of people hurrying out.

Every few seconds, a crump heralded another bomb, followed by other sounds – the shower of bricks and crashing of glass. The cries of someone hurt. Cook tuned the sounds out. Focus on the job in hand – getting the crowd out of the pub, into the shelter.

A nearer thud. The air in the pub condensed, suddenly resolving into a thick soup of brown fog. A liquid sound from above as slates slid from the roof, crashing onto the road. Now, the door jamb in Cook's hand lost all solidity, and he took an awkward step to the side, struggling to stay on his feet.

A new sound got everyone's attention, slowing the crocodile as all eyes were raised to the sky. A whistling sound. Louder than the sirens, louder than the explosions, cutting through all of it. Like hearing your lover calling to you across a crowded room.

'Keep moving!' Cook shouted, pushing an elderly man who'd stopped in the doorway, his half-finished pint still in his hand. The man didn't want to leave, didn't want to step outside. But the pub was only an illusion of safety.

The whistling got louder by the second. Everyone stopped. What was the point of running when the bomb had your name on it?

This one was going to be a direct hit. Cook knew. Everyone knew. The way you knew when you threw a cricket ball from the boundary line, aiming at the stumps in a desperate attempt at a run-out – knowing as soon as the ball left your hand, that it was going to hit its target.

The whistling was deafening now. Frankie was still inside, grabbing his presents. The ball rolled off the bar and Frankie followed it, under a table, chair legs getting in the way.

'Frankie,' Cook said. 'Time to go.'

The boy grabbed the ball and turned back to Cook, looking to him for comfort. Somehow, against all the odds, Cook had become someone the boy trusted. Looked up to. More fool him.

Gracie gathered the day's takings from the till.

'No time,' Cook said.

The whistling sound filled their ears. They were too late. Gracie gathered Frankie in a hug, and grabbed for Cook, the three of them holding each other in the last seconds of their lives.

There was a heavy thud. They braced for the explosion, but it didn't come.

Gracie met Cook's eyes. She breathed out, a ragged breath.

'We should go,' he said.

Gracie turned off the gas lamps and gave the place a once-over. She fished in her pocket and came up with a piece of chalk, which she used to write on the front door.

GONE TO SHELTER

'For Ruby,' she said.

'Where's the shelter?' Cook asked.

Gracie nodded down the passageway.

'Hundred yards,' she said.

'You think we'll make it?' Frankie asked.

Cook had learnt something in the last war. The Great War. If you said something calming with confidence, it gave people comfort. It turned out he had a gift for it, sounding calm and confident. Combine that with a bit of common sense and you turned out to be right, more often than not. Worse case, you'd avoided panic.

'Keep out of sight and we'll be all right,' Cook said. 'Besides, it'll be dark soon. They can't aim their bombs when it's dark. Once we're in the shelter I reckon we'll be all right.'

Gracie smiled, as if someone had given her proof that the worst was behind her.

But Cook was wrong. It wouldn't be all right, and the worst was definitely not behind them.

14

The shelter had been put up in the middle of the public garden, interrupting gravel paths and rose-beds. A small park, enough to give the residents of the island the sensation of standing on a bit of grass, smelling a flower. Better than nothing. Presumably a donation from a well-meaning benefactor. Someone who'd made good, wanting to give back.

Cook stood at the entrance to the shelter, helping the old and infirm navigate the dark, low entrance. Some had shopping bags – a bite of food, a bottle of something to get them through. Not much bedding. A short visit while the bombers passed. A routine they'd all got used to over the past year.

The shelter was a low structure. New brickwork. A freshly painted wooden sign was screwed onto the outside, by the door.

PUBLIC SHELTER
FORTY OCCUPANTS
FURTHER CAPACITY AT ST STEPHEN'S

The signwriter had drawn an arrow pointing to the right, towards the church.

Cook was a tall man, and he had to duck under the lintel. Once inside, his hat scraped against the underside of the rough concrete slab that formed the roof.

The shelter wasn't the worst Cook had ever seen, but that wasn't a fair comparison. On the Western Front, this shelter would have won awards. But this wasn't the Western Front. This shelter had been designed by men who had the advantage of every insight gained from the last war. The effects of blast waves on structures. The likelihood of being hit in a sustained bombing campaign. The features and conveniences people needed if they were forced to spend any amount of time huddling for their lives.

With all that knowledge, a design had been commissioned, no doubt. That design had been through committees, attended by experts. Engineers would have weighed in. Former soldiers, veterans who'd spent years huddling in ditches, up to their eyes in mud. Accountants weighed pluses and minuses when it came to costs. Then the tender had gone out. Builders selected. Inspections made, to ensure the government got its money's worth.

Unfortunately, Cook reflected, as he studied the shelter with his expert eye, the accountants had done too fine a job. Costs had been weighed against benefits, and all the benefits had been found unnecessary. Perhaps an element of retribution. A generation of men who'd survived the worst, couldn't bring themselves to make conditions better for the next lot.

The shelter was entirely lacking in creature comforts. The ground was mud. No chairs. No benches. No bunks. Worse, no sanitary provisions. Forty people were to spend the night, but the only concession to bodily functions was a galvanised steel bucket in the corner. All in all, a badly designed building, thrown up with the minimum amount of effort and money. A token, meant to give people the feeling that the government had done something for their protection, with precious little protection being provided.

'Don't stand there,' he said to Frankie, who was near the door. 'Something goes off outside, that door'll squash you flat against the wall.'

Frankie took a quick step away from the door.

Cook looked up into the darkness, to where the wall met the roof. He pushed his fingers up into the corner.

'What?' Gracie asked.

'This roof slab's not fastened to the walls,' Cook said. 'If anything shifts, it'll flatten us. Like a house of cards.'

The wall was no better. Cook ran his finger along a seam of mortar between the bricks and a trail of sand came away at his touch.

'Who built this?' Cook asked.

'ARP,' someone said, from the corner. 'Beaumont and that lot. They've been putting them up all over the borough.'

Beaumont, Cook thought. The smartly dressed gent who'd brought the cricket ball. Great minds, and all that. He looked around to see if he was here.

'He scarpered,' the voice from the corner said. 'Like a frightened rabbit. Disappears at the slightest hint of danger, our Mr Beaumont.'

Gracie set her basket down on the driest patch of ground. She took out a bottle of whisky, cracked the seal, and took a drink. She passed it to Cook. He took a sip, and handed the bottle on.

'Where's that sister of yours got to?' Gracie said, in the direction of Frankie.

'Where's she coming from?' Cook asked.

'Green Park,' Gracie said. 'She works in the Lyons.'

'Do they run the buses during a raid?' Cook asked.

'They have to,' Gracie said. 'People have to get home, raid or no raid. Besides, there's been alarms every night.

If all of London ground to a halt every time a plane flew over . . . But even if they did, she'd walk if she had to.'

The ground shook as a bomb landed nearby. There was a shower of dust from the concrete roof.

'Let's see if we can find her,' Cook said. 'Could use a walk.'

15

They cut through the docks, a guard giving them a nod and letting them in through a wrought-iron gate. Inside the walls of the vast compound, Gracie gave a running commentary of each wharf and warehouse they passed. She had all of Frankie's enthusiasm for the docks and the island. Cook saw where the boy had got it from.

In the old days, Gracie said, a ship would come in and it would be loaded with a bit of everything. Dockers would be carrying tea one minute, spices the next, even gold. But that was history. Nowadays it was efficiency itself – each ship specialised in one product. Each warehouse likewise. Gracie listed them off with each looming building they hurried past – cacao, sugar, cotton, spices, fresh-cut pine from the vast Canadian forests. The largest warehouse on the long southern side of the basin held enough wheat for the whole country for several months, assuming enough got through the U-boat blockades in the Atlantic. Cook knew a bit about the wheat trade, it had decimated domestic prices in the decades between the wars. A lot of good men had lost their farms, waiting for things to turn around.

The steel drawbridge at the far end was up. Cook assumed Gracie would get it lowered. A favour for a local, or perhaps a bribe. An old friend with a long history of mutual assistance. But Gracie hurried past the bridge, the rusting metal roadway left pointing towards the sky.

They followed the water's edge to the Thames, just visible between a row of smaller, older warehouses. The original docks, Gracie said, before the modern ones replaced them. Another wrought-iron gate, this one unattended, opened with a screech, and Cook followed her down a narrow alley, both his shoulders brushing against walls black with mould. At the end of the alley, a wooden staircase led down to the foreshore, and a floating dock where small boats bobbed in the waves.

Gracie stepped expertly into the nearest boat, a small craft, grey wood planks for seats and an outboard motor on the back. Cook followed suit, tried not to let the side down. Gracie had made it look easy. The boat hadn't even wobbled as she'd stepped on board. Cook found it wasn't as simple as he'd hoped. He must have put his foot an inch too far to the side, because the whole thing tilted as if it was going to capsize, but Gracie shifted her weight to counter-balance Cook, a glint in her eye.

Cook sat, gingerly, on a plank that spanned the boat, conscious that he was raising the centre of gravity with his mere presence.

'First time?' Gracie asked, with a grin.

*

Gracie kept the boat close to the north bank of the Thames as they motored under Tower Bridge, past the tower itself – the Norman keep almost a thousand years old, its white stone glowing in the moonlight.

'Traitor's Gate!' she shouted cheerfully, above the noise of the engine. Cook eyed the barred gate warily. He could feel the despair of the men and women who'd been taken through there on their final, one-way trip.

From behind them, further east, Cook watched as black smoke rose into the evening sky. Specks of light glinted in the smoke. The longer he looked, the more things resolved. He could make out bombers, black specks flying in formation. The higher, looping specks must be fighters, ours or theirs. Cook wouldn't have wanted to be in a bomber, relying on your comrades high above, waiting to get the job done so you could turn for home. Give him solid ground beneath his feet and a rifle any day, no matter how desperate the mission.

Gracie tied the boat off at a dock on the far side of Blackfriars Bridge, opposite the Oxo Tower. They cut through the Inner Temple, its gardens and courtyards entirely unflustered by the war. It was late on a Saturday but smartly dressed, grey-faced men hurried between law offices, bundles of legal documents in their hands. Everyone was dressed lightly, suit coats held in crooks of arms. The newspapers were already calling it an Indian summer.

Cook felt like an intruder, but Gracie clearly knew where she was going. She led Cook through passageway after passageway until they emerged next to a dingy pub, opposite the black stone gatehouse to the Royal Courts.

Traffic was light, heading west towards Trafalgar Square. Buses passed them, and Gracie peered anxiously into each one.

'She could be up top,' Cook said.

But Gracie shook her head as if he didn't understand.

Cook peered into buses as they hurried past, curious about the mass of humanity, living lives he had no knowledge of. Growing up in a small town, he'd got used to knowing people's business, recognising them on the street. Here were thousands of people passing each other in complete anonymity. A lonely place. Cook's eyes settled on a row of shoppers sitting next to each other on a bus, studiously ignoring each other, reading their papers.

They crossed Trafalgar Square and took an alley next to the National Gallery, up through Leicester Square. Gracie cut through the crowds without slowing, a woman on a mission.

But the momentum was lost at Piccadilly Circus. Traffic was stopped, and police constables were directing traffic down Haymarket or up, along Regent Street.

Gracie hurried across the road, trying to squeeze past a wooden barrier, but she was stopped by an ARP warden – a civilian with a steel helmet and an armband.

'Road's closed,' the warden said. 'Bomb damage.'

Behind the warden, Piccadilly was eerily quiet. The road and pavements were empty, apart from a few parked cars. In the distance, Cook could make out what looked like the remains of a bus.

A direct hit, by the look of it.

16

The Lyons restaurant was busy with the evening crowd. Cook hadn't been in this branch, but since all branches were exactly the same, he felt a sense of déjà vu. Lyons were taking over the tea shop business with ruthless efficiency. Cook had read an article. They had a team of people who did nothing other than count the seconds it took a waitress to carry a pot of tea from the counter to the table, that kind of thing. The tone of the article had been scathing. Taking the human element out of the experience and all that, but it was evidently working.

A harried waitress nodded them towards a table just vacated, plates scraped clean of the evening special – pie and mash.

'We're here for Ruby,' Gracie said.

'You're here to eat, or you're not here,' the waitress said. Cook knew sergeant majors, veterans of several years on the North-West Frontier, who could have learnt a thing or two from her command presence.

'Tell Ruby her mum's here,' Gracie said, as she allowed herself to be guided to the table. Cook followed.

'Two specials,' Cook said. 'And tea.'

Mollified, the waitress left them to go and put in their order. Gracie craned her neck to look around the crowded restaurant.

'Looks busy,' she said. 'Must have kept her late.'

Cook didn't respond. He was thinking about the reason they'd had to take a detour around the backstreets. Piccadilly closed. The wreckage of a bus. A civilian target, a couple of miles away from anything remotely military or tactical. Hitting the docks was one thing – denying vital food and materiel had always been a cornerstone of military strategy – but outright targeting of civilians was beyond the pale. Even Hitler had said it was a line he wouldn't cross.

'A long way to come every day,' Cook said.

Gracie shrugged. 'She says she likes it better up west.' She looked around at the clientele. 'She couldn't wait to get off the island, ever since she was a kid.'

She folded her arms, watching the waitress bringing their tea. Cook was impressed. The clock-watchers had done a fine job.

'You're looking for Ruby?' the waitress asked as she set out the tea things.

'She's meant to get off early today,' Gracie said. 'Her brother's birthday. He's come up from the country.'

'Tell her I said hello,' the waitress said.

'When's she get off?' Gracie asked.

'She doesn't,' the waitress responded. 'To get off, she'd have to get on. She hasn't clocked on for two weeks.'

'You're having a laugh,' Gracie said. 'I saw her leave this morning, had her outfit on just like yours.'

'Look,' the waitress said, softening. 'You can have the tea on me. If you want the pie and mash that'll be the regular rate. But I'm telling you. Ruby doesn't work here any more.'

'What shift d'you work?' Gracie asked.

The waitress shook her head. 'Time sheet's in the staff room,' she said. 'Her name's above mine, so I see it twice every day. Once when I clock in. Once when I clock out. She hasn't been here for two weeks.'

The waitress left them, the mystery not important enough to merit losing precious seconds of serving time.

'She goes out every morning in her uniform, same as all these,' Gracie said, looking around at the staff. 'Comes home at God knows what time, stopping out with friends she says.'

'Maybe she's changed to a different branch,' Cook said. He leant back to allow a different waitress to deposit two plates of food. The pie was steaming. The pastry was done perfectly. He could tell, just looking, he was going to enjoy it.

Cook caught sight of an elderly couple standing in the doorway. Something odd about them. They were dressed in indoor clothes, coats hurriedly shrugged on. Pullover on the man. Red pinafore on the woman. They'd been settled in for the evening and something had caused them to hurry out, unexpectedly. One thing they didn't look like was a couple of people who'd stepped in for a cup of tea. They were looking around, on a mission.

The waitress intercepted them. Cook couldn't hear the conversation, but it was clear the woman in the red pinafore wasn't being fobbed off by the officious waitress. She looked like she wanted something. The way she was standing in the doorway, other customers pushing past, coming and going.

Cook watched as a man emerged from a blank door behind the serving counter. He wasn't a waiter, more of an office type. White shirt with a black band around the right sleeve. Kept his cuffs out of the ink as he was doing the books.

The man approached the woman and listened attentively. He shook his head, but the woman stood her ground. He looked in solidarity to the waitress, then gave way, nodding slightly. The waitress made a gesture, letting the woman pass. They all headed back through the restaurant, a little crocodile of four people, threading through the tables.

Cook stood up.

'Drink up,' he said, to Gracie.

Cook followed the party of four. He ignored the complaint of the nearest waitress, filling a tray with cups and saucers at the service counter, and pushed past. He reached the featureless door just in time, stuck his foot in it while he waited for Gracie. He could hear footsteps ahead of him, climbing the stairs, and as soon as Gracie reached him they followed. The staircase was utilitarian, not for customers, black scrapes on the walls at waist height from deliveries. A gouge in the plaster showing thin wooden strips behind it. An unloved space.

At the top of the stairs, a plain corridor gave a couple of options. Two doors, one on the right and one on the left. Cook heard voices behind the door on the left and pushed it open.

'Staff only,' the man with the white shirt said, as Cook stepped into the room. It was some kind of canteen. A tea urn on a melamine counter, a tray of upturned mugs, a bottle of milk. Several chipped tables with uncomfortable chairs, each table with an overflowing ashtray and a collection of the day's papers.

'We're here for the same reason as her,' Cook said, nodding at the woman in the red coat.

'You know Irene?' the woman asked.

'Ruby,' Cook said.

The woman burst into tears, and her husband gathered her into him, glaring at Cook.

'Ruby left,' the manager said.

'Our daughter hasn't come home,' the woman in the red pinafore said. She was facing the manager but she made sure to address Cook as well, not sure who was most able to get things done.

'She always gets home at twenty past six,' the man added.

'Perhaps she took shelter when the raid happened,' the manager said.

The manager looked at Cook as if for moral support. He looked like he'd much rather be timing waitresses and weighing slices of cake than dealing with this odd interlude.

'Is it true Ruby hasn't worked here for a couple of weeks?' Cook asked.

'She was rather rude,' the manager replied. 'Said only an idiot would stick with this job when there's real money to be made. You can tell her I didn't appreciate it then and I still don't appreciate it.'

'Did she clear out her things?' Gracie asked. Cook noticed a row of coat-hooks and cubbyholes. It reminded him of being at school. Hang your coat up, put your bag in a cupboard with your name on it. A place for everything and all that.

Cook stepped closer to the row of coat-hooks. Each hook had a name card inside a brass holder. Easy to slot in a new card at the top, or take the old one out. Several were blank. He saw Ruby's hook. No coat. No bag. Worth a try. He'd thought maybe she'd have left something if she'd stormed out in a hurry.

The woman in the red pinafore had said her daughter's name was Irene. She had the hook next to Ruby's. A coat hung on the hook.

'Your daughter's coat's still here,' Cook said. 'Would she have left it here when she came home?'

'No,' the woman said. 'She always carries it. Rain or shine.'

'She'll be nearby then,' Cook said. 'Having a drink with someone.'

'She wouldn't,' the woman said.

Cook didn't press the matter. A mother wouldn't want to think of her daughter like that – a young woman out in the city, meeting people, going for drinks, the things young people had done since the dawn of time.

Besides, it was beside the point. Ruby clearly hadn't been here.

'We should get back,' Gracie said, and Cook agreed. He thought of Frankie in the shelter. Was it too late to catch a train out of the city? Back to the relative safety of the country?

Coming to London had been a mistake.

17

Margaret had the dark on her side, and she was familiar with the space. The low rafters, the protruding nails that dotted the underside of the roof. Let him come.

The door creaked, and a shaft of light intruded.

She felt the secret place in the chimney breast. The pistol was wrapped in oilcloth. She'd taken it out into the woods, late at night. Firing it had been a risk, but she'd needed to know it worked, for when the time came.

'Lady Miriam?' It was unlike him to use her title. He was usually at pains to ignore it, keep her in her place.

He stepped into the attic, a pistol in his right hand. He held it out from his body, as if it were a torch. A tactical error, if he hoped to leave the room alive.

'Or should I say Lady Margaret?' he said.

Margaret waited in the dark. A few steps closer and she'd be able to lunge at him. Grab the gun. It would be fifty-fifty who'd win the resulting struggle.

'I hope I didn't interrupt your evening communication,' he said. He didn't step forward. He was waiting for his eyes to adjust to the dark. She'd underestimated him.

'I'm not here to fight,' he said. He sounded amused. 'Although I have the sense you'd make a worthy opponent.'

He stepped back, into the doorway, his silhouette blocking most of the light.

'I'll be waiting downstairs,' he said. 'We have things to talk about.'

He left, then paused.

'My men are outside Frau Wassenberg's room,' he said. 'Waiting for my order. In case you're thinking of disappearing.'

*

He was sitting in front of the fire, a glass of wine in his hand. Another glass sat on the polished oak table, waiting for her. A plate of bread and cheese, neatly sliced. A folded napkin.

Margaret walked behind him. She could have swept a blade across his neck, or put a gun against his head. But he didn't turn. Margaret pictured the SS guards in the house, waiting for the order. She heard Bunny's voice.

There will come a time when you have to sacrifice innocent people, in order to complete your mission. What will you do?

There was only one acceptable response. The mission takes priority. The ends justify the means.

Margaret sat in a leather armchair, smoothed her dress over her legs. She took the glass and sipped the wine. He raised his glass and drank.

'So,' he said.

The pendulum in the ancient clock on the mantelpiece marked the passing minutes, a sombre knocking sound with each swing. More of a tock than a tick.

'I don't like you,' he said. 'And I'm sure you don't like me.'

Margaret watched him. He smiled after each statement. He was pleased with himself. He'd written this speech in advance. Polished it. Practised it. Assessed each word for the desired effect.

'You've lied to us. You pretended to be someone else. You made up a story when that was surely to be discovered, and you abuse our hospitality by transmitting our most secret information back to your people.'

He smiled, pleased with his delivery. Margaret was looking forward to killing him, if only to stop the damned smirk.

'You trade on your old friendships, as if going to kindergarten with someone means they owe you their life. Your activities here will undoubtedly sentence your friend to death, sooner or later. When I put all of this together I can only conclude that you're a person with no sense of right and wrong. The most dangerous type.'

'I'm not sure I have all that much patience for being lectured on ethics by a member of the SS,' Margaret said, pouring herself more wine. She tried the cheese. It was excellent.

'I want to help you get back to your beloved England,' he said. 'And when you're there, I want you to do something for me. Something easy for you. Painless. Something with no cost to your position.'

'Or I could kill you now and get back to England by myself,' she said.

'Perhaps,' he said, 'although I'd suggest that you underestimate me because you despise me. You trust in your own training but you don't give mine any weight. I have to tell you, everything your people did to you, mine did to me with more . . . enthusiasm.' This time the smile was more forced. There was a pain there, she saw.

'So let's pretend we're both the people we once were, before we were turned into weapons,' he said. 'What do you say?'

Margaret was running through scenarios. Scenario one, at the top of the list, was to kill him, slip into the chateau, kill the guards threatening Frau Wassenberg, then make her escape. Its biggest flaw was what would happen the next day. She'd be gone, her friend would be vulnerable.

There'd be recriminations. Revenge. Punishment. Scenario two was to let him talk. Agree to his demands. Accept his help getting back to England. There'd be doubts about her when she did show up back home. The possibility of her being a double agent would be discussed. But still, she'd be home.

'I'm listening,' she said.

18

The water was choppy, small waves hitting the front of the boat as they made their way back downriver. Ahead, the sky was orange. A false sunrise, caused by the blazing docks. A flock of pigeons wheeled above them, confused by the light.

Cook thought about the wreckage of the bus. They'd had to detour through the backstreets alongside Piccadilly, the main road closed. As they'd crossed the top of Sackville Street, he'd looked down to the other end of the road. An ARP warden had been laying blankets on the ground, covering bodies.

Cook pictured a busy bus. A young woman running to catch it. Jumping on as it pulled away. A lone bomber, an excitable Luftwaffe pilot, either gone rogue, or following a new kind of order – a deliberate attack against the civilian population.

But why would Ruby be running along Piccadilly if she didn't work at the tea shop? Enough of a question for Cook to keep quiet. Let Gracie run through her own thoughts, in her own time.

If Ruby *had* been on the bus, they'd find out sooner or later. How would it be done? A telegram? A policeman, most likely, tasked with delivering the news. They'd have special training. A script developed. Hundreds of thousands on the first night of proper bombing they said. There'd be some kind of pre-printed government notice – a condolence from Churchill.

They passed back under Tower Bridge. It had been two hours since they'd left to find Ruby, and still the bombers were coming. Gracie pointed at the nearest formation. Bombs fell delicately, like seeds from a dried seedhead, glinting as they reflected the setting sun. Cook heard a distant rattling, like a sewing machine. Short bursts. A flare of light in the sky – one of the bombers was hit. The plane, still little more than a dot in the distance, dropped out of formation, towards the skyline, a thread of smoke trailing behind it.

It went out of sight, behind distant warehouses far downriver. A puff of smoke went up, then the sound, following behind. An explosion.

Soon, all Cook could hear was their own outboard motor, and the planes. The drone of the bombers drowned out all other sound from the city.

Still the planes came, and still the bombs fell.

Gracie nudged the tiller, taking them in towards the shore. Cook made out the spire of the church almost invisible against a pall of thick, black smoke. It seemed like the whole island was on fire, and the closer they got, the fiercer the heat.

Cook looked for defensive gunfire. Where was the ack-ack? Had there been a plot to take out the gunners on the ground? A co-ordinated attack? Perhaps parachutists, dropped earlier in the day, or spies lying low, ready for the invasion.

A Spitfire dropped out of a thick cloud, directly above them. It circled furiously, trying to shake off a pursuer. It flew back up the river, underneath Tower Bridge, then lifted back into the sky, almost vertically. Rejoining the fight.

And still the bombers came.

19

The long gallery spanned the river. Built by a long-dead queen. Two hundred feet long. Mullioned windows overlooking the gently flowing river, luminous in the moonlight. Black and white chequerboard tile floor inviting the eye forward. Once a gallery, now a causeway between Nazi-occupied France and the remainder of the country – a nominally free France stretching south from the Loire to the Mediterranean and the Pyrenees.

Two guards at the far end of the gallery blocked Margaret's passage to freedom, one a young man, the other older. Local men given a choice, a German uniform or a one-way journey in a cattle car to Poland.

The young man got up from his chair and stood his ground. He wasn't concerned. Nothing in his orders had suggested the possibility of danger from an aristocratic woman. She looked lost. Probably looking for the toilet.

Margaret was in two minds. Knife, or gun. In her right hand, behind her back, she held Schmidt's Luger. She'd checked the ammunition. Six rounds in the cartridge. One in the chamber. Safety off.

In her left hand, inverted, hidden behind her wrist, a commando knife. A French model, similar in design to the Fairbairn Sykes model she'd been trained with. Two different designers coming to the same conclusion based on function. A long, two-sided blade. Narrow. Deep enough to penetrate to the vital organs. It had been left in the attic for her, along with the radio.

The gun was preferable in all aspects, apart from secrecy. She put a sway into her step as she closed the distance – too many glasses of wine with dinner. Everyone knew women couldn't hold their drink. She could hit the bull at fifty yards, but shooting at the club was different from shooting in anger. The closer she got, the better. But a doubt lingered. The gunshot would surely rouse others in the chateau – women and soldiers alike. The knife would allow her to slip away quietly, her absence not discovered until the morning, when the local girl who 'did' for her at the farmhouse opened the old oak door to find Margaret gone.

She could leave her options open until the last second, but one logistical problem presented itself. She was right-handed. She could, in theory, use the knife in her left hand, but it would be sub-optimal. These may be local men, likely with minimal training, but it seemed like tempting fate.

Margaret kept her eye on the younger sentry. She staggered slightly, over-egging it perhaps. But the sentry seemed to buy it. He perked up. She could see him thinking it through. The lady might fall. A gentleman like himself might need to carry her to her bed, render aid. His rifle was slung over his shoulder, like they'd shown him. He stepped forward to meet her.

Margaret hurried now, faster than before, almost skipping. The other sentry, the older man, shouted a warning.

Confused, the young sentry pulled his rifle and raised it to his shoulder.

'*Arrêtez!*' he shouted. Margaret raised the pistol and fired.

The sentry staggered, like someone had hit him with a sledgehammer. He tried to turn but his body wasn't working.

Margaret fired again. A second flash from her gun, then a third.

He fell, dead before he hit the floor. Behind him, the older man raised his hands, his rifle still hung over the back of his chair. Margaret levelled the Luger at his face. He should have fought back. Should have levelled his gun at her, tried to take her down as she ran, firing, towards him. It would have taken the decision out of her hands.

Margaret froze. Shooting the young man as he'd levelled his rifle at her had felt justifiable. Shooting an old man with his hands up was different.

'*Madame*,' he stammered. '*S'il vous plaît.*'

A shot rang out from the far end of the gallery. The guard fell to the floor, his blood already pooling on the black and white tiles. Margaret risked a look back. Schmidt saluted, then stepped back into the shadows.

Margaret hurried down the spiral staircase, running her hand down the central stone column. Distant shouts told her she wouldn't be alone for long. Schmidt had been very clear on the matter – once she made her escape, she was on her own. Get caught, and face the consequences.

At the bottom of the stairs she stumbled into a dank entranceway. Two coats hung next to a narrow outer door – grey oak boards held together by thick iron bands. She turned the handle, trying to remember if she'd heard the jangle of keys as the older sentry had fallen, his eyes watching her in his last seconds.

The door was locked.

Shouts echoed from the stone staircase above. Hurried footsteps echoed down the spiral, gaining on her.

She tried the door again, pulling it, willing it to be unlocked, but there was no movement.

She had one bullet left in the gun. Bunny's advice had been clear. Once your cover's blown, don't let them take you alive. Better a quick death at your own hand than the agony of interrogation. Better for England. Better for you.

She tried the door one last time, pushing instead of pulling. It burst open and she struggled to stay on her feet. The river bank was clear of undergrowth for ten feet, then the dark wall of the woods beckoned. She ran into the darkness.

They didn't follow her. The rules were clear, and they knew how to follow rules, especially the junior ones. Besides, the dark woods, this side of the river, were not a safe place for a German soldier.

20

Ruby felt the scratchy wool blanket around her neck and pulled it tight. Her mouth felt dry, like she'd been out late, drinking.

A key turned in a lock, then the creak of a rusty hinge. She wasn't at home, she realised, opening her eyes.

It was dark. Darker even than her room with its blackout curtains. She felt a breeze, then the door closed. A match flared and she squinted as an oil lamp glowed. A small enough light, but almost blinding against the darkness.

He picked up a tea tray. He'd put it down on a wooden chair, next to the door, while he'd lit the lamp. Now he brought it to her. Set it down on a bedside table. Like she was in hospital. The tray had a faded picture of a coronation on it. Ruby's mum had the same design. He'd brought two cups of tea, delicately balanced on saucers. A small plate – two slices of brown bread with a scraping of margarine, and a jar with two sticks of celery.

'It's happening,' he said, 'he's bombing London.'

No need to ask who *he* was. Hitler. The man who'd dominated everyone's thoughts, every conversation, for the last year. When's he going to invade? What will he stop at? Who's going to stop him if we can't?

Ruby sat up, confused. Under the blanket, she was dressed in a nightie. It wasn't hers. Silk, she thought. Who'd put her to bed? Who'd undressed her?

'I should go,' she said. 'Mum'll be worried.'

'I telephoned,' he said. 'Told her you're safe.'

'She'll need help,' Ruby said.

'The best thing you can do is stay safe,' he said. 'They're hitting the docks. Your mum was heading out to the shelter. Everyone's sheltering. Same as us.'

He put his hand on the blanket where it covered her leg, halfway up her thigh.

'Have some tea,' he said. 'I'll come and see you later.'

'Where are you going?'

'Got to keep an eye on things,' he said.

'I think I'd like to leave,' Ruby said.

He looked annoyed. She'd said the wrong thing.

'Thanks for the lift,' she said, 'and the tea, but I should be with Mum. Frankie's come up.'

His hand didn't move.

'No,' he said.

Ruby waited. It didn't really make sense.

'In the morning, then,' she said. 'When we get the all clear.'

'No,' he repeated. He took his hand off her leg, and stroked her cheek, pushing a strand of hair off her face.

'You're going to stay,' he said. 'We'll shelter together. Keep each other company. Make the best of it.'

She shrunk back. A flash of annoyance on his face.

'You think I should have left you out there, to die in the raid?' he asked.

'It's not that,' she said.

'You don't think you owe me even an ounce of gratitude?'

He let his hand drop from her face, brushing her shoulder, then lower, to the curve of her breast.

'Don't,' she said.

His hand moved quicker then. Her face felt like it had been pressed against a frying pan, seared hot, before she even realised he'd hit her. The crack echoed in the small space, the domed Anderson shelter, corrugated iron arching over the bed.

'I'm sorry,' he said.

Ruby was rigid. Even breathing felt like an act of will.

'I'll be back later,' he said. 'I'll be good to you. I promise.'

21

Gracie brought the boat into Shadwell Basin, followed the canal through a canyon of warehouse walls into the sudden open space of the vast Eastern Dock.

To their right, the northern side of the dock was an inferno. Gracie kept the boat as far from the flames as she could, but still the heat was unbearable. Cook held up his arm to protect his face from the worst of it, smelling burning wool from his sleeve.

The water was low, the locks at either end of the complex chain of docks and canals had been left open. As Gracie brought them into the southern wall, Cook looked up. They were ten feet below the level of the quay. Holes in the slippery dock wall made for a rudimentary ladder, covered with green algae.

A cloud of black smoke engulfed them, blown across the water from the northern quay. Cook squinted, trying to protect his eyes. The stinging was intense. It felt like the fire itself had reached across the water and pierced his eyelids. He had a desperate urge to dunk his head in the water, but when he looked down he saw a slick of oil on the surface.

'Pepper,' Gracie shouted, as an explosion from one of the warehouses sent a shockwave across the dock. Her eyes were red, and streaming from the smoke.

'Oh Christ,' Gracie said, forgetting the pepper smoke. Cook turned to follow her gaze. A huge ball of blue flame rose into the sky. More blue flame poured out of a warehouse, gushing around stone columns, spilling over the dockside, cascading onto the water. An erupting blue volcano.

'Get out,' Cook said, pushing her up, reaching for the nearest handhold in the dock wall. 'Now.'

The rungs embedded in the wall were slick. Cook waited as Gracie made her way up. He allowed himself a look back, expecting the blue flame to extinguish when it met the water, but instead it was spreading, an expanding semi-circle of fire crossing the water as fast as thought. Cook grabbed the slippery rungs, and pulled himself up, out of the boat.

In an instant, the flame was below him.

*

Thick smoke, alive with glowing embers, filled the air as Cook and Gracie threaded their way to the pub. Cook held his handkerchief over his mouth and squinted his eyes.

'Sugar wharf's gone up,' Gracie shouted, over the roaring of the flames. She nodded towards a tall warehouse at the end of the street. Three fire engines were doing their best, three squadrons of volunteer firemen had their hoses on it, but the water was evaporating before it could even land on the building. Cook pushed Gracie out of the road as a ringing bell heralded the arrival of another engine, but it wouldn't be enough. They needed a hundred hoses to make a dent. The smoke smelt like burnt toffee. It got through the handkerchief, into Cook's eyes, into his ears.

Gracie coughed, doubled over. Cook stopped. Waited for her coughing to subside. She spat black phlegm onto the pavement.

'We'll be doing the same to Berlin soon enough,' Gracie said.

'Two wrongs don't make a right,' Cook said. But he could tell Gracie didn't believe him. He wasn't sure whether he believed it himself.

A bomb landed nearby. A big one. Cook felt the shock-wave through the ground – the eerie sensation of a solid turned to liquid, the pavement rippling like a child making waves in a skipping rope. A symphony of breaking glass followed. Then a moan.

'Mother?' A man's voice. An old voice. Weary. Weak. Thin – the strength gone from the lungs. 'Where are you, Mother?'

Cook and Gracie paused, waiting to see if there would be a response. But no response came.

'Mother?'

Gracie led Cook through a maze of alleys, trying to locate the voice. Hard to hear over the roar of the fires and the drone of the bombers and the thump of the bombs.

'Mother,' the old man said, this time sounding weaker.

Gracie stopped at a gate, leading into a yard, a few square feet of concrete, and a reeking outhouse.

'I'm scared, Mother,' the voice said.

The back of the house was gone, peeled off, like a doll's house, everything on display. Upstairs, a bed hung halfway off what was now a sloping ledge. In front of them, a mess of bricks and rubble.

'Stay in bed, Father,' a muffled voice called out. A no-nonsense voice. 'I'll be there in a minute. I'll bring you a nice mug of tea. Lots of sugar.'

The rubble moved, causing a tiny landslide of broken tiles.

Cook dropped to his knees and pulled away a brick, then another. He saw a hand. He thought it was disembodied. But the fingers moved. He swept a mound of dust away, pulled more bricks, and revealed the arm it belonged to.

'You're all right,' Cook said. 'Keep wiggling those fingers to let me know you're still there.'

'It's gone dark,' the woman said. 'Think something knocked me on the head. And I can't move me legs.'

'Annie? It's Gracie Reynolds. We'll get you out, don't you worry.'

'Is that you, Gracie? Bless you. I've got to get Father's tea on. He won't understand.'

Cook looked up to the bed, threatening to fall out of the upstairs room.

'Mother?' the voice called again.

'Think me leg's stuck,' Annie said.

Cook felt among the remaining bricks. There was a beam, two-by-fours nailed together to make a cheap lintel, carpenter's marks still visible now it had been exposed. It lay across the old woman's ankle. Cook couldn't see the foot on the other side. Worry about that in a minute. Job one was to get the beam off her. Get her free.

He felt the beam, gave it a tug, a test to see if there was any give. It was heavy, but he thought he could move it.

'I'll pull this up, you drag her out,' he said.

Gracie grabbed the woman under the arms, prompting a scream.

'Sorry!' Gracie said.

'*Ça ne fait rien,*' the old woman said. A saying the Tommies had brought back from the last war.

'San Fairy Ann indeed,' Gracie responded.

Cook tensed his arms.

'Ready?'

'Ready,' Gracie said.

'Ready,' Annie said.

Cook pulled. The slight give he'd initially felt turned out to be about a quarter of an inch, then he felt something more solid.

'Mother!' the old man called from out of the ether.

'Don't you move, Father! I'll be there in a jif!' Annie called out. Then, to Cook – 'Come on, lad, get it done.'

Cook had, he felt, been trying to get it done. He tried again. Harder. A fierce burst, grunting with the effort.

A shower of glass and dust fell onto Cook's head. A dagger of intact glass, a foot long, landed at his feet.

'Bit more,' Gracie said.

Cook didn't like giving up, but there was only so much a man could do. He let his arms relax, shook his head.

'Gracie,' he said, 'get over here.'

Gracie shuffled over and took her place next to Cook.

'Watch out for the glass,' Cook said, with a quick look up. There was a potential waterfall of jagged shards above them. Like one of those machines on the pier that held a teetering overhang of ha'pennies.

Gracie grabbed the beam and gave a grunt, her shoulder muscles stretching her coat with the effort.

'That's not going anywhere,' she said.

'We can do it,' Cook said. 'On three.'

Cook counted. 'One,' he tensed his arms, Gracie did the same.

'Two . . .'

'Mother . . .' the voice from above was weaker.

'Three.'

Cook pulled. He felt a muscle in his back give. The beam moved, then more. A crunching noise as a chunk of masonry slid way, then it was free.

'Thank God!' Annie whimpered. 'Don't move, Father!'

Shouts from the alley heralded the arrival of more men. Two of them, tin hats with ARP stencilled on the front.

'What have we got?' the one in front asked, as he stepped into the yard, crunching on glass.

'Father's upstairs,' Annie said. 'Gracie's just got me out from under half the back wall.'

'You should be in the shelter,' the ARP warden said, as Cook stood up. 'Can't have civilians running around, getting in the way.'

'Who's in charge?' Cook asked.

'Beaumont,' the ARP warden said.

'Where is he?' Cook asked.

The warden looked at his mate, who shook his head.

'On patrol,' he said.

Cook knew the look. It was the look of a man who's learnt the truth about his superior officer, after all the training, and the marching, and the blowing of whistles, when the shots start firing and the bombs start falling.

22

Frankie found the first mushroom next to the shelter. It was still warm. A heavy lump of shining metal, with a stalk and a flattened cap. A tiny version of the real mushrooms Cook had shown him in the fields around the farm.

He found more at the edge of the park. As he stooped to pick them up, putting them in his pockets, he heard the clink of metal on concrete, and then a soft thud as something landed in the grass nearby.

The thing in the grass was a bullet. Just as shiny, and just as warm. The shape was unmistakable. The ones that bounced off the roof of the shelter were mushrooms – the impact shaping the soft metal.

Bullets – mushrooms – either way they felt valuable, so Frankie put them in his pocket.

A light was showing from the hermitage warehouse. After a year of the blackout, Frankie wasn't used to seeing such a bright light outdoors. He took the alley past the pub, towards the warehouse. As he got closer, he could see what had happened.

The front wall had taken a direct hit. There was an electric light inside, hanging at the end of a wire.

Frankie looked up into the clouds, imagining a German pilot seeing the light. He'd turn his plane, zero in on the target. One of those Stukas, the type that screamed as it dived.

Frankie clambered over a pile of rubble – big chunks of masonry, covered with so much dust it was like fallen snow.

He couldn't find a light switch. It must have been on the front wall. The wall that was now just so much dust.

A bomb came down in the river on the other side of the warehouse. It made a satisfying plonk, like when Frankie threw a large pebble into deep water. Then the ground shifted, and before he knew it he was up to his ankles in the dust, as if quicksand wanted to swallow him up.

Frankie hurriedly pulled his feet out of the dust, and stumbled back down onto the street.

But the light was still burning. It wouldn't do.

He picked up a stone. A good size for throwing. Not too big, but with enough weight to fly true.

He looked around, feeling guilty. He was in the right, but it felt wrong.

He threw the stone. It went wide. Now he was glad nobody had been watching.

He hunted for more stones – stocked up with a few. But the next throw hit the target. The light went out instantly.

A car crunched on broken glass, and Frankie took cover behind the rubble, still feeling like he'd done something wrong.

It was a black car, with writing on the side. Big letters in white, like they'd been made with some kind of sticking paper.

ARP

The car door opened, and Frankie slid further behind the debris. It was Reynolds.

Frankie felt a pang of fear. He knew it was wrong to feel like that about his own father, but he couldn't help it.

He'd never actually seen his father hurt anyone, but every time he was near him it felt like something bad was going to happen.

Reynolds lifted a wooden box from the passenger seat of the car, and carried it into the warehouse. The metal sliding door screeched behind him, until it clanged shut.

23

The ARP headquarters was in the church cellar. A musty storage space in peacetime, an ancient, iron door separating the room from the crypt proper, where they buried the former priests, or so everyone said. Not a place anyone would choose to spend any time in, but a place presumed safe from the worst of the bombs. Enough space for a camp bed, so whoever was manning the station could get some sleep when things were quiet. A large-scale map of the district was pinned to the wall, not that anybody ever looked at it. Everyone who'd grown up on the island knew every street.

Most of the space on the desk was taken up by the wireless set. Transmitter and receiver. There'd be a message every fifteen minutes when things were quiet. And things had been quiet for almost a year. Then, suddenly, they weren't.

Beaumont had put up with a year of abuse. Tinpot dictator, he'd been called, all for doing his job, making sure people were obeying the blackout. When his team of volunteers had shut down the high street for a rehearsal of a gas attack, half the people ignored them, walking through their war game as if they knew better. Beaumont had lain awake that night, praying for a gas attack. Put them in their places. Everyone had been given the gas masks, shown how to use them, but most of them still didn't believe in the threat.

But that was all changed now. Now the bombers had arrived, Beaumont was a man whose time had come. Tonight, as the bombs rained down, he was the most powerful man on the island, just because he'd raised his hand a year and a half ago when they'd asked for volunteers.

The radio squawked. Kathleen, one of Beaumont's more competent volunteers, picked up the receiver and listened, noting down the message.

'Two high explosives, Limehouse.'

Useless information. Out of their jurisdiction. As if they didn't have enough to worry about already. Half the island was burning.

Beaumont knew, on a purely theoretical level, that he should be out there. The training had been very clear. See and be seen. But what good could he do? The volunteer fire wardens were doing what they could. He could do more here, co-ordinating. Keeping things under control.

There was a commotion at the door. Beaumont looked up from his desk. It was the farmer. The one who'd brought the cricket bat.

'That shelter in the park,' Cook said. 'It's not safe.'

'Course it's safe,' Beaumont said. 'Only built a few months ago. Government specification.'

'You've got to close it,' Cook said. 'Get people out.'

'Get them out of the shelter?' Beaumont asked, as a shower of dust fell from the ceiling and a bomb fell nearby.

'It's going to come down,' Cook said. 'You need to put a sign up. Boards across the door. I'll do it if you've got the lumber.'

The phone rang. Kathleen picked it up, listened.

'They want to lower the bridge at Shadwell,' she said. 'Get more fire engines onto the island.'

Beaumont was aware all eyes were on him. It was his decision. But it was an impossible one to make. Not enough information, and conflicting priorities. Keep the waterways open, the latest bulletin from the government had made very clear. But that had been before the island had been turned into a target for the whole of the Luftwaffe.

'What shall I tell them?' Kathleen asked.

'The bridge stays up,' he said.

Kathleen relayed this order. There was shouting from the other end. Beaumont leant over and cut the line.

'There's no right choice,' he said.

The phone rang again.

'Wait,' Cook said.

Kathleen looked to Beaumont for confirmation. The ARP man opened his mouth to respond, but then he heard it. The sound they weren't meant to hear.

They all strained to listen, above the ringing of the phone and the roaring of the fires. Filtering out the distant screams and the crashes as another warehouse succumbed to its injuries and collapsed inward.

It was a normal enough sound. A peaceful sound. Sleepy Sunday mornings in quiet country villages. Holidays. Celebrations. A sound that nobody in England had heard for months, since the order went out. No church bells until the invasion begins.

Father Ryan ran down the stairs, an ARP armband over his vestments.

'I heard the bells from St Mary's,' he said. 'It's happening.'

Cook followed the priest up the stairs from the crypt. Above ground, the bells were deafening. No attempt at a tune, just a discordant peal.

Beaumont and Kathleen joined Cook and the priest.

'Look!' Kathleen said, pointing to the dark sky.

Cook followed her arm, and then he saw it. A parachute.

'Get the rifle,' Beaumont snapped, and Kathleen disappeared, back down the stairs.

Cook scanned the sky for more. They wouldn't just drop one man. If this was the invasion, there'd be thousands more on the way.

A searchlight picked out the parachute. Cook pictured the crew, manhandling the large light. The light flickered off its target then found it again.

There was no parachutist. Instead, the parachute was supporting a large cylinder. Hard to judge the size at such a distance, but it looked like it was the size of a small car.

'Bloody hell,' Kathleen said. Then – 'Sorry, Father.'

'Bloody hell indeed,' Father Ryan replied.

24

Cook ran towards where they'd seen the parachute come down, through the warren of alleys. Beaumont, the ARP man, followed behind.

They turned a corner and there it was. An unremarkable hole in the road at the end of the alley, with what looked like a lake of silk puddled on the road next to it.

'What if it goes off?' Beamont asked. He looked back down the road, the way they'd come, as if hoping someone would come along and take the problem away from him.

Beyond the hole, a large yellow-brick building loomed. Four storeys high, towering over neighbouring houses.

'What's that building?' Cook asked.

'St Patrick's,' Beaumont said. 'Lying-in hospital. Two hundred beds.'

Cook took a step forward, but Beaumont put his hand on his arm.

'I can't let you,' he said. 'Procedure. I've got to call it in.'

Cook took another step forward, out of Beaumont's reach. He looked at the hospital. Thinking about what Beaumont had said. Two hundred beds. Two hundred women and babies. Nurses. Doctors. Any one of them worth more than a farmer who'd chosen to use up all his nine lives in some of the most dangerous places known to man.

25

Cook kept his eye on the hole. Watching it had no practical purpose, of course. Either the bomb would go off, or it wouldn't. But it seemed like the sort of thing you'd want to keep your eye on. Perhaps there'd be warning signs. A sudden burst of smoke, or a flash from an initial detonator. Something that might give a man time to hurl himself to the ground.

Beaumont had done his disappearing act. Gone to call the powers that be. Cook wasn't hopeful. The island was cut off from the rest of the city. There'd be a pen-pusher at the other end of the phone line. Procedures to be followed.

Cook looked up at the looming building. Every window was open, heads peering out, watching. Two hundred beds. Women and children. Doctors and nurses.

A door opened near the pool of silk. A matron, surveying the damage.

'What's going on here?' she asked, in a tone that suggested Cook was somehow at fault.

'Bomb,' Cook said.

'A dud?' the matron asked.

'UXB,' Cook said. The first time he'd heard the term, it had sounded alien, like something from a science fiction novel. But the press had taken to it. Short for Unexploded Bomb.

'How long to get everyone out?' Cook asked, glancing up at the open windows.

'Impossible,' the matron said. 'I've got three women in labour as we speak. Ten in critical condition, can't be moved. We'd need ambulances for the rest of them.'

'Can't get ambulances in,' Cook said. 'Bridges are all up.'

'You'll have to do something about it,' she said.

Beaumont returned, out of breath.

'Got to leave it,' he said.

'We can't,' Cook replied.

'ARP say it's the army's job. I called the army. They do bomb disposal. I told them what we saw. The parachute. They said it's not a bomb, it's a mine.'

'What's the difference?' Cook asked. It sounded exactly like the army. Preferring to split hairs about terminology rather than get the job done.

'Mines go in the sea,' Beaumont said. 'Float there, waiting for a ship to come close. Then they explode. Army said to call the navy. Navy's in charge of mines.'

'What did the navy say?'

'Their mine disposal experts are all in Portsmouth. And they're busy.'

Cook looked up at the open windows, and then at the hole.

'Keep everyone back,' he said.

'I can't allow you to go near it,' Beaumont said.

'I don't answer to you,' Cook replied, walking away from Beaumont, away from the smell of fear he exuded.

Towards the hole in the road.

26

The hole was ten feet deep. Even slowed by the parachute, the bomb had burrowed its way into the ground. Designed to cause maximum damage when it eventually went off.

Cook heard ticking. Possibly the metal contracting or expanding. Or possibly a timing device.

The bomb was an inanimate object, but Cook had the impression it was watching him. Waiting.

'Got a light?'

Cook turned in surprise. Frankie's father, Reynolds, the man who only hours earlier had been holding a knife in Cook's face.

Reynolds winked. From another man, it might have been a friendly gesture, but Cook saw a coldness in his face that spoke of anything but friendliness. Reynolds fished in his pocket for a box of matches and lit up.

'You got Beaumont out of his burrow,' Reynolds said, nodding back to the end of the road, where a crowd was gathering behind the ARP man.

'You should go back and join him,' Cook said. 'This thing could go off any minute.'

'Could do,' Reynolds said. 'Could go off instantly, or after a minute, or any time after that.'

But Cook stayed, and Reynolds stayed with him. Bloody-mindedness, perhaps.

'So what's your plan?' Reynolds asked.

'Try and defuse it,' Cook said. 'Must be some kind of detonator. Failing that, dig it out, carry it further away from the hospital.'

'You might not get very far.'

'Every yard's a few less dead civilians,' Cook said.

'You done this kind of thing before?'

'No,' Cook said.

'Fancy your chances, do you?'

'It's designed to be armed by someone in a dark aeroplane, flying miles up in the sky. I gather it's cold up there. You'd be wearing gloves. Fumbling around. So there's going to be some kind of arming mechanism that's pretty accessible. If they can arm it, we can disarm it.'

'Got any tools?' Reynolds asked.

Cook shook his head.

'Blow the whole place up if you get it wrong,' Reynolds said, looking at the hospital.

'Got any better ideas?' Cook asked.

'Not much of an ideas man,' Reynolds said. He reached into his pocket and pulled out a roll of fabric. He opened it, like a magic trick – turning the roll into eighteen inches of material, packed with tools, each tool held in place by a loop of elastic. Pliers. Screwdrivers. Things that looked like dental implements.

'Royal Essex,' Reynolds said. 'Sappers. Four years of mucking about in the mud, messing about with these kinds of things. Putting them places. Taking them away from other places.'

'So what's the plan?' Cook asked.

'Plan?' Reynolds replied. 'There's no plan. Like as not this thing goes off as soon as we touch it.'

Cook looked into the hole. The bomb looked back.

'Best get it over with then,' Cook said.

27

The bomb was even bigger up close. Reynolds was underneath it. He'd gone in first, dug himself a hole to the side of the bomb. He had his cheek pressed against the casing, his arms stretched around it. From the expression on his face, he was trying to locate something on its far side.

'Where'd you put it, you fucking Kraut bastard?'

Cook slid down into the hole after Reynolds.

Reynolds looked back at Cook – awkward in this cramped position. He smiled, tilted his head as he performed some kind of operation with the hand hidden on the far side of the bomb. There was a scrape of metal, then a tinkle of glass.

Reynolds froze.

'That's not good,' he said.

More tinkling glass. Reynolds grimaced. He shut his eyes.

Seconds passed. Nothing happened.

Reynolds opened one eye, squinting at Cook.

'Get your hand around the other side,' Reynolds said. 'I've got the detonator, but I can't pull it out. You'll have to do that.'

With Reynolds lying to one side of the bomb, there was nowhere else for Cook to stand.

'Get up on top of it,' Reynolds said. 'It's not going anywhere.'

Cook carefully climbed onto the bomb, feeling the heat of the metal beneath him.

'Down there,' Reynolds said, gesturing with his head.

Cook reached his left hand down, felt Reynolds's fingers. He was holding something the size of a jam jar.

'Got it,' Cook said.

'It's going to unscrew,' Reynolds said. 'Might have an anti-tampering device on it, so if you hear it click, stop what you're doing.'

'What would trigger it?' Cook asked.

'If you turned it the wrong way. Could be they've made it so you're meant to turn it clockwise, so anti-clockwise arms it. Kind of a bomb-maker's sense of humour.'

'I thought the Germans didn't do humour,' Cook said.

'Everyone who makes bombs likes a laugh,' Reynolds said. 'You have to, otherwise you'd go loopy, messing around with these bastards all day.'

'So I should turn it clockwise?' Cook asked.

Reynolds grimaced.

'Up to you,' he said.

Cook closed his eyes. Clockwise or anti-clockwise. No way to make a high-quality decision.

Cook turned the jar-sized device anti-clockwise. It turned smoothly – precision engineering from a German factory. He paused to reset his grip. Turned it again.

Click.

Cook felt it. A switch, disturbed. Moving from one state to the other. From on, to off. Or from off, to on.

Cook waited for the world to end. He hoped it didn't, which surprised him.

Nothing.

He pulled the jar-shape out from its recessed housing, felt Reynolds fumbling with pliers.

'Sure you've never done this before?' Reynolds asked, as he snipped a bundle of wires between the detonator and the rest of the bomb.

'Anything you sappers can do,' Cook said. 'It's not like they had entry exams.'

'Where were you?' Reynolds asked.

'Wherever they told me to be,' Cook answered.

'I heard you stayed in, after.'

'Didn't know how to come home,' Cook said.

Reynolds paused, like he was considering a wise-crack, but held his tongue.

'Do you need any help?' a voice from above. It was Beaumont, looking down into the hole. Reynolds met Cook's eye, and winked. He threw the detonator up to Beaumont.

'You want to be careful with that,' Reynolds said, 'take your hand off if it wants to.'

28

When the flashbulb popped, half the people in the crowd flinched. Frankie, face still smeared with grime, had been posed on a pile of rubble. A smart young man in a suit had handed him a Union Jack on a stick and told him to wave it.

Half the crowd had flags. Most held them listlessly by their sides. A few got into the spirit, cheering when Churchill stepped from his car. A flying visit, surveying the damage. More than a few onlookers had things to say under their breath. The early editions of the papers had told one version of the story. The docks had been the target. The rest of London had been largely untouched.

Someone passed Cook a paper. The front page was dominated by a picture of Tower Bridge, a column of smoke behind it.

COWARDLY RAID ON LONDON DOCKS
FEW CASUALTIES
LONDON CAN TAKE IT!

Cook looked at the crowd, most of whom sullenly watched Churchill as he made his inspection. London may or may not have had an opinion on whether it could take it, but the islanders knew what taking it meant. The island was finished.

'Where are we going to go?' a brave voice rang out. A uniformed police constable took a step towards the trouble-maker, and the bravery evaporated.

Churchill returned to the safety of his armoured car. A wise move, Cook thought. He'd been curious to see the great man in person. He looked tired. Must have spent the night waiting for the invasion, as they all had.

One thing was certain, another few nights like the one they'd just survived, and there wouldn't be much left to invade.

29

Cook and Frankie sat on the train, Cook facing the direction of travel. The boy opposite.

The window was an excuse not to talk, a moving picture constantly evolving as the stations passed by. First the suburban stops, then the tunnel under the North Downs. Then a succession of country towns. Oxted, Hever, Eridge, Crowborough, Buxted, a litany that had seen Cook through a lifetime.

Rabbits scattered as the train passed. The fields were stubble, the harvest finished and the new farming year not yet underway. Cook was glad to see defensive fortifications being built. A line of concrete bunkers – octagonal shape, gun slits facing south. He was disappointed, but not surprised, to see they were putting them in the wrong place. Directly in the line of attack. Better off to the side, hidden, set up for enfilading fire, diagonally across the line. Cook wouldn't want to be the poor mug sitting in one of those buildings, firing his Bren gun at an advancing Panzer. Waiting for the darkness as he looked down the length of the tank's gun. Man versus artillery. They'd tried that in the last war. Proof of man's inability to learn from experience.

They walked up the lane, past the oast-house, the quiet a physical presence after the sirens and the bombs. London was finished. All the experts had proven it, in the run up to the war. Tons of explosives per square mile. Population density. The tolerance of a population to remain sane under intense bombardment. They'd taken everything they'd learnt from the Western Front, applied it to a civilian population, and the results had been clear. No point in wasting too much time and money on bomb shelters. Better to go straight to the finish line. Invest in mental hospitals for the insane, and coffins for the dead.

Presumably the men in charge had other plans. Plans they kept quiet. A new capital. Edinburgh perhaps. Or Canada. Take the government, the royal family, the gold, the scientists – get them all safely across the Atlantic. A far more defensible position, great oceans on both sides. Neutral America to the south. Let Hitler do his worst with London.

Not what Cook would have chosen, if he'd been asked. But men like Cook were never asked. They were told.

They climbed over the stile, onto Cook's land. Cook breathed it in. The dry soil in the warm evening air. Smelt like home.

They stopped in the shadow of an ancient oak as a small aeroplane flew low overhead. Cook put his hand on the boy's shoulder.

They waited, listening to the plane. Cook didn't think they were in any danger, but better safe than sorry. As the sound of the plane receded, he stepped out from the cover of the tree and scoured the sky, but in the deep blue of the gathering evening it was like looking for a dark needle in a dark haystack. One of ours, he hoped, returning from France. If it was up to him, they'd be dropping supplies and people, building up a network of operatives. People like him who could disappear into the countryside, keep away from the German occupiers, make a nuisance of themselves. Unlikely to turn the tide of the war, but enough to tie up German resources. Make it costly to keep France occupied.

A fox barked, and Cook heard a rustle in the undergrowth. A rabbit, making sure it wasn't too far from its burrow.

Going to London had been a mistake.

*

Mum was watching for them, Cook could see her face in the kitchen window, looking out across the field. She knew how long it took from the station to the farm. Would have been standing there seventeen minutes after the arrival of every train that day. She'd had plenty of practice during the last war. Waiting for her son to come home. That, or a telegram. And now there was the boy, too. One more person to worry about.

She fussed over them both, put a plate of bread and jam on the table, Frankie's favourite. Two mugs of tea, sugar for Frankie. Uncle Nob took his tea by the fire. Elizabeth hovered in the corner. They'd have been waiting just as much as Mum. Fearing the worst.

Cook had been right to help Reynolds defuse the bomb, but he'd got the calculus wrong, he now realised. He'd weighed his life too cheaply, thinking only of his own feelings about death – feelings he'd been living with for longer than he could remember. But somehow, without him noticing, he'd taken on responsibilities. People counted on him, people who hadn't asked to be put in that position.

The old refrain was going through his head. Going to London had been a mistake. A mistake he'd do his best to avoid making again.

30

Margaret looked out through the plexiglass cover as the engine revved and a great cloud of smoke engulfed them, then dissipated. Her first time in an aeroplane. The pilot had been waiting at the pre-planned location, smoking a cigarette, talking with a French farmer as if making a secret flight across the Channel to pick up an agent was just another day's work. The farmer was holding a bottle of Scotch, she'd noticed when she'd arrived, and the pilot wedged a bottle of wine into his cockpit as they'd climbed in.

She wondered how they'd take off in the bumpy meadow, no more than a couple of hundred yards of grass until the looming trees, but the pilot seemed confident enough. He revved the engine again, until she could feel the small machine straining, held by the brakes presumably. Then they were off, stumbling across the pasture, impossible to imagine breaking free of gravity. Then, as if they were picked up by some invisible hand, the bumpy ground became less of an issue, and suddenly they were aloft, the line of trees still a threat, but the ground no longer slowing them down. The pilot was awfully quiet as he pulled the stick back, and despite the roaring engine all she could hear was his breathing, and the almost inaudible coaxing – *come on girl, come on* . . . And then Margaret opened her eyes, not realising she'd closed them, and outside all was blackness, the hum of the engine reassuring her that she was not, in fact, dead, and a disconcerting feeling in her stomach providing something else to worry about.

'Try not to throw up!' the pilot shouted back to her. 'Gets me in a pickle with the ground crew.'

The flight over occupied France took forty minutes that felt to Margaret like two lifetimes. She was accustomed to dealing with tense situations, but being strapped into the back of a tin can like this was almost more than she could bear. It was the feeling of powerlessness. Not a feeling she liked. Not one bit. Then they were over the Channel, the thin sliver of sea all that was holding back Hitler from the successful completion of his grand tour, and Margaret started to think they'd make it. Now they were over Sussex, and she finally felt she could breathe again.

For a moment, the clouds parted and moonlight illuminated the countryside below. Margaret squinted to see if she recognised anything. But it was impossible. Every tree, every field, every farmhouse, all looked alike from up here. Nevertheless, she couldn't tear her eyes away.

Cook would be out there. Making plans. Getting the job done.

Margaret wasn't one for dwelling on the past, but her time with Cook had been . . . What *had* it been? Love, perhaps. Yes, she allowed. But love had only been a part of it. Being part of a team. Pulling together for a common cause, each making the other better. Margaret was used to being the smartest one in the room. She saw things others didn't see. She laughed before anyone else did when watching a revue – her mind joining the dots and predicting the punchline a fraction of a second before the rest of the audience. She'd become reconciled to being alone, in that respect. The men she'd known had been companions, amiable for the most part, but tiresome, needing work. Cook was different. As smart as her, in his own way. Niceties not required. No work needed. Like coming home to a quiet room.

The pilot shouted to Margaret but she couldn't hear the words. She realised her ears were ringing from the continual assault of the engine noise. Having got her attention, the pilot pointed out of the right-hand side of the cockpit.

What she saw shocked her.

London was burning. The River Thames snaked away to their right, silver in the moonlight. On both sides of the river, flames rose from fires that looked like they were consuming the whole city. Huge columns of smoke rose, blocking out the stars.

'Why aren't the guns firing?' Margaret shouted to the pilot. Anti-aircraft guns had become part of the background, firing on bombers throughout the summer, their distinctive four-beat rhythm – pom pom pom pom – a reassuring sound against the drone of the enemy attack.

'Our fighters are up there, trying to get behind the bombers,' the pilot shouted. Margaret squinted to see if she could see planes in the darkness. Was that tracer fire she could see, like fireflies in the distance?

'I can't see them,' Margaret shouted.

'That's the problem,' the pilot shouted. 'It's too dark for the fighters, but the guns can't fire because they're up there.'

The Westland Lysander touched down lightly on the tarmac, propellor buzzing. The pilot manoeuvred the plane off the runway and steered towards a quiet part of the airfield. A car waited, barely visible in the dark, raindrops glistening on the windscreen.

The pilot cut the engine and climbed out. He turned to help Margaret but she was already behind him, clambering out of the cockpit, down onto the struts and the curved wheel-covers.

'Welcome to Croydon,' the pilot said, with a grin. 'I'll be in the pub with some of the boys if you fancy a drink.'

The car door opened.

'That's very kind,' Margaret said. 'But I rather think I've got plans.'

Margaret sat in the back of the car, her ears still ringing, as they cruised through an endless succession of suburban towns. Purley. Streatham. Brixton. All dark in the blackout, buses looming out of the drizzle at the last minute, pedestrians taking their lives into their own hands with every dash across the road. In the plane, there'd been the frisson of excitement that they might get shot down by an over-enthusiastic home defence unit, or encounter a lost German fighter, but those odds were, in reality, incredibly low. Here on the streets, in the blackout, it felt like every mile without deadly incident was a lucky escape.

'What's the mood over there?' Bunny asked. Just like him, Margaret thought. No pleasantries. No hint of concern for her welfare, no recognition of what she'd been through on his behalf.

'They're angry,' Margaret said. 'When they heard you'd bombed Berlin it was like you'd thrown a rock at a wasp's nest.'

'Goering sent everything he had against us,' Bunny said. 'Every bomber, every fighter, every pilot on the roster,' he said, looking out of the window. 'Killed almost two thousand people.'

'Is it true we've already done worse to Berlin?'

Bunny looked at her, as if trying to decide how much to trust her.

'Their strategy of bombing our airfields was working,' he said. 'Another day or two and they'd have broken the RAF. Then they'd have had free rein.'

'Was it you?' Margaret asked. 'Throwing the rock at the wasp's nest?'

Bunny didn't respond.

'Two thousand people killed in one night,' Margaret said. 'How long do you need to rebuild the RAF?'

'Couple of months,' Bunny replied.

'What if the people of London decide they don't like being used as a diversionary tactic?'

'We're rather hoping they don't,' Bunny said, a typical understatement. 'We've modelled it all out. We think there's a fifty-five per cent chance it brings everyone together. Blitz spirit, we're calling it. All the press are on board.'

Margaret thought he was being optimistic. Easy to play with public opinion when the public don't have any power, the poor down in the docks for instance. Give it a few nights of bombing over Knightsbridge – that would be a different matter. But she kept quiet. She'd learnt that about Bunny. When he was lecturing, you let him carry on. Same for most men, in her experience.

'The French gave up France to save Paris,' he said. 'We're taking the alternative view. We think it's rather easier to rebuild a city than it is to retake your country.'

'It sounds like you've thought it all through,' Margaret said.

'We're going to put you up in one of our receiving facilities,' Bunny said. 'There'll be lots of recent arrivals from the continent. We thought you might be able to make yourself useful helping us sort them out – let us know which of them have swastika armbands in their sock drawer.'

It was what she'd expected. They wouldn't just set her free. She was suspect, now. Tainted. Impossible for anyone to know which side she was on. 'Make yourself useful' sounded like code for 'stay where we can keep an eye on you until we decide how much we can trust you'.

'Facility?' she asked. It had an unpleasant ring to it. A prison. Or a remote island. The sort of place meant to wear down a person's sense of self. Show them that everything they once had, once were, could be taken away.

'Bit of a zoo, I'm afraid,' Bunny said, 'with all the comings and goings. Shouldn't be any real danger.'

'I can handle danger,' Margaret said. She could even handle discomfort, but given the choice, she'd rather not. She'd heard they were using Holloway. God knows what they'd done with the regular inmates – volunteered them all into the army perhaps.

The car took a sharp right turn and suddenly they were crossing the river, the blazing docks casting an orange glow on the interior of the car, casting Bunny into the shadows. Where he belonged.

'We can debrief tomorrow,' Bunny said. 'I'll meet you for breakfast.'

Margaret didn't want to imagine what breakfast would be like at a prison, even a prison repurposed for 'recent arrivals from the continent'.

The car pulled up. Margaret hadn't been paying attention to the route. Besides, she'd never got to know London particularly well. Even though she was a member of the country's ruling class, most of her upbringing had been at a remove – in Switzerland and India. London had always been seen through the lens of a storybook, or a flickering newsreel.

The driver hopped out and opened the door on Bunny's side. Bunny climbed out, making an effort of it. He looked older than when she'd first met him, even though it had only been a year since he'd first approached her and asked if she'd be interested in 'doing her bit'.

Margaret climbed out of the car, expecting the worst – some kind of impenetrable fortress, high brick walls and barbed wire. She realised she knew the street. She'd been here before.

Margaret had come to the Empire for tea with her aunt, the very first time she'd come up to London. At the time she'd barely glanced at the surroundings. Apart from anything, it was far less opulent than many of the grand buildings on the Bombay waterfront she'd grown up in. Even so, she found herself remembering her aunt – a kind woman who'd done her best, all things considered.

'No bag,' Margaret snapped at the hovering bellboy. He clicked his heels and made himself scarce, as Bunny escorted Margaret through the revolving door, the bomb-proof tape marring the effect.

They stood in the lobby. Bunny put his hands on Margaret's shoulders, gave her a grimace. Like being dropped off, your first day at boarding school. Don't get into trouble. Don't embarrass us.

'You'll want to explore, of course,' Bunny said. 'But don't go too far.'

'Am I allowed out?'

'Of course!' Bunny pretended to laugh. 'You're not a prisoner. Far from it. You're a returning hero. We don't want to lose you. You're one of our most valuable assets.'

For a man whose business was lying, Bunny was shockingly bad at it.

'Do you want to give me any parameters?'

'I don't know if we need to go that far.'

'So I could take a train to the country?'

'Nobody's going to raise any eyebrows if you want to go shopping in Mayfair, or up to Oxford Street. Go to a show at the Café de Paris. That kind of thing.'

'I'm not a Londoner,' she said. 'You're describing the monopoly board, but I don't know where those places are.'

Bunny squirmed. It seemed he was determined not to be the strict headmaster. Not quite his modus operandi. More the kindly uncle.

'Call it a quarter-of-a-mile radius,' he said. 'Nothing worth seeing beyond that anyway.'

'Expenses?' she asked.

'We've set you up with an account. Don't go wild, it all goes through my budget and there's hell to pay if we have to explain to the PM why our people are having champagne sent to their rooms.'

'Anyone you want me to keep an eye on? While you're keeping an eye on me?'

'Keep your eyes and ears open. The more you can prove your worth, the quicker this whole thing is apt to go.'

Bunny caught the eye of the man on the desk, who passed him a room key. Bunny, in turn, handed it to Margaret.

'Try and keep out of trouble,' he said.

'I always do.'

31

One week later
Saturday, 14 September 1940

The telegram came at six. Just after tea. A few minutes earlier and the delivery boy could have had a slice of bread and margarine.

Bess had wanted an evacuee as soon as she'd heard about the scheme. Heaven knows she wasn't getting any younger. Seemed like only yesterday she'd been holding her own newborn baby in her arms, a boy furious with the world from day one. The first wave, back in '39, John had put his foot down, said he couldn't have a young child running around the place. So she'd given up on the idea, even if she hadn't agreed with him. Hadn't done *him* any harm growing up on a farm. One of those city boys, they'd love the chance.

John and Frankie, the lad, had taken a while to get used to each other. Frankie hadn't taken to farming life at first, confounding all of them. You'd have thought every boy's dream was to be allowed free rein over the woods and the fields. But something about the open spaces had bothered the boy. It had been Margaret who'd finally brought him out of himself, the same way she'd brought John back to life, after all he'd been through.

But Margaret was gone.

Bess took the telegram, thanking the boy and sending him away with a farthing for his trouble and an egg for his mother. She stood by the sink, where she could see out over the nearest field. John and the children were playing a game. French cricket.

Nob watched her from his armchair by the fireplace. When she finished reading she couldn't look him in the eye, had to wipe her face.

*

Cook was bowling. Elizabeth stood in the middle, the cricket bat held defensively in front of her legs. He gave her an easy one and she went for it, almost knocked the leather off. Frankie chased the ball through the long grass, running into the setting sun like his life depended on it.

Cook watched Mum walking from the farmhouse. A heavy tread. She had a piece of paper in her hand. Cook would have wagered that paper was trouble.

Frankie was running in from the outfield, stopping half-way to throw the ball. A decent throw. The ball smacked into Cook's hand. He lifted it to his face, smelt it. Something good, and pure. The smell of the grass, the leather, a hint of linseed oil from the bat. The sound of swifts wheeling above.

He read the telegram. Looked at Mum, and then at the boy. 'I'll tell him,' he said. 'Later.'

No need to interrupt the game. If Cook could go back to his own childhood, spend another few hours out in the fields, as the sky darkened. He'd give a lot for that. The older he got, the more he believed it.

The news could wait.

*

Bill Taylor, Cook's farm manager, said his goodbyes, setting off on his walk home in the perfect evening. Elizabeth ran upstairs, getting ready for bed. Good to see her playing. Taking part. She was only a couple of years older than Frankie, but life had aged her too quickly.

'Frankie,' Cook shouted, calling the boy in from the farmyard. 'Cup of tea for you.'

Frankie was flushed from running around. He didn't want to come in. Didn't want the day to be over.

'Got some news from London,' Cook added. That got the boy's attention.

Cook looked at the telegram as the boy stood by the kitchen table, juggling with his cricket ball. Nob sat in his armchair. Always watching.

There wasn't any way to soften it, Cook realised.

'It's bad news,' he said.

Frankie looked confused, suspecting some kind of prank.

Cook shook his head.

'Your sister. Ruby.'

32

The church was full. Frankie's mum worked her way down the aisle, holding hands, thanking. Like she was comforting them, instead of the other way around. Father Ryan followed, keeping a professional eye on her, keeping his distance.

It was bigger inside than Cook had expected. Ancient stone blackened by soot, bright beams of light through the stained-glass windows. Could have been any church, anywhere in the country, apart from the smells. Fish, tar, spices, and most of all – smoke. It reminded Cook of his time in Hong Kong, a lifetime ago. Two island ports on opposite ends of the earth, linked by a non-stop procession of ships. Something Hitler didn't understand, if he thought he could intimidate Churchill. Britain wasn't just an island across the English Channel. It was a spider in the middle of a web that spanned the globe. The largest empire the world had ever seen. Hitler may have taken most of Europe, but he'd still run short of the resources Britain could depend on.

Cook sat on the unyielding pew, calculating how quickly they could be on their way. There'd be some kind of gathering, back at the pub. An hour there, to be polite. Let the boy be with his people, then excuses made, back across Tower Bridge. The 17:08 from London Bridge if all went well. The 17:33 if they got caught up. Home before dark. Cook was aware of his responsibility – he'd promised to look after the boy, keep him safe from bombers, but here he was, once again sitting in the heart of the lion's den.

It was a short service. Father Ryan evidently knew his flock, knew they wanted comfort but not preaching. Cook appreciated a clergyman who didn't try to labour the point.

A short walk from the church, back to the pub. Washing hung from gantries spanning the high street. Only a week since Cook had been here, but the days and nights since hadn't been kind to the island. More buildings were gone than left standing. The streets were empty. Many who'd survived the bombs had fled. Relatives in the country, or elsewhere in the city. Only the die-hards remained, and the men who relied on the docks for work.

Gracie had made sandwiches, neighbours chipping in their rations. Cook took a cup of tea from the barmaid, gave her a sombre nod of thanks.

'How's Frankie taking to the country life?' the priest asked.

Cook nodded, looked about for Frankie. He'd spent the service fiddling with his cricket ball. Hadn't let it out of his sight since he'd got it.

'It was hard at first,' Cook said. 'For both of us.'

'Gracie tells me you've been a good influence,' the priest said. 'It's a great comfort.'

Cook didn't know what to say. Gracie rescued him.

'Got a job for you,' she said. 'Before you head back.'

33

Margaret had always enjoyed a late breakfast in a hotel. The luxury of it, watching the world go by, reading the paper, being waited on. But after a week the novelty had worn off.

The toast was cold. A tiny pot of butter, barely enough for a scrape. She cut it into soldiers and cracked her egg. It was hard boiled, and cold. No use trying to dip the soldiers. Still, she was lucky, she knew that. Millions of people on both sides of the Channel would have woken up hungry and would be going to bed hungry.

But really, how hard was it to boil an egg?

Bunny was late. A deliberate tactic, make her think she wasn't important, not a priority.

He took his seat and the waiter brought another pot of tea, fussing with the cup and the saucer and the jug of milk and the extra pot of hot water until Bunny waved him off.

'That chap there,' Margaret said, waiting for Bunny to take a discreet look at a well-dressed man in his forties, red hair barely tamed by what looked like a whole tin of Brylcreem, breakfasting with a better-dressed woman in her sixties. 'He's a fraud. His suit's too clean. Looks like he bought it last week. Came down from Manchester or some such place, got a wife back there. Now here he is, taking his tea with the Countess of Gwynedd. She knows he's a sharp – she wasn't born yesterday, so what's going on?'

Margaret paused to let Bunny take a good look at the emerging situation.

'You tell me,' Bunny said.

'She thinks he's going to get her a good price for her necklace,' Margaret said. 'No other reason to wear pearls to breakfast. He'll have a friend somewhere who'll take them and provide a valuation. While the supposed valuation's taking place, they'll swap the necklace with a fake. Give the fakes back to the countess, then disappear. She's too embarrassed to go to the police, and he goes back to Manchester with a few hundred pounds.'

Bunny nodded politely and sipped his tea.

'Not really what we trained you for,' he said.

'I've met about twenty Nazis since I arrived,' she said. 'Would you like me to have a list typed up?'

Bunny pretended to consider it. Margaret watched him. Waited.

He finished his tea. Poured more hot water into the pot. Waited for it to brew.

Margaret pretended to ignore him. Two old friends, watching the world go by.

'How would you feel about going back to Sussex?' he asked, as if the thought had just occurred to him.

'Why would I do that?'

'Why wouldn't you?' Bunny asked. 'You and Cook. He's good for you, you know.'

Margaret felt a flush of colour in her neck, her body betraying her. She hoped Bunny saw it as anger.

'I've done everything you've asked,' she said. 'I'm wasted down there and you know it.'

'I know no such thing,' Bunny said.

'You'd have me playing the farmer's wife,' she said. 'It's like having a racehorse and using it to pull a cart.'

'I'd have you smack in the middle of the invasion zone,' he said. 'Even if Hitler doesn't invade this autumn, we've got no idea what his plans are next spring. And if he doesn't invade, we're going to have to start thinking about a counter-attack. Either way, Sussex is in the thick of it, and I can't think of a better place for someone of your talents.'

'You'd have to make it up to me,' Margaret said.

'No I wouldn't,' Bunny said, with a twinkle in his eye. 'This is exactly what you want. You're just too pig-headed to come out and ask for it. Everything has to be a battle.'

Margaret drank her tea.

'I'll think about it,' she said.

'Well, there is one thing,' Bunny said. Margaret braced herself.

'There are some people who worry about you,' he said. 'You've done too good a job of playing both sides. I take full responsibility of course, but it's something we have to deal with.'

'What do these people want?' Margaret asked.

'I'm not sure there's anything that would convince them, I think it's more a matter of giving it time,' Bunny said.

'They sent you here with a request,' Margaret pressed.

Bunny sipped his tea.

'I'm assuming you had to make certain promises in order to get away,' he said.

Margaret looked at him, impassive.

'There'll be a handler,' he said. 'Someone who'll make contact with you. I'm sure they can't wait to hear what kind of intelligence you're able to gather and pass back. The girls at Bletchley have picked up some chatter – the Germans have got high hopes for you.'

'You should be a novelist,' Margaret said. 'I hear Peter Fleming's making a go of it. You should pick his brains. You'd make a fortune.'

Bunny leant forward. He lowered his voice.

'We need you to give us a name,' he said. 'One of their operatives, undercover in London. They're out there, sending their little signals back. London's leaking information like a sieve. Just give us one of them. A show of faith.'

'If any of what you said is true, then me giving up one of their people would be a giveaway that I wasn't to be trusted. Not that I'm an expert in this kind of thing, but I'd assume you'd like to have me as one of their trusted sources. Feeding them just the right kind of wrong information.'

Bunny beamed.

'I knew you were the right choice, that first time we met,' he said. 'There's ice in those veins. Just like your father.'

Margaret didn't respond. If Bunny thought comparing her to her father was any kind of compliment, he was mistaken.

'You give us a name,' Bunny said. 'We'll watch them and nab them for something unconnected. Parking ticket. Library book overdue, that kind of thing.'

'What if I say no?' she asked. 'What if I think this is a silly idea, concocted by silly men who think this whole thing's a game?'

Bunny winced. He put his hand on hers. His grip was surprisingly firm.

'Don't mistake this for a request,' he said. 'If the wrong people get the wrong idea about you, your days of champagne and trifle will be over like a shot, and you'll be somewhere with bars on the doors for the rest of the war.'

Margaret took her hand back. She was glad she'd drawn him out. Better for everyone.

'I'll see what I can do,' she said.

'Marvellous!' Bunny was instantly the loveable uncle. 'And make sure you enjoy yourself! Go to the theatre. Do whatever it is young people do when they're in town.'

34

The police station in Bow Street was strategically situated. The perfect location to keep an eye on the hustle of Covent Garden market, a hundred yards away. The blue lantern was dark, thanks to the blackout. That, along with the darkened windows, gave the place an air of being out of business. Not the impression Cook would have wanted to give, in a city on the edge of going feral.

'I'll wait here,' Gracie said.

Inside, there was a crowd of people gathered around the front desk. A young desk sergeant sounded like he'd been repeating the same information for a while.

'If you need help finding shelter,' the desk sergeant shouted, 'the nearest rest centre's Soho baths on Wigmore Street.'

Nobody moved.

'If you're looking for someone gone missing, your first stop should be hospitals. Start with St George's if your loved one was last seen in this vicinity.'

A young mother, baby in arms, pushed her way back out through the crowd, past Cook, to the exit.

'If you're looking for the home repair allowance, talk to your local ARP warden.'

'They told me to come 'ere,' a red-faced labourer replied. 'Said your lot was giving out five quid for materials.'

'I've got no money here,' the desk sergeant said, firmly. There was a collective moan from much of the crowd, who had evidently been sent here on the same understanding as the labourer.

'Who's in charge?' the labourer asked. It was a reasonable question, Cook thought.

'In charge of what?' the sergeant replied.

The labourer looked around as if it was obvious.

'The whole lot,' he said. 'They've known the bombers was coming for years. All the blackout stuff, all the gas masks. Someone must be in charge.'

The desk sergeant, trying to avoid the discussion, caught Cook's eye.

'I'm here for Ruby Reynolds's things,' Cook said. 'She was on the bus last week, near Piccadilly Circus.'

The sergeant nodded and shouted back, through a door.

'Ruby Reynolds,' he shouted. 'Next of kin for the belongings.'

'What about my savings?' an elderly woman at the front of the crowd asked, quietly.

'What happened to your savings?' the desk sergeant asked, not unkindly.

'We went down the shelter like we was told, and when I came back someone had been in the house and taken my savings,' she said. '*And* the piece of fish I'd left out for me tea.'

The sergeant brightened. Finally, his body language seemed to say, a customer he could help. He reached below the desk and produced a sheaf of paper. Small print, densely packed. Spaces for information. He handed it to the woman and pushed a pencil across the counter.

'Fill this in,' he said.

'Will I get it back?' she asked.

'What, the fish?' someone in the crowd joked. He was rewarded with a ripple of laughter.

'Tell us the amount,' the sergeant said, 'and if we nick someone with that exact amount on him, we'll let you know.'

'Unlikely,' opined the self-appointed commentator. 'He'll be right off down the pub.'

A constable appeared at a connecting door behind the counter with a brown paper bag. He handed it to the desk sergeant, who checked the label, then passed it to Cook.

Cook looked inside the bag. The remains of a black coat. 'That's it?' he asked.

The sergeant shrugged. He looked tired. Soot in the creases around his eyes. He cradled his right hand on the counter. A nasty burn on the palm.

'Were you there?' Cook asked.

'Not that one,' the sergeant said. 'He's kept us busy though.'

'Check it's hers,' the sergeant said, as Cook turned to leave.

Cook took the coat out of the bag and shook it out. It was a thin raincoat, scuffed at the elbows, hand stitching around the collar. A name written on the label: Ruby Reynolds.

'I heard there wasn't a body,' Cook said.

The sergeant looked him in the eye. Shook his head.

'There wasn't anything,' he said. 'Surprised that survived. Must have been caught on the blast. They said it was across the street.'

Outside, Gracie took the bag.

'That it?' she asked, pulling out the coat.

'Direct hit,' Cook said.

Gracie was quiet.

'She wouldn't have felt anything,' Cook said. 'In the army, they used to say a bomb like that, the blast wave moves faster than your brainwaves. You're gone before you know it.'

Gracie thought about this for a second.

'You reckon that's right?' she asked. 'Or just something they say.'

'I reckon it's right,' he said.

Gracie fingered the coat. She brought it to her face and breathed it in.

'I'll get it taken in for Frankie,' she said. 'He'll need a coat for the winter.'

A siren wailed into life. Within seconds it was joined by more. Cook looked east, towards the docks. Dots in the sky already growing larger.

'I wanted Ruby to go with him,' Gracie said. 'Get her away from all this.'

'You didn't know the bombs would come,' Cook said.

'Not just the bombs,' Gracie said. She looked around. 'All of it.'

35

Cook made the decision to stay the night. Safer to take shelter than try to get across town, and no guarantee the trains would be running.

The public shelter was still standing. Cook still didn't like the look of it. It was leaning, for a start. The top of the wall was a foot further back than the bottom. And above it all, the concrete slab roof looked like it was waiting to fall.

'This isn't safe,' Cook said.

Nobody inside seemed moved by Cook's assessment. Forty pairs of eyes blinked at him in the darkness.

'When this thing comes down, anyone's left inside they'll be flat as a pancake.'

A bomb landed nearby, and the blast pushed Cook into the shelter, then sucked him out again as air rushed back to fill the void created by the explosion. He braced his arms against the door of the shelter, as the roof slab made a sickening, grinding sound. In the gloom, there was suddenly a crack of light where there shouldn't be.

'One more like that and we won't have to have this debate any more,' Cook said. 'Let's go.'

Still no response.

Gracie peered in. 'Come on! You heard the man! Shift your arses out of there!'

There was grumbling, but people started moving.

'Quick smart!' Gracie shouted.

It was the whistling sound that broke the deadlock. A bomb with their names on it. Falling straight towards them, getting louder by the second. Suddenly, everyone was up and moving.

Cook stepped inside, his hand on the rough concrete roof, willing it to stay put while forty people shuffled out. It didn't feel right to be outside, safe, while others were in danger. Something he'd learnt from his old CO, always make sure you're the first on the battlefield, and the last to leave.

'Move your arse!' someone shouted.

'I've forgotten me blanket!' from outside. Someone half-way out, trying to push their way back in.

'I'll bring the blanket,' Gracie's voice rang out. 'You get clear of the doorway, let the rest of us out.'

After a few seconds that felt like hours, the crowd began moving again, while the screaming bomb got louder and louder. A direct hit, surely, Cook thought.

There was a loud splash as the bomb went into the water. A muffled explosion, and the ground moved. Dust rained down from the concrete slab, and pinpricks of light suddenly emerged from the brick wall.

Another explosion nearby rocked the shelter as Cook stepped out. Unearthly screams pierced the night. A sound of pure terror and agony, louder than if a hundred people had been suddenly hit.

'Stables,' Gracie said.

Cook waited for the last stragglers, while the horses screamed. Cook thought it was the worst sound he'd ever heard.

36

'Nobody's coming in,' the guard said. He held a shotgun at his waist, levelled at the crowd. He was scared, and he was right to be.

'You move yourself out the way right now Jim Brown,' a woman shouted. 'There's a bloody war on, didn't nobody tell you?'

Jim Brown, with the unenviable task of holding off what looked like it could turn into a mob, took a step backwards. Cook didn't like the way his finger curled around the trigger.

He was guarding a stairwell. A small brick building behind a formidable iron fence. Beneath the stairwell, according to Gracie, was one of the safest spaces on the island – a cavernous wine cellar, built to hold thousands and thousands of barrels of the finest wine. Some of the richest people in the country maintained stocks there. Hence the security. Strictly no admittance, the signs said. Jim Brown was there to enforce that rule and he looked like he meant business.

'How many shells have you got loaded?' Cook asked.

Jim Brown looked at him, and Cook saw panic in his eyes.

'I'll make it easy for you,' Cook said. 'The answers range from a minimum of none to a maximum of two. Let's say it's two, all right?'

The young man nodded.

'So what's your plan? You fire both shells, kill a few people. What do you think's going to happen after that?'

'I'll tell you what's going to happen after that—' someone shouted from the crowd.

Cook held up his hand.

'Nothing's going to happen because Jim isn't going to fire his gun,' Cook said. 'Jim's a good lad. He's got to do his duty, but he can't go around shooting half the island. So he's got a problem, and we've all got a problem.'

'If I let you in, you have to promise not to nick anything, and you have to keep it a secret,' Jim said.

There was a general muttering. Jim raised the gun into the air, away from the crowd. As soon as the gun was out of the equation, the crowd surged, past Jim, through an iron gate, down a spiral staircase cut into the stone wharf.

'I'm telling the boss this was your idea,' Jim said to Gracie.

'Tell him what you want,' Gracie replied. 'At least we'll be alive to tell the tale.'

Cook stepped aside as the crowd flowed in. He wasn't ready to shelter yet. He was thinking about the building they'd left. A death trap. If he didn't do something about it, others would find it and take shelter.

Gracie waited with him, watching back along the route they'd just taken.

'What's wrong?' he asked.

'Haven't seen Frankie,' she said.

37

Annie sat on a pile of bricks and watched her island burn. Born and raised here. Seventy-five years. Only left once, when they'd taken her and the other children for a day in the country. She crossed the bridges once a week to go up to the market, but she never felt right until she was back on the island. The docks had provided work for Father, never quite enough to pay the rent and put food on the table but somehow they'd survived. Children had come and gone. Many of them had died within weeks. Just visiting, the other women used to say, little mites too weak to draw breath. But it had been a good life, all things considered.

Father sat next to her, shaking. He was cold. Since their house had been blown up they'd been living rough. The young folks from the ARP had told her to go to the rest shelter, given her two coupons for tea. When she'd asked where she was meant to spend the night, they'd looked at each other and smiled, as if she were an imbecile. Stay put, they'd said. Someone will know what to do.

Not their fault. They were doing their best. Helped her get Father safe. Made sure the gas was turned off. Then they'd rabbited. Plenty more piles of rubble to dig through. Coupons to give out.

She'd done the best she could, found a bombed-out warehouse with a bit of roof left. But it wasn't enough. No place for a fire. No place to keep anything that the rats wouldn't get at.

She clutched her gas mask. The papers had been very clear. Any day now, the Germans would gas the city. Millions would die. Annie wasn't scared of dying. She didn't think there'd be an afterlife. She wasn't stupid. Not like she'd be in heaven, reunited with her babies. It would be like going to sleep. Sometimes she thought she could do with a long sleep.

But she couldn't die yet, not while Father needed her. He'd been fading for a long time. If she was honest, he'd been gone for a long time. The man who'd hefted crates twice his size, who'd taken her up West to the pictures the day he'd proposed to her, who'd carried her over the threshold of their tenement flat, promising to look after her as long as they lived. If he was still in there, she hadn't seen him for a couple of years. Now he was like one of her babies, needing feeding, and changing. She'd hated him at first, for leaving her. But she couldn't hate him any more. Not his fault, she told herself, when it got so bad she had to step outside and grit her teeth and give out a silent scream.

A cloud of yellow smoke rose out of a distant warehouse. She'd seen the bomb come down. Watched the flames consume the roof of the building. An odd sight, seeing a wall come down that had been her horizon for half her life. Now the smoke was drifting towards her. She could already taste it, making her cough.

Gas.

'Got your mask, Father?' she asked. She knew he wouldn't respond, but it was her habit. Give him the chance to redeem himself. Show he'd been hiding in there all along.

He coughed, and looked at her. His eyes were streaming, the gas already swirling around him.

She put the mask on his face but he pushed it away.

'Don't want it,' he said.

She held it to his face, struggling with the leather straps. He pushed again, hurting her. Still a trace of his old strength.

'I said no!' he yelled, giving her the back of his hand as anger flashed across his face. All traces of her husband gone.

She recoiled, and he saw then what he'd done. His face screwed up, the tears arriving in an instant.

She tried once more, raising the mask to his face, but he shook his head.

She held him to her chest. Comforting him. Hating herself for the anger she'd felt as he'd pushed her away. Not his fault.

Not his fault.

The gas was getting in her chest.

She threw the mask away, the glass eyepieces smashing as it landed on the rubble.

'Come here,' she said, holding him. Doing her best to comfort him.

She felt him pull away, but she held tight. Kept his face pushed into her chest. Taking care of him this one last time, before they both went to sleep.

He struggled harder, but the fight was gone out of him. She was coughing now, the gas working its way into her lungs. She hoped it wouldn't hurt too much.

Eventually, he stopped struggling, and she held him more, the way she'd held her babies when their short visits had come to an end. She closed her eyes and let the tears come.

38

Cook heard an incongruous sound, over the wail of the siren, and the rumble of the bombers. Children laughing. Cheering. Even more incongruous, but unmistakable, he heard the crack of a well-struck cricket ball, followed by the smash of broken glass.

Sounded like they were in the park. Near the shelter.

A lone bomber rumbled in from the south. Must have come up over Kent or Sussex. Cook kept a wary eye on it.

A Hurricane chased the bomber, lining up behind it, the rattle of its eight guns, a second or less for each burst. The Hurricanes only carried enough ammunition for fifteen seconds of firing, a pilot had told him.

The Hurricane must have got his target, because Cook saw a plume of smoke erupt from the bomber. But still it kept on its way. Crossing the river, over the island. The bomb bay doors opened. Bombs tumbled out, looking weightless.

The first one hit a street away. Cook ducked into a doorway as the second one crashed through a roof. A window blew out, spraying glass across the street.

The next two bombs landed with two crumps – one, then another. Cook felt the shockwaves through the narrow streets.

Then he felt another shockwave. Something else, hitting the ground. Something heavy. A crump, without a bomb.

Cook ran. He knew what it was – something heavy enough to shake the ground like a bomb, something just as deadly.

The roof of the shelter. Several tons of concrete, left unattached to the badly pointed brick walls.

The park was a maelstrom of dust and flying leaves. The air was gritty, getting in his eyes. Cook squinted against the sharp dust, kept his mouth closed and held his hand over his nose.

The shelter wasn't there. Or rather, in place of the shelter was a pile of rubble. The brick walls had gone outward, and the concrete slab was flat on the ground, a crack across it, but otherwise in one piece.

Cook hurried towards it.

A flash of colour caught his eye. A distinctive shade. Red leather, sewn around a cork ball, hand stitched and polished. Stamped in gold with the maker's mark. A Dukes cricket ball.

Cook picked up the ball. It was warm and sticky, the way it would be if a boy had carried it around all night.

Cook picked up three bricks mortared together. As he grabbed them, they came apart, the mortar that should have been joining them little more than sand.

Cook grabbed a chunk of concrete and threw it behind him, the adrenaline giving him extra strength. If he could find where the doorway had been, there was a chance. He threw brick after brick behind him, clearing a space, all the while looking for any sign . . .

'Frankie?' Cook shouted. He didn't expect an answer, and he didn't get one.

Then he saw it. A hand. A child's hand. Ivory pale, covered with a fine layer of dust.

39

Cook saw the chain of events perfectly well. Money had been paid for a job to be done. Some of that money had been spent. Some hadn't. A natural occurrence, like water flowing from high ground to low, some of it making it to the sea, some of it soaking away en route. In Cook's experience, government money soaked away easiest. Less oversight. No business manager keeping an eye on the bottom line. Just a civil servant whose duties were discharged once the cheque had been written and paperwork collected.

Cook let the anger flow through his body. Better that than the alternative. The voice that Cook knew would have to be reckoned with at some point.

This is why they sent him away to the country.

The bombers had been inevitable. Everyone had agreed. The knockout blow against London. The biggest city in the world. The fattest target. Impossible to defend.

The bomber will always get through.

Half a million children sent to the countryside. With all the mistakes and terrors that had come with it, still a good idea. The right thing to do.

You were trusted with his care. And all you had to do was keep him in Uckfield, keep him safe on the farm.

That voice would be reckoned with. For the rest of his life, most likely. But right now, in the moment, Cook had another conversation running through his head. A conversation with the man who'd murdered an innocent young lad, through greed or stupidity. Cook didn't care about the details. His anger was righteous. It demanded satisfaction. Justice, even.

When he reached the drawbridge at the eastern end of the island, an old man in a black coat and a black flat cap emerged from the hut at the side of the bridge.

'Get that down,' Cook said.

'Not sure it'll work,' the man said.

'Get it working,' Cook said, the tone of his voice not inviting further discussion. The bridge keeper looked at him as if he was thinking of arguing, but thought better of it.

The bridge lowered with a grinding sound that suggested it was performing its last trick, something in the mechanism destroying itself as gravity brought the roadway back down to its resting position.

The ARP girl in the church basement had given up Beaumont's address without complaint. A quiet road, once-grand houses in various states of genteel decay. Beaumont's house was at the end, set back from the road, a private location.

A low brick wall along the pavement had small dark holes in the top layer of bricks, every six inches, from where the iron railings had been removed for the war effort. Cook drank with a man in his local who worked in a scrapyard. Told him all the metal that had been donated was useless.

Behind the wall, a thick hedge, and behind the hedge, Cook could make out the rooftops of a substantial house.

The railings may have gone, but an imposing wrought-iron gate remained. A stone footpath led from the gate to the front door. Lawns led around both sides.

Cook pulled a black metal handle that hung by the front door, and a bell rang inside the house. He waited. He'd walked from the destroyed shelter in righteous anger. But now he found himself standing on a doorstep, cap in hand, like a travelling salesman.

No one came to the door. No sound of footsteps on the stairs, no scrape of chair on floor. Cook stepped back and looked up at the house. Nothing. He stepped forward and pulled the handle again, let the bell ring, then repeated the action. Insistent. He stepped back and looked up at the window.

The ARP girl had said Beaumont had been fleeing the city at night. Epping Forest, she'd said. A coward's way out.

Cook gave the doorbell another tug. The bell jangled deep in the house.

It was a fool's errand, but he wasn't ready to admit it. He walked to the side of the house.

The back garden was long. A hundred yards at least. A hundred and fifty perhaps. A line of poplar trees at the far end. Lawn mown with perfect diagonal stripes, flanked by carefully sculpted flower-beds. Halfway down, a fenced vegetable patch. Then, beyond the sprouts and cabbage, right at the back, an arch of corrugated metal.

The grass was covered with a fine powder, looked like snow. Cook left footprints in his wake. Nobody had walked this way since the dust had settled.

He threaded his way through the vegetable patch – neatly laid beds edged with stones. There was a tool shed to the right with a standpipe next to it. Easier than trekking up to the house every time you wanted to water your seedlings. A nice set-up. If you were going to live in the city, this would be how to do it, assuming you had the money.

The shelter was half buried. From ground level it stuck up about three feet. Grass had been laid up to the sides, leaving a small section of exposed metal. Steps down, cut into the soil and laid with flagstones. Two flowerpots, one either side of the door. A decent effort to cheer the place up.

Cook hammered on the door. Imagined Beaumont cowering inside, waiting for the invasion.

'Beaumont?' he shouted.

Cook waited. Knocked again. Louder. A waste of time – the shelter couldn't have been much more than six feet wide and ten feet long. If someone was knocking on the door and you were inside, you'd know about it, no matter how soft or loud they were.

Cook tried the handle.

It was locked. A brass padlock.

Why would you lock a shelter? If he was going to build a bomb shelter, he'd want a clear path to it, no zigzagging through a vegetable garden, and he'd want the door unlocked all day every day, knowing that the time you forgot the key would be the time you really needed it.

Cook looked back at the house. No movement. He tried to summon the anger that had brought him here, but it was gone. He felt sick, the departing adrenaline leaving his stomach in knots.

With the anger gone, the guilt returned.

This was your fault. You had a job to do – protect the boy – and you failed.

40

Annie stood on the end of the wooden dock, the one that stuck out into the Thames. She'd loved coming here as a girl, some of her best memories, when they'd dangle their feet in the water, the boys showing off, jumping in. The sun on her face, the smell of the river, the sheer busyness of it all – ships coming from the far ends of the earth, and the island the centre of it all.

She'd seen an elephant once, walking off a clipper all the way from India, bound for the new zoological gardens. All the things she'd seen.

Her apron pockets were heavy. She'd gathered bits of rubble on her way. An easy enough task – the island was one big pile of rubble. The canyons she'd grown up in, between warehouse and tenement, now mostly gone.

The tide was halfway out. It would be a big drop down to the water. She hadn't thought about that. She'd never liked heights. Still, once it was done, she could sleep.

There was a boy down on the foreshore. He was looking out at the water.

She'd wait until he left.

But he didn't leave. He took a step forward, into the water, never mind his shoes and socks. He took another step, the water swirling up over his short trousers.

'What you doing?' she shouted. But the boy didn't hear her. He took another step into the water.

Annie hurried back along the dock, then down the slippery stone stairs, green with algae. She waded out into the river and grabbed the boy. It was the lad from the pub. Gracie's boy.

'Going for a swim?' she asked him. He looked up at her as if he'd just woken up.

'Let's get you home,' she said.

41

Cook stood back as a chair flew out of the pub, through the open door. It landed with a crash on the street.

Cook took stock. He didn't have any weapons. If a looter was inside, he'd have to rely on surprise.

He took three quick steps to the door and strode in.

Another chair flew towards him, and Cook caught it with a smack of wood on palm.

'Sorry, love, didn't see you come in.' It was Gracie. Standing in the midst of the dust-covered interior, she looked ready for battle. A fresh turban covering her hair and a fresh apron. Thick rubber gloves on her hands.

'Would have been easier if there'd been a direct hit,' Gracie said, gesturing at the destruction.

The inside of the pub was coated with the same dust that covered every inch of the island.

'They took the clock,' she said, gesturing at the mantelpiece, where an empty space gaped like a missing tooth. Cook thought of the kind of person who'd steal from his neighbour at their darkest hour. If that was the city, Hitler was welcome to it.

'Was it valuable?' Cook asked.

'It was ugly,' she said.

She looked past Cook, as if expecting someone else.

'Where's Frankie?' she asked.

A creak at the door heralded another arrival. It was Beaumont.

'Where've you been?' Cook asked.

Beaumont ignored Cook. He was juggling something in his hand. A red cricket ball.

'Where'd he leave that?' Gracie asked.

Beaumont didn't reply.

'You'd better sit down, Gracie,' he said.

She stared at him.

'Don't you dare,' she said.

Beaumont nodded, turned to Cook. 'You shouldn't have brought him back,' he said.

He was two steps away. Two steps that Cook took with no conscious thought. Two steps for every part of his civilised mind to shut down, to give way to rage.

'Cook!' Gracie shouted.

Her hand was on his arm, and he dimly registered her voice, shouting his name. When the fog cleared, Beaumont was in front of him. His face was purple. Cook's hand was wrapped around his throat, simultaneously pushing him against the wall and choking him.

Your fault, he'd said.

'How much did you skim off?' Cook asked.

'Let him go!' Gracie pleaded.

'How many other shelters like that?' Cook pressed.

The door swung open again.

'Found this one on the beach.'

Frankie stepped out from behind Annie's skirts, ran past everyone and disappeared upstairs.

Cook let go of Beaumont. As soon as he was free, the ARP man ran, the door slamming behind him.

'You all right, Annie?' Gracie asked. The old woman was shaking. Gracie pulled a chair over and sat her down.

'Where's Bertie?' she asked.

'He's gone,' Annie said.

'Where you been stopping?' Gracie asked. It had been a week since her and Cook had pulled Annie and the old man out of the ruins of their house. She'd assumed they'd been taken care of.

'Here and there,' Annie said. 'Got a cup of tea?'

Gracie nodded to Dottie. 'Get the kettle on,' she said, then knelt down in front of Annie.

'You'll stop here,' Gracie said. 'No arguments.'

'I thought it was gas,' Annie said. 'They said there was going to be gas.'

42

Frankie had his sister's coat wrapped around his hand, wielding it like a whip on nettles that had the temerity to lean over the footpath.

The train back from London had been slow, shunting back and forth, a long detour through the suburbs – the main line out of action due to a UXB.

'That's not a very respectful thing to do with your sister's coat,' Cook said.

Frankie ignored him, swiped the coat at a particularly thick patch. Cook held his tongue. Shouldn't have said anything in the first place.

'You should ask your mum to come and visit sometime,' Cook said.

Frankie shrugged.

'She wouldn't like it,' he said.

Cook briefed his mum and Uncle Nob while Frankie was washing his hands before tea. The service. The police station. The journey back.

When Frankie came down for tea, nobody quite knew what to say.

'That's a nice coat,' Mum said.

Frankie shrugged.

'That'll see you through the winter,' Mum said. She'd started it, she was going to see it through. She was good like that. Besides, the boy was less likely to be openly hostile to her.

'Let's see it on you,' she said.

'Let the boy eat his tea,' Cook said.

She fanned out the coat, holding it for Frankie to step into.

'Go on,' she said.

Frankie stood up. Shrugged the coat on.

'Must have cost a few bob,' Mum said. 'You look like Humphrey Bogart.'

Frankie put his hands in the pockets, drew the coat round him like some kind of spy in a flick. He sat down, keeping the coat on.

'Shall we put the news on?' she asked. 'See if there's any more bombing?'

As soon as the words were out of her mouth, she froze, aware of what she'd said. But Frankie didn't seem to notice. He was fidgeting, his hands deep in the pockets.

'What've you got?' Mum asked.

'There's a hole in the pocket,' Frankie said, looking up while his fingers explored the lining of the coat. Hunting for treasure.

He pulled something out with a flourish and put it on the table. It was a white piece of card.

'What's that?' Mum asked.

Frankie turned it over.

'Nothing,' he said, then dug into the coat again, hopeful for more treasure.

Cook picked up the card. It had a safety pin stuck on the back. On the front it had the logo for the Lyons tea room. And a handwritten name. Cook frowned. He'd been expecting it to be Ruby's name, but it wasn't.

'Who's Irene?' Mum asked, taking the card and peering at it through her thick glasses.

Frankie shrugged.

The name rang a bell, Cook thought, and then he remembered. The couple in the Lyons, the night he and Gracie had gone to collect Ruby. They'd been there on a similar errand to Cook. Looking for someone. Looking for their daughter.

Cook thought of the two pegs in the staff room. One with a coat. One without. Two pegs, next to each other. Two missing girls. Only one of them working at the Lyons the day the bus got bombed.

'Think I'll go up to London tomorrow,' he said.

'Again?' Mum asked. Even Frankie seemed curious.

'Probably nothing,' Cook said.

Cook drank his tea, and ate his bread and jam. He thought of a young woman, leaving work after a long day. Rushing to catch the bus. Reaching for a coat. Two coats, the same design. Grabbing one, hurrying down the road. Dropping her name tag into the pocket, jumping onto a bus.

Probably nothing, he'd said. But he didn't believe that. He didn't believe that at all.

43

The siren was earlier than usual, although Ruby worried that her sense of time was slipping. It was difficult to keep track without windows.

She sat on the bed, a thin wool blanket pulled taut over the sheets. Hospital corners. Important to keep to a certain standard. At home, she'd have left her bed unmade, but here it seemed like a defiance. Show him he hasn't got through to you. Hasn't beaten you.

Not yet.

Ruby's assessment of her current situation was bleak. She was going to die in this Anderson shelter. And the stupid thing was, she'd known. She'd known the second she'd seen him near the Empire. She'd always known, right from the start.

He was coming. He'd put in concrete steps leading down to the entrance and his slippers scraped on them, bits of grit he'd picked up from the gravel path, leading down from the house.

Of course, he must be thinking the same thing. He couldn't let her go – he'd hang for this – and he couldn't keep her here for the rest of her life. So he, too, must have been thinking about when, and how, he'd end it. End her. So it was going to be him or her, one of these days. She'd see her moment, and she'd take it.

Not today. He was still like a kid in a candy store, as the Americans in the pictures would say, his eyes roving over her body, then his hands. The cat that got the cream, her mum would've said. Ruby had never much listened to her mum when she was a child, but now she was a grown-up, out in the world, she found her mum's aphorisms coming to her, and more often than not they were bang on.

He carried the tea tray into the shelter and locked the door behind him. A brass key in a brass padlock. Put the key on a hook by the door. A little game, letting her see the means of her escape, torturing her with the hope.

'Lot of bombers tonight,' he said, as he set down the tea tray on an upturned apple crate. 'Heinkels, mostly.' The tray had two cups, one for her and one for him, and a sandwich, for her. He had his own meal up at the house. Got to keep her strength up, he liked to say. She thought back to the first night, when he'd slapped her. How it had shocked her. It seemed like a lifetime ago. A lifetime of being locked in an underground bunker with a man who raped you every evening, straight after tea.

She ate slowly. Not much to write home about. Two thin slices of brown bread and an even thinner slice of cheese. No butter. Not even margarine. There was a slight bloom of mould on the corner of the bread this evening, but she ate it, slowly, trying not to gag.

'I saw your mum,' he said. Ruby tried not to show interest.

'It was your funeral,' he continued. 'Good turnout.'

She finished the bread, sipped the tea, washing it down. The tea was too sweet for her, but she drank it anyway.

'The boy was there. They let him come up. Time off for good behaviour,' he joked.

Ruby looked up, before she remembered not to.

'Hardly recognised him, turning into a country lad. New clothes and everything. There was a brute of a farmer brought him up, must be the one who's looking after him.'

He stood up and took his jacket off. Hung it on the hook by the door.

'No,' Ruby said.

'What's that?'

'Leave me alone,' she said.

He smiled. 'I didn't know you felt like that.'

His fist felt like a brick against the side of her head. The pain was bad, but the shock was worse. The outrage.

He had his hands on her. No pretence now. No false civility.

She couldn't breathe. She was face down on the camp bed, suffocating. She tried to arch back, make some room, but his hand was holding her head. He was sitting on her back, both of her arms pulled back. He was like a dead weight.

'Going to have to teach you a lesson,' he said. He let go of her head and she gasped for air. He ripped her knickers off and forced his fingers inside her. One of his nails was broken. She could feel it.

From a long way away, she heard the siren, muffled by the earth that had been piled up around the shelter. She felt the ground shake. A bomb, perhaps. She willed the bomber towards her, praying for a direct hit. Something to kill her before *he* did.

44

The number nine bus wound its way through Piccadilly Circus. Eros was boarded up. A symbolic gesture, Cook thought. If it got hit by a bomb, the boards nailed around it were unlikely to do much to protect it. The statue itself was bronze, designed to last for centuries. They could level the whole city, and the statue would still be there. But Cook understood the power of symbols. If he was Churchill he'd be doing the same thing – box up the statues. Get some balloons up in the air, even though the bombers flew thousands of feet higher. Make it illegal to light a cigarette on a dark street on a dark night, even though the pinprick glow would be invisible to that bomber, up in the heavens. All of it theatre – give the people something to do. Make them feel part of it. The blitz spirit, the papers were calling it.

He'd started the journey at the Lyons tea room. Noted the time. Strode out into the street with the pace of someone leaving work and hurrying home. The manager had given him the address – anything to get rid of him. A bus had come along at the right moment, just as Cook had approached the stop, and he'd jumped on, grabbing the metal post on the rear platform as the bus pulled away into traffic.

He got off at Tower Hill, remembering the boat trip with Gracie, past the Tower of London.

He bought an A to Z at a newsagent's, careful not to take too long, didn't want to mess up his experiment. It was a book of maps, the whole of London, printed on rough wartime paper. As he strode up Tooley Street, he checked the requisite page. He was crossing a threshold – the first bus had been on one of the earlier pages devoted to central London – the maps a larger scale, easier to read. Now, he had to turn to page fifty-two, a smaller scale, the print smaller. Cook had to squint to find his destination. Avondale Street. Whitechapel. Another bus.

The house was on a quiet residential street, running parallel to a row of small shops. A nice neighbourhood, all things considered. Tiny front gardens, six foot square. White doorsteps, immaculate, whitened with chalk every morning. Lace curtains at every window, bought on tick most likely, paid off weekly when the tallyman made his visit. A place where appearances were important, where it was better to be in debt for your whole life than to have the wrong kind of curtains.

Cook checked his wristwatch. Forty-two minutes, door to door. If Ruby's former colleague had got on the bus that had been bombed, that would have meant she was expected home just after twenty to six.

He knocked at the door, feeling the weight of his mission hanging on his shoulders. He was the bearer of bad news. The destroyer of hope.

The mother opened the door a crack, peering out at him. She was wearing the same red pinafore. She recognised him, and her face lit up. There it was, he thought. Hope.

Cook sat in the parlour, opened up in his honour.

She poured tea. A white teapot with images of Victoria's coronation. Gold leaf around the spout. Mother and father, waiting for news of their only daughter.

'Have you heard anything?' she asked, unable to hold back.

'I wanted to ask you the same thing,' Cook said. 'Whether you'd heard from Irene.' Empty words, unnecessary. Every tock of the mournful clock on the mantelpiece screamed it.

Cook had come to make sure of two things. First, the journey. They'd told the manager what time she was expected home. Cook had assumed she'd have left at five. But assumption was the mother of all errors, as his old CO Blakeney used to say. So he'd had to check.

Secondly, Irene's continued absence. If he'd been right about her staying out for a drink with a young man, she'd have been home by now. But she wasn't home. Cook could feel it in every corner of the house. The absence of joy. The emptiness of a house where a man and a woman had lived hard lives, done what they could to give their daughter a chance.

'What time would Irene get home, after work?' Cook asked. He knew the answer, but he wanted it said out loud, one more time.

'Twenty to six,' she said.

'Couple of minutes later,' her husband said, 'unless there wasn't any traffic.'

Cook sipped his tea.

'I think your daughter took the wrong coat,' he said. 'It was on the hook next to hers. It was the same type of coat. Same colour. Same design. She was in a hurry. Wanted to get home. She left at her usual time, ran along the road, and got on the number nine bus.'

45

Cook left the couple with their grief. They had questions he didn't have the answers to. Half pretending not to believe him. Pretending to themselves.

There was a smell of autumn in the air, a smell Cook associated with the fields and the woods. Even here, in the heart of the city, brown leaves crunched underfoot. There was a chill in the air, and a softness in the light. Soon it would be Michaelmas, the start of the farming year. Normally Cook would be making plans with Bill Taylor, his farm manager, laying out this year's plan. Contracts with the working men to be renewed, hiring to be done.

This year was different. Some things remained – the fields still had to be ploughed, crops sown, plans made. But most of the labourers were gone – the first of them had volunteered, then conscription had taken many more. Farming was a reserved occupation, meaning many of the men could have got out of their service, but most wanted to do their bit, as Cook had done when it was his time.

There was a bus waiting at the stop. Perhaps the driver recognised Cook from the outbound journey. Cook shook his head when the conductor waved at him, and the bus pulled away. Cook needed to think. He thought best when he was sitting in a pub, sipping a pint. Second to that, when he was walking. He'd be in a pub soon enough, so for now he walked. He had the book of maps in his pocket, but he didn't need it. A column of black smoke rose up from the docks, and as the sky darkened in the early evening, Cook could see an orange glow from a fresh crop of fires.

Cook walked, and thought. About a smoldering bus, reduced to fragments of steel. About a girl, running from the tea shop, eager to get home, to her mother and father. About another girl, one who'd escaped the tenements and the canyon-like alleys of the island, who'd got a job up West, but who'd stopped showing up. A girl who'd lied to her family, setting off each morning dressed in her waitress uniform.

None of it was Cook's business. He'd tell Gracie his suspicions – that Ruby hadn't been on the bus, that she was therefore most likely alive. The rest was between a mother and her daughter. Cook had plenty to do. A farming year to prepare for. Men to hire. Crops to get in the ground.

He crossed onto the island at the far end, over the drawbridge that had been lowered at his insistence when he'd thought the ARP man had been responsible for Frankie's death. The bridge keeper was stripped to his waist, arms deep into the engine that drove the mechanism. He glared as Cook passed.

After the bridge, the road bent sharply to the right, adhering to a curve in the river on the far side of the warehouses. There was a pub squeezed in on the corner. The World's End, a faded sign proclaimed, a picture of a sailing clipper, all sails billowing, sailing into a red sun.

A hundred yards along the high street, another interruption to the otherwise monolithic wall of warehouses. A pawnbroker, brass balls entirely blackened by smoke. The window had been cleared of grime – the shopkeeper anxious to let everyone know he was still in business. Probably busier than usual, with half the population of the island needing cash to replace things lost in the bombing.

The window was filled with everything an islander might own – a composite picture of a life amongst the warehouses. Sunday-best suits alongside workers' overalls. Baling hooks. Frying pans of varying sizes and condition. A candelabra, no doubt a space left on a mantelpiece in an unused front parlour. And a clock. An ugly clock, carved mahogany, a souvenir from the Black Forest. A clock that had been taken from Gracie's pub.

The bell tinkled as Cook opened the door. The space inside the pawnbroker's shop was as cluttered as the window display. Shelves on every wall were crammed with bric-a-brac, none of it of any value to anyone other than its owner. This wasn't the sort of place a stranger would step in and make a purchase – the items were simply held as security against a high-interest loan made to their owner, designed to be repaid the next payday.

There was a man behind the counter.

'I'm here for the clock,' Cook said.

The man had a ledger opened in front of him, as large as a newspaper. He ran his finger down the most recent entries until he found what he was looking for.

'Half a crown,' he said.

Cook had enough money in his pocket. Paying the man would be the shortest way to resolve the situation. He could return the clock to Gracie, tell her his news about Ruby. The all-round conquering hero. She'd give him another free pint.

But paying for something that had been stolen didn't sit right with Cook. Especially something stolen during an enemy raid. Looting was punishable by death for a reason. It was the thin end of the wedge. Let people think the rules of law no longer applied and you'd already lost, invasion or no invasion.

'I'm not here to pay for it,' Cook said. 'I'm here to take it back. It was stolen.'

The man behind the counter stared at him. A man used to every kind of approach, from begging to threatening. He'd have a weapon close to hand, and he'd be willing to use it.

Cook turned his back on the man and reached into the window display. He picked up the clock. It was even uglier than he'd remembered. A small brass plaque on the back:

With Regards
9 September 1928

'I could let you take it,' the man behind the counter said, 'only I've got no guarantee you represent the rightful owner. I could be abetting a further theft. Compounding the error, you might say.'

Cook turned back to the man, and found himself facing the barrel of a tommygun. A fine weapon, imported from America. An automatic rifle, capable of firing twenty rounds per second from its drum-shaped magazine. Designed, too late, for use in the trenches. First shipments from the Thompson factory went out on Armistice Day, which meant a glut on the market at a time when governments and armies had no need for more weapons. Subsequently, a favourite of organised crime organisations, who needed something easy to use and reliable, and American police forces alike, if the Hollywood prop masters were getting their details right. All things considered, the 'trench sweeper' was overkill for an encounter with a single unarmed assailant in a small, enclosed space.

Cook felt a grudging respect for his adversary. The gun was a clear statement of intent. No messing around with threats of broken legs, or telephone calls to the powers that be. It presumably worked wonders on belligerent dock-workers who wanted to argue about the price offered for a pair of boots or a baling hook.

But Cook wasn't a dock worker. There'd been a time when he would have been intimidated by a man standing four feet away from him, pointing a three-foot-long gun in his direction. But that very natural reaction had been anticipated by the men who'd trained Cook, who'd drilled the correct response into him until it was instinct, and who'd sent him out to use his training in the mountains above the Khyber Pass.

'You're going to murder a man over half a crown?' Cook asked, taking a step towards the counter, bringing the gun into arm's reach.

The man didn't answer. He allowed his eyes to flick past Cook, over his shoulder, to the door. Some kind of cavalry on its way. An alarm triggered.

'You're going to get yourself killed over half a crown?' the man asked.

'You got it set to full automatic?' Cook asked. 'Make sure you hold it down as you fire, otherwise it'll creep up. You'll fire two rounds into me and a hundred and ninety-eight over my head, into whoever's across the road, having their tea.'

'You'll be just as dead,' the man said.

'I'm thinking about your neighbours,' Cook said. 'My life's not worth much. More than half a crown, but that's for me to worry about. But I can't let you fire that gun into the street.'

The doorbell tinkled behind Cook. The cavalry had arrived. Must have been close by. A tactical error on their part. The shop was small and narrow. Whoever came through the door would find themselves standing behind Cook – a straight line between the gun, Cook, and the newcomer. If the gun fired, everyone in front of it would be dead.

Cook knew of two ways to deal with a long gun pointed at you from a frontal position. Left hand or right hand. Sweep the barrel away, then twist to the side. Grab the arm holding the gun, then put an elbow into your assailant's face, aiming for the chin but an eye or a cheekbone worked just as well. The only decision was which hand to use.

Cook's left arm was already spoken for, cradling the ugly clock. Which cut down on decision-making time. His right hand was the only one available, so it was the one he used. He stepped towards the gun, batting the barrel away to his left, while pivoting his body in the same direction. Once he was side-on to the counter, he jabbed the man's chin with his right elbow – jarring for Cook but much worse for the recipient. Like being hit with a metal bar, definite damage to the teeth and jaw. Concussion likely. Momentary knock-out almost always the result.

The tommygun clattered to the counter as the man went down. Cook reached forward and guided the man's head away from the edge of the counter. He'd already inflicted life-altering damage. Anything worse seemed out of proportion. Cook had been taught time and again that combat wasn't cricket, but he'd seen enough killing. Seen enough, and done enough.

The bell above the door jingled again, a second visitor, just as Cook was guiding the man into a crumpled heap on the floor behind the counter.

'What's this?' Cook recognised the voice. It was Reynolds. Frankie's father.

Cook turned to face him. Reynolds was flanked by another man. Two jingles from the doorbell – two men. Everything accounted for. Both Reynolds and his man had their right hands in their pockets, ready to produce weapons should the need arise.

Cook raised the clock, held in the crook of his left arm.

'This got misplaced,' Cook said. 'Thought I'd return it.'

'That was here?' Frankie's father asked.

'*Was* being the operative word,' Cook said.

Frankie's father looked angry. He whispered something to his man, who shook his head. Cook recognised the situation. When your boss is angry, and he asks if you've got anything to do with it, denial is always the best response.

'A mistake, no doubt,' Frankie's father said. He pulled a sheaf of banknotes from his pocket, peeled off a pound.

'Let me,' he said, proffering the money.

'No need,' Cook replied. 'We resolved the dispute without money changing hands.'

Frankie's father stepped forward and looked over the counter. He looked back at Cook.

'Looks like you've saved me the trouble,' he said. 'Lee should have known better than to take that. Everyone on the island knows it's Gracie's.'

Frankie's father made a gesture to his man, and he left hurriedly, the doorbell clanging behind him.

'How's she doing? About Ruby?' Frankie's father asked. 'Must be taking it hard.'

Cook followed Reynolds across the road, back to the pub he'd passed. The World's End. It was crowded, the air thick with smoke. Reynolds had a corner table. Two beers, half drunk, claimed the places, and when Reynolds sat down he sipped from one of the glasses. Cook wondered how he'd been alerted about the trouble across the road. A boy, running in with the news? A telegraph? And what did that make the man sitting across from him? Was Reynolds some kind of enforcer? The way he'd taken control in the pawnshop, Cook thought that unlikely. More likely an owner.

A barmaid brought Cook a pint, and Reynolds nodded to the remaining chair. Cook sat, checking his surroundings. He didn't like being forced to sit with his back to the crowd.

'I don't think Ruby was on that bus,' Cook said.

'Say more.'

So Cook told his story, about the coat, and the pegs in the Lyons – one with a coat and one without. The parents looking for their daughter.

'So you don't know she's alive?'

'I don't know anything,' Cook replied. 'Everyone thought she was on that bus, so they thought she was dead. If she wasn't on the bus, but she hadn't come home, would you think she was dead?'

Cook watched as Reynolds thought it through. He didn't want to let himself hope, if it was going to be taken away again.

'We should tell Gracie,' he said.

'Didn't expect to see that again,' Gracie said, as Cook hefted the clock onto the mantelpiece. She didn't sound particularly enthusiastic about it.

'Is it true, about Ruby?' the barmaid asked, as she put three glasses and a bottle of whisky on the table.

'I think so,' Cook said.

Reynolds opened the whisky and poured three glasses.

'Has she stopped out like this before?' Reynolds asked.

Gracie was polishing the bar, a thick wax that smelt of linseed, reminded Cook of cricket bats and summer.

'Not since that lad went off to France.'

'What if he came back?' Reynolds suggested.

Gracie shook her head.

'Didn't get off the beach at Dunkirk.'

'You sure?'

'Since when did anyone on this island do anything that wasn't known by every other bleeding person.'

Gracie took a glass. Reynolds had poured generously, but she didn't pause – downed it and put the glass back in front of him, wanting more.

'Thank you,' she said to Cook. 'I can't tell you.' She shook her head. 'I'm going to give her hell when she walks in though.'

'What's this?' – a new voice. Cook turned to see Beaumont, the ARP man.

'You got the clock back?' he noted, with an approving nod towards the mantelpiece.

'Cook found it,' Gracie said. 'He's got some good news. Reckons Ruby wasn't on that bus. So she's all right.'

Beaumont took a stool at the bar, nodded to the barmaid who brought him a glass. Cook didn't like him being there. Sitting above them, slightly apart. It could have been deference, not wanting to join the family unit, but it felt to Cook like he preferred to keep his distance.

'You got proof of that?' Beaumont asked.

'I'd say the best proof'll be when Ruby walks in through that door,' Gracie said.

'Quite,' Beaumont said. 'But what if she doesn't?'

'The odds suggest she's alive,' Cook said. 'Several million people in the city. A few hundred killed every night, do you reckon?'

'Few thousand,' Beaumont retorted. 'I can't share the exact details.'

'Call it three thousand,' Cook said. 'A quiet day on the Western Front. Three thousand out of three million, that's a ninety-nine point nine per cent chance of surviving each night of bombing. So the starting assumption should be that she's alive.'

Beaumont didn't answer. One of those men who didn't like to be proved wrong.

'You said Ruby had a boyfriend?' Cook asked.

'Arthur,' Gracie replied. 'Went to France last year, soon as war broke out.'

'She ever hear from him?' he asked.

Gracie shook her head.

'Not that she told me.' She picked up a chamois, buffing the wax off the bar.

'What if he came back?' Cook said.

It didn't feel right, watching someone else work.

'You got another one of those?' Cook asked.

Gracie reached beneath the bar and threw Cook a chamois – older, scrappier than the one she was using.

Cook took the other end of the bar. The soft leather grabbed on the wax, took a lot of work to push it. Gracie made it look easy.

'Wouldn't be the first time a young soldier comes home from war and heads straight for his young lady,' Cook said. He had to choose his words carefully. Usually in this situation he'd been chasing the soldier, and everyone concerned had been very clear on the soldier's motives. Talking with the young woman's mother was a different matter, he realised.

'Maybe they got married,' he said. 'You could check the registry office.'

'Arthur's a good lad,' she said. 'But Ruby wasn't interested. Not really. He'll take over his dad's milk round and that'll be it. Ruby wanted more than that.'

'She'll show up,' Beaumont said. 'You know what young people are like. Bet she stopped out with a friend.'

'You got a phone down your place?' Gracie asked. 'We'll call you, when she turns up.'

'No,' Cook said, thinking about returning home without an answer – the job only half done. It didn't feel right.

'Here's our number,' Gracie said, writing on a slip of paper. 'Just in case.'

Cook took the paper, put it in his wallet. He could borrow Doc's phone, call once a day until Ruby was found safe and well. He realised he hadn't told Frankie the good news yet.

48

The dairy was less than a hundred yards from the pub. An iron gate from the high street, leading into a small courtyard, high brick walls on both sides. Cook smelt the cows, knew he was in the right place. The stalls were at the back of the courtyard, incongruous. Four cows, a stall each, along one side. Milking pails and bottles stacked on the other side, around an enamel sink. A small operation, still using the old ways. It wouldn't have lasted in Sussex. Dairy farms had been going mechanical for the last decade. Herd sizes had been increasing. Not a bad way to make a living, until the War Ag had stopped most of it in the drive to turn England arable and reduce dependence on grain from the colonies.

A young boy was washing returned bottles, doing a good job of it from what Cook could see.

'Are you Arthur?' Cook asked. He knew from experience that families of soldiers got defensive if you asked them where their son was. Better to come at it somewhat obliquely.

'He's not here,' the lad said. 'Off fighting Jerry.'

'You his brother?'

'Who's asking?'

Cook liked the lad, admired his spirit.

'I'm from the Ministry for War,' Cook said. 'There's been a mistake with his paperwork. He hasn't been getting enough pay. If we can sort it out your mum and dad can get what he's owed, and I won't have to tell my boss about the mistake.'

'Dad!' the boy shouted, without moving from the sink.

The boy's dad took a minute to appear. Looked like he'd been asleep. Out before dawn with the milk deliveries. One of the things that had held Cook back from the business himself, driving a cart around town before anyone was up. More of a delivery boy than a farmer, he'd told himself, even as those farmers who went into the business made good money, delivery boys or not.

'This bloke's looking for Arthur,' the boy said. 'Trying it on with a line about extra pay. Thinks I was born yesterday.'

The man looked at Cook for a long second. He nodded to the door he'd come from.

'You'd better come in,' he said. 'I'll get a brew on.'

Cook sipped the tea. It was strong and sweet. The man had stirred three sugars into each mug without asking, his hand shaking – knocking the teaspoon against the mug. Not many places in the country you'd get enough sugar for that. Didn't hurt having Tate's refinery just down the river.

The radio was on. Lord Haw-Haw, broadcasting from occupied Europe with news of how fantastic it was all going to be once the Führer was running the show in England.

'Who'd you say you are again?' the man asked. He held his own tea with both hands. He'd only half filled his mug, but even so it spilled over the top as his hands shook.

Cook told him about Frankie being evacuated, which he knew about, nodding along. He knew about Ruby.

'The number nine bus, I heard,' he said, shaking his head. 'Fucking Germans. Least in our day it was all over there.'

'Where were you?' Cook asked.

'Wherever they told us to be. Most of the lads round here signed up. Wanted to get away, do our bit.'

He put his mug down and put one hand over the other, stilling the involuntary movement.

'Doesn't ever leave you, does it?'

'The war to end all wars,' Cook said.

'I'll tell you what I told everyone else who's asked,' the man said. 'I haven't seen him since he walked down that road with his kit bag, setting off for Portsmouth.'

He reached behind to a cluttered bureau and pulled out a piece of paper.

'This was the only letter I got,' he said. 'From . . . Amiens.' He made a face as he read the place name, like Englishmen do when they know they should be pronouncing a French word in the French way but don't want to show off their ignorance by getting it wrong. 'Five months ago. Before Dunkirk.'

'You haven't heard from him since?' Cook asked.

'No,' the man said, his face set like a mask. Quite possibly the least convincing lie Cook had ever been privy to.

'Did he have plans to settle down with Ruby?' Cook asked. 'After all this?'

The man warmed up.

'Course he did,' he said. 'Lovely girl, always helping out. She was out of Arty's league. She could have her pick.' He shrugged. 'Arty's a good lad though. Hard worker. Solid. Sensible. He'd take care of her.'

He got up and riffled through a stack of old papers. When he found what he was looking for, he brought it back to the table. A yellowing copy of a local paper.

'Look at them,' he said. There was a picture of a young couple, milking pails at their feet, smiling up at the camera. Even through the low-quality picture, no more than a collection of dots on poor-quality newsprint, Cook got a sense of Ruby. She was grinning, a lock of errant hair across her face, happy in the moment.

'Can I borrow this?' Cook asked. 'Might want to show it to some people.'

'Bring it back?'

'Of course.' Cook folded the page and put it in his wallet, along with the telephone number from Gracie.

'You reckon he might have made it home and gone to pick her up?' Cook asked. 'Train up to Gretna Green, quick marriage. Hypothetically speaking.'

The man looked at Cook, trying to decide. He shook his head.

'You seem like a good bloke, looking out for Ruby. And I'd tell you if there was anything I knew about her. But I haven't seen Arty since he shipped out. God's honest.'

The boy poked his head in the door.

'Better be going if we're going to get a place,' he said.

The man nodded. Explained to Cook.

'Dickins and Jones on Oxford Street,' he said. 'They've got the best shelter, but you've got to be there before six to get in line.'

49

Cook followed the man and the lad, both of them carrying bundles of bedding. He kept back as far as he could. The lad seemed sharp.

The lad's father had done a good job of acting distraught about his son, but he knew he wasn't left behind. Haw-Haw's radio programme had been on, running through a list of names – British soldiers who'd apparently turned up in prisoner of war camps. Impossible to know if it was true or not, but if you were missing someone and you were desperate for news, you'd listen, and you'd listen very carefully.

But the father hadn't been listening, which meant one thing. The father knew the lad wasn't sitting in a POW camp, or working as slave labour in a German factory.

The boyfriend wouldn't have come home if he'd gone AWOL. Too much risk someone would be sniffing about. So he'd likely be lying low, somewhere in the city. Somewhere his dad and brother could meet him, bring him supplies.

The man and the boy walked up to the high road and waited at the bus stop. A problem for Cook. He couldn't very well join them. There were only a couple of others waiting. It would be impossible for Cook to run up to the bus even at the last minute without alerting them.

The answer presented itself as two buses came along at once. Both number nine, both headed for Mortlake. Cook hung back, around the corner, watching as the man and the lad got on the first bus. He watched them up the stairs, and stayed hidden until the bus pulled away. Then he hurried to the stop as the second bus pulled in. It didn't stop entirely – no need as the first bus had picked up all the passengers, but Cook raised his hand as he jogged to the stop. The bus slowed enough for Cook to jump on.

'Where to?' the conductor asked.

Another problem. The fare depended on the length of the journey, but Cook didn't know where he'd be getting off, even if he was able to keep an eye on the bus in front.

'How far to the end?' Cook asked.

'Seven pence,' the conductor said, pulling out a ticket overlaid with a seven. He used a device to punch a hole on the start point and the end – Mortlake – and gave it to Cook.

The roads were quiet heading into town, and the two buses travelled in convoy, close enough that Cook worried he'd be seen if either the man or the lad decided to look out of the back of their bus. He kept to the lower floor, towards the back, where it would be hardest for them to see him. At each stop, he kept tabs on who was getting off, and was fairly sure he'd have seen them.

The number nine would go to Piccadilly Circus, then along Piccadilly, past the Lyons, then on to points west – Knightsbridge, Kensington and so on. The return version of the route the bombed bus was taking. If the man and the lad were going to Oxford Street, they'd get off at Piccadilly Circus, then either walk up Regent Street, or switch to another bus. If it was Cook, he'd have walked. The stopping and starting of the buses was annoying, and he got the feeling he'd get further if he was on foot, travelling at his own pace.

Everything was going smoothly until the bus drivers made it more tricky. Coming along Fleet Street, the bus in front pulled over. Cook's bus didn't slow. No one on board had 'pulled the cord to alert the driver that they wished to alight, and after the first bus scooped up the people waiting, there was no other reason to stop. Cook's bus sailed past the first one, and he turned his head away from the window, in case the man or the lad were looking out.

Now he was in front, in plain sight if the man or the lad were looking out the front of their bus. If he wanted to get off, he'd make the situation worse – walking to the platform on the back of the bus, standing there in full view. He got up and moved further to the front, into the shadows.

Piccadilly Circus was up next, according to the map posted above the windows. The man and the lad would be getting off, heading up Regent Street. Their bus was directly behind his.

He stayed on his own bus until the next stop, halfway along Piccadilly. When the following bus went by he tried to see inside. If the man and boy were still on it, he couldn't see them. Most likely they'd got off at the last stop, to walk up Regent Street.

Cook realised he was across the road from where Irene's bus had caught it. Easy enough to identify, going by the blown-out windows in all the surrounding buildings, boarded up now. The road had been repaired with a fresh topcoat of asphalt – the crater gone. Cook's shoes crunched on the pavement, an odd sound, like he was walking on sandpaper. The paving slabs glittered with glass dust.

Further down the road, Cook saw the sign for the Lyons tea room. What *had* Ruby been doing, if she hadn't been working there? If he could answer that, he'd be a lot closer to working out where she'd gone.

50

The Lyons was as busy as ever. Cook had to wait ten minutes to get in. Everyone in the queue had a story to tell about the bombings, comparing notes about where they'd been on what night, what they'd heard, what they'd seen. There was a clear hierarchy. Seeing a bomb yourself was essential – if you'd seen one you had a story worth listening to. If you'd felt the blast, even better. Hearing one was second best. From the thirty-odd people in the queue, it seemed everyone in London had personally seen a bomb, and most had felt one. Stories were told with a giddiness, a sense of exhilaration at having faced the worst – the thing that every Londoner had been dreading for more than a year.

The same surly waitress seated Cook, evidently disappointed that she had to waste a table for two on one person. Cook did his best to make up for it with his order. Tea, kidney pie and mash, apple pie and rice pudding. Last time he'd been here, he'd had to dash off and leave his food. He felt like he was owed a generous meal.

The waitress was one of four on duty. None of them spent more than ten seconds with a customer, Cook noticed. They moved quickly and efficiently between the tables, shuttling stainless-steel teapots and refills of hot water. It was an impressive display of logistics.

'You're Ruby's friend,' Cook's waitress said as she dropped off his tea things – teapot, extra pot of boiling water, small jug of milk, a tiny saucer holding two sugar cubes.

'Good memory,' Cook said.

The waitress flicked her eyes around, checking to see who was watching.

'Drop your cup on the floor,' she said, under her breath.

Cook understood. She needed cover. Couldn't stand chatting with the customers without an excuse. He reached across the table for the teapot and knocked his teacup to the floor. It smashed on the hard lino.

'I'm sorry,' Cook said, bending down to pick up the pieces.

The waitress took a cloth from her pocket and knelt down, putting her head alongside his.

'You didn't hear this from me,' she said. 'But you might want to check out the bar at the Empire. From what I hear Ruby's been doing a roaring trade.'

51

The farmer had been looking into things. Acting like some kind of detective. He said he'd be going back to his farm, but he didn't seem like the kind of man who liked giving up. He had a quiet confidence. Brought back memories of an old sergeant major, used to stand at the top of the trench, pushing the men into no-man's-land, then running alongside them as if the bullets wouldn't ever hit him.

He filled the car from the ARP supply tank. He'd have to adjust the books, average out the usage, but that would be easy. He'd come to the realisation at an early age that he was smarter than most people. He thought quicker, and he saw things they didn't see. Another thing he'd realised, most people play by the rules, and don't think outside those lines. You could get a girl into your car, for instance, and they'd see you being a gent. Giving a girl a lift. Maybe picking up your daughter. Maybe you were sent to collect her.

East India Dock Road was covered with ash, like it had snowed. Glass crunched under the tyres, and he kept his fingers crossed he wouldn't get a puncture. Be just his luck.

The great East India Dock on his right was a floating graveyard – burnt hulls listing against each other. The stink of it was incredible. Burnt rubber and burnt meat.

Ships from all ends of the empire, all that way just to end up twisted metal.

The seafront at Southend was blustery. A cold wind whipped off the North Sea, bringing the smell of salt and seaweed with it. Even a bit of snow in the air, he fancied, carried all the way from Norway.

The beach was covered with barbed wire, but a few patches of sand were accessible. A few brave souls had set up windbreaks, temporary walls of bright striped fabric, held up by sticks hammered into the ground like oversized cricket stumps.

The seafront offered dozens of shops to choose from. All the same – little stands of postcards, fishing nets, buckets and spades. The season was coming to an end and the shopkeepers watched him eagerly each time he slowed. He picked the only shop with other customers in it – a well-dressed couple with two children. A day's holiday by the sea.

He bought a couple of postcards. One of the pier, one of the front – looked like it had been taken from an aeroplane. They sold him a couple of stamps to go with the postcards and he bought a pencil as well. Thinking ahead. No point in having a postcard and a stamp if you find you've got nothing to write with when the time comes.

He was fully aware that one day the game would be up. He'd make a mistake, get seen by the wrong person, take the wrong girl. But he didn't feel like it was coming any time soon.

He should sell up, make the move to the country a full-time thing. He liked the thought of that. Those farming girls, all fresh rosy cheeks and plump round bodies, always enough food in the house. The problem with these East

End girls – skin and bone most of them. Halfway to starving to death. Not much to catch a man's eye, to get his blood stirring.

Ruby was different. She always had been. Always been able to catch his eye, get him thinking about things he shouldn't be thinking. Still, what was a man supposed to do.

She had it coming, when you thought about it like that.

52

The Empire was a hundred yards along Piccadilly, back towards the bus stop, towards Piccadilly Circus.

Cook stood across the street, under the awning of an art dealer on the corner of Albemarle Street. A tramp had made his home in a closed-off doorway. Cook felt awkward invading the man's territory, so he strolled ten feet up the side street, away from the main road. Two telephone boxes huddled together as if for protection. Cook stood next to one of them with the air of a man contemplating a phone call. He was being foolish, he realised. Nobody cared which street he stood in or what buildings he looked at. One of the few advantages of the city. You could stand where you wanted, and watch what you wanted, and nobody gave a monkey's.

Cook had an excellent vantage point to watch the front of the hotel. It wasn't that he was expecting Ruby to come out, exactly, but there was always the chance.

What *was* he doing? A young woman had gone out to work and never come home. Hardly the first time, and unlikely the last. When Cook had delivered the news that Ruby hadn't been on the bus, even her own mum had seemed content that the girl would show up.

So why was he lurking in a side street like a criminal, rather than striding up to the door of the hotel?

It wasn't a simple matter, Cook told himself, watching people coming and going from the hotel. For a start, there was a doorman controlling the only obvious access point. Dressed in a fine suit in the colours of the hotel's livery, complete with top hat, the doorman seemed to possess a preternatural understanding of who he should open the door for. As Cook watched, people walked to and fro, past the hotel entrance. Most of them had no business with the place. Some did, however. Cook watched as an elderly gentleman, dressed in a shabby suit, walked towards the door from the direction of the park. Without any communication from the gentleman to the doorman, the latter stepped out of the way of the door, held it open, and guided the gentleman into the hotel.

Cook wasn't an idiot. He knew what was going on. The Empire was a place for a certain type of person. The gentleman was an example of that type. Cook was not. He had been many things, a soldier, a farmer. But he was not the kind of man who walked into a place like the Empire as if he belonged there. He didn't even know, he realised as he stood there, whether he'd be let in. Cook was startled to realise he was feeling something akin to fear. Fear of transgressing one of England's most inviolate rules. A rule that never once needed to be spelt out, but one that was implicitly understood by every one of the King's subjects, in every country of the empire – a quarter of the world's population, from the slums of London's East End to the tea plantations in India.

Know your place.

53

Cook walked back along Piccadilly, as far as Hyde Park Corner. He stood at the edge of the pavement and raised his hand. A black cab passed by on the opposite side of the road, waited for a gap, then swung around in a tight U-turn, pulling up next to Cook.

Cook climbed into the cab, fumbled in his pocket for some coins. He leant forward to the driver.

'Up the road. The Empire. Pull up like we're in a hurry.'

'The meter won't even get running,' the driver complained.

'Half a crown if you put some effort into it,' Cook said.

The driver's eyes lit up.

'Hold on,' he said.

The driver took his charge seriously. He sped along Piccadilly like he was on the speedway at Brands Hatch and completed another tight U-turn, much to the complaint of every other car on the road, earning him a cacophony of horns. He slammed on the brakes outside the Empire, wrong-footing the doorman, who had to hurry from the front door to offer assistance.

Cook climbed out, ignoring the doorman who had managed to get to the car in time to grab the door for the last couple of inches of its arc. He crossed the pavement to the steps of the hotel, in the shade of the famous awning. It was only a few yards but it felt like a mile. A second doorman clicked his heels and held the heavy brass door open. Cook felt a bead of sweat trickle down his back. It was a warm afternoon, but not warm enough to account for the sweat.

Know your place.

Cook breathed deeply, calming himself, as he strolled through the foyer. Going over the top had felt only marginally more dangerous.

The foyer was as grand a place as Cook had ever been. It was cooler than the hot street. Something to do with the marble floor and high ceilings, he assumed. Like stepping into a cathedral – a space designed to intimidate.

There was a desk in front of him, manned by an elderly man in a uniform that looked vaguely naval. It matched the doorman. In fact, the men looked similar. Cousins, perhaps.

Cook slowed, but only enough to get his bearings. He was under scrutiny, and the slightest hesitation would reveal him. From hotels he'd been in before, he presumed the bar would be located close to the main entrance. The clientele might be different here, but they'd still like a drink.

An immaculately uniformed maître d' intercepted him at the double doors that opened out into the bar.

'I'm late for a meeting with General Blakeney,' Cook snapped, walking past the maître d'. 'Is he here yet?'

'No sir,' the maître d' replied, stepping in front of Cook, an expert manoeuvre that spoke of years of guiding and blocking people who enjoyed going through life feeling like they were neither guided nor blocked.

'I'll need a table, somewhere quiet,' Cook said, scanning the busy room. There was a bar in the centre. A U-shape, dominating the space. The rest of the large room was given over to small tables, white tablecloths and silver candlesticks. About as far as you could get from Cook's local pub while still being recognisable as a place a man might get a drink. On either side of the grand room, huge chandeliers hung from the mirrored ceiling. Not something you'd want to be underneath in a raid. The whole space was a deathtrap. Perhaps it added to the sense of joie de vivre – if the patrons at the bar and seated at the tables were concerned about the prospect of sitting underneath several hundred pounds of glass, they were hiding it well.

'Of course, sir,' the maître d' replied. 'When the general gets here, who will he be looking for?'

Cook tapped his nose. 'Careless talk,' he said.

'Quite right,' the maître d' said, with a discreet bow of his head.

The maître d' led him to a table in the corner. To Cook's satisfaction it was away from the windows.

Cook ordered from a young waiter. It didn't take him long to return, gliding around the tables with a pint of beer on a silver tray.

'Will you be staying with us, sir?' the waiter asked.

'No,' Cook said.

The waiter pulled a slip of paper from his inside pocket, placed it on the table in a small leather folio.

'Whenever you're ready, sir.'

The waiter left, and Cook took a sip of his beer. He'd look at the bill once he'd enjoyed the drink. Cook knew his limitations, knew that when he saw the price it would make him angry, take away the enjoyment of the thing. Better to delay that reaction. For now, he was in, and he had a beer in his hand.

He could, of course, walk up to the front desk or the bar and asked about Ruby Reynolds, a girl from the docks who'd left her job as a waitress at the Lyons to come and try her luck at the hotel bar, but he had the strong impression that line of enquiry wouldn't get him very far.

Better to do his own reconnaissance. See what he could find out.

That was the thing with reconnaissance, in his experience. Until you did it, you didn't know what you might learn. But one thing was certain, if you didn't do it, you wouldn't learn anything.

54

He looked pleased with himself, Ruby thought. He'd been clever. Wanted to tell her about it. Like a little boy coming home from school.

He pulled a paper bag from his pocket and the smell made her stomach growl. A bacon roll. Still warm by the smell of it.

'Brought you a present,' he said. He put the bag on the floor by the door, took his coat off and hung it on the hook.

'Got a job for you,' he said, showing her the two post-cards. Beach scenes from Southend.

The postcards were a good sign. Good for her. It meant he was worried. It meant somebody out there was looking for her, and he'd had to come up with a way to deflect them. But if she wrote them, telling everyone she was all right, she'd be putting the power right back in his hands.

'Why would I do that?'

He held up the bag. The smell of the food made her stomach growl.

He took the bacon roll out of the bag. Looked at it. Took a bite.

She tried to resist. She wasn't going to die of starvation. Not for a while. But try telling her stomach that.

He took another bite. Her food, disappearing in front of her.

Where there's life, there's hope, her mum used to say. That was one of hers. Keep your strength up. That was another one.

He raised the roll to take a third bite.

'All right,' she said. He smirked, and she hated herself for giving him the satisfaction. But her mum was right. Where there's life, and all that.

He made her write the postcards first. The pencil was hard, one of those ones that scratched the paper without leaving much of its lead behind.

He dictated the first one:

Don't worry about me. I'm all right. Met a chap. Might be away for a bit.

Tell Frankie I'm sorry I missed his birthday.

She edited his wording slightly, hoping he wouldn't notice. He'd said 'Tell Frankie' but she slipped in the word 'our'. Her mum would know something was wrong. Ruby never referred to Frankie that way. It was a nuance her mum would see in an instant. She finished up with a doodle. A whimsical touch but something that perhaps someone would recognise. She tensed as she handed the postcard back, wondering if he'd be angry at her embellishments, but he took it without looking.

She ate the roll, trying to make every mouthful last, in the end licking the waxed paper clean of grease. Maybe Mum would notice her message, maybe she wouldn't. But she liked the feeling of having done something. Maybe it was the food, making her feel like things were looking up. A little voice told her she'd given in to him, but she told that voice to shut up. Told it she'd made a good choice. Live to fight another day.

He raped her after she'd eaten. Took his clothes off, got into bed with her. Almost apologetic. Didn't look her in the eye.

Ruby watched him getting dressed, afterwards. A domestic enough scene – a man pulling on his vest. Buttoning his collar.

He was in a hurry to escape, his shame rising off him like the stink of his sweat.

'It won't always be like this,' he said. 'After the war we can go somewhere, be together properly, like husband and wife. A farm in Wales. You can grow vegetables and I'll tend the sheep.'

He pulled on his trousers, pulling the braces over his shoulders. He reached for his pullover, folded neatly over the back of the chair.

Ruby had a chance, she realised. A slim chance, but better than nothing. She saw it coming, quite clearly. He'd put both arms in the sleeves. Put the pullover over his head, arms up, like a little boy being dressed by his mother.

He put his arms in the holes, noticed her watching him. He stopped.

'What?' he asked.

'Nothing,' Ruby said.

He thought.

'You're right,' he said. 'Too warm for this. I'll leave it for you in case it gets cold tonight. Don't want you catching a chill.'

It was too much to bear. Lying there, her stomach in knots. All for nothing. Ruby launched herself from the bed and flew at him with a shriek.

He was fast. Faster than his physique suggested. He stepped out of her way and grabbed her, slamming her into the metal wall. She felt something go in her shoulder – a sharp pain like she'd been stuck with a red-hot needle.

'There there,' he said, calmly, albeit through gritted teeth.

She kneed him between his legs. Didn't hold back. He gasped and for a second he loosened his grip on her arm. She pulled away and made a retreat to the far corner of the shelter, trying to ignore the shooting pain from her shoulder, preparing herself for whatever was coming.

But he didn't advance. He stepped backwards.

He pulled the door open.

'Come on,' he said.

She eyed him, warily. What kind of trick was he playing on her?

He grabbed her by the wrist, pulling her outside.

They were in the middle of nowhere. There was a house in the distance but nothing else. Just trees, and fields, and sky. A flock of birds took off from a distant tree.

'Look,' he said, nodding at a rough patch of ground down the side of the shelter.

'What?' she asked.

'What do you see?'

Ruby saw stinging nettles, some brambles – a few blackberries. Then she went cold, realising what he was pointing at. The earth had been disturbed in places. It had sunk, and nettles grew instead of grass. The shapes were recognisable. Six feet long. Two feet wide. Spaced a few feet apart.

Graves.

She counted them. Five in total, varying ages judging by the weeds. The oldest was entirely overgrown. The most recent was still earth.

'In case you're wondering how good you've got it, and how bad it can get if you don't play along,' he said. He kept his voice calm, like he was telling her about the weather.

'And it wouldn't just be you,' he said. 'There's others you care about. The boy, for a start.'

Ruby couldn't bring herself to look at him. She nodded.

'I love you,' he said. 'I know you didn't mean to hurt me, and I forgive you. We're meant to be together, Ruby, you and I. You've always known that, same as I have.'

After he left, locking the door behind him, she listened as his boots crunched on the gravel path, the sound fading to nothingness. Then it was just her and the crows.

Ruby was scared. More scared than she'd ever been in her life. She'd been managing to tell herself it was all some kind of misunderstanding. A momentary thing that would end. But now she'd seen the graves, she knew exactly how it would end.

55

It took Cook an hour of reconnaissance and two pints to fully establish what was going on.

The U-shaped bar was busy on all sides – thirty or forty drinkers at any one time, standing or sitting at high stools. Young women back from a day of shopping. Elderly matrons, watching out for the honour of said young women. A solid number of military men – the RAF represented most strongly, but Cook saw both army and navy dress uniforms. Most of the military personnel were his age or older, careerists who presumably worked nearby at the Admiralty, the War Office, or Adastral House. Others were young men, in town to let off steam.

Some of the young women didn't fit in. Cook counted six in total, but he focused on two of them, on his side of the horseshoe bar. Both were dressed in an approximation of a young heiress, but even a casual observer could tell they hadn't got it right. Their make-up was too loud. The colours of their clothes ever so slightly brighter than the bright young things surrounding them. Cook wasn't a fashion critic – he couldn't think of an item of clothing he owned that wasn't some variant of brown – but he knew enough to notice things that didn't fit. As he looked around the crowded bar, filled with soldiers, civil servants, and the great and the good from across Europe, the girls stood out. Presumably by design. Like a colourful window display.

Cook watched a young couple standing at the bar. A pilot officer and one of the young women, leaning in, a cigarette in her mouth, so the pilot officer could light it for her.

'Drinking alone?' a woman's voice disturbed Cook's reconnaissance. Without asking for a reply, the woman took the other seat at Cook's table. She had a drink in her hand – a large cut-glass tumbler liberally filled with whisky.

'You don't belong here any more than those girls do,' she said. 'I've been watching you.'

She was American, judging by her accent. It made her sound like a movie star. Cook gave his best impression of a smile, trying to hide his annoyance at being disturbed.

The woman held out her hand. 'Eleanor Goodrich. *New York Herald*. How about you?'

Cook took her hand. They shook.

'Douglas Jardine,' he said. Jardine had captained England's cricket team, brought home the Ashes from Australia. Goodrich seemed unaware, and Cook immediately felt guilty for making her seem foolish in his eyes.

Cook wasn't sure he'd ever met a real journalist, let alone an American one. Eleanor Goodrich was dressed like she was ready for an expedition. White linen shirt, khaki waistcoat, liberally supplied with pockets. He couldn't see below the table and hadn't been watching when she'd sat down, but he guessed she'd be wearing khaki trousers and desert boots.

'Who do you write for?' she asked. 'I'm open to collaborations, but only if I get the lead byline.'

'What do you think the story is?' Cook asked.

'So there *is* a story.' She smiled. She looked across the crowded room to the bar.

'You've been pretty focused on the bar,' she said. 'I thought at first you were eyeing up those working girls, choosing which one you wanted. But you don't need to sit all the way over here to do that. Most of the men who've come in to pick up a girl dive straight in, from what I've seen.'

'How does it work?' Cook asked. 'I presume a man doesn't simply walk up to the girl and ask the going rate?'

Eleanor cocked her head, reassessing the man in front of her.

'You tell the bartender you're interested in some company,' she said. 'He's the go-between. A veneer of decency if you will. You pay him for an expensive drink that never gets delivered, then you go to your room. A few minutes later, one of the girls follows you, and Bob's your uncle. They call them the Hyde Park Harriers, apparently. The girls, that is.'

They both watched. Another airman was in close conversation with the barman. A pound note changed hands.

'What kind of stories do you write?' he asked.

'Human interest,' she said. 'What it's like to live in London. The blackout. The bombs.'

'You won't see much of that in here,' Cook said.

'London's a drain,' the woman said. 'Everyone in Europe ends up getting sucked in, and everyone who ends up in London ends up here.'

'You should be careful,' Cook said. 'I'd imagine if you hang around places like this talking to strangers, people might think you're a spy.'

'I'm not a spy, I'm an American. We're neutral.'

'So how do you go about getting information for your stories?' Cook asked. 'You just walk up to them and start asking questions?'

'In fairness it usually works better than this,' she said.

Cook nodded. 'All right,' he said. 'I'm looking for a girl. Her name's Ruby. She's missing and her family are worried. Thought I'd ask around.'

'I'd say you need to talk to one of the girls at the bar,' Eleanor said, 'instead of skulking back here. One of the things I've learnt in my line of work – if you don't ask questions, you don't get answers.'

'I'll bear that in mind,' Cook said.

'How much money have you got on you?' she asked. 'They won't talk for nothing, they've got jobs to do. You'd be better off hiring one of them, but they're not cheap. Two pounds for half an hour, from what I heard. And you'll need a room here. Do you have one?'

Cook didn't answer. He was beginning to regret telling her what he was doing.

'I'll get you one,' she said, looking at the girls at the bar. 'Which one do you want?'

'No need.'

'Don't be silly,' she said. 'You're paying, by the way, but I'll do the awkward bit.'

She got up, excited by her mission. Cook put his hand on hers, firmer than politeness would allow.

'Really,' Cook said. 'No need.' He put an edge into his voice.

She took her hand back and stared at him, flushing pink.

'Just trying to be helpful,' she said, backing away.

56

Cook gave it another half an hour, making sure the American woman had disappeared. She'd hurried away from his table without looking back, made her way into the lobby. Off to write a story about the dreadful manners of the English, no doubt.

'Another one, sir?' It was the waiter, hovering discreetly over Cook's shoulder.

'Yes,' Cook replied. 'And I have a question.'

'I can do you a drink, sir, but I'm not very good with questions.'

'I'm looking for a girl,' Cook said.

The waiter glanced towards the bar, as if the answer was self-evident.

'A specific girl,' Cook said. 'Name of Ruby.'

'I'm sorry, sir, I don't sell information. Just drinks.'

Cook took his wallet from his pocket. He'd seen this kind of thing in films. Never thought he'd be trying it out.

'How much for the information?'

'Perhaps you might like a bottle of champagne?'

'How much?'

'One pound, six shillings,' the waiter said.

'Fine.'

'I'll have it sent to your table, sir. Would you like an extra glass? In case you find your young woman?'

'Tell me about Ruby,' Cook said.

'Sir?'

'I asked about Ruby and you made me buy the champagne.'

The bartender looked blank.

'I'm sorry, sir. Don't know a Ruby. Is she a resident at the hotel? Perhaps the concierge could take a message to her room?'

Cook fumed. He felt like a country bumpkin who'd been taken in – like a tourist caught by one of the conmen on the street, promising a prize if you could identify which walnut shell hid the pea.

*

The champagne was delivered, and Cook drank it slowly, savouring his annoyance with the American and the waiter. He was getting nowhere.

He should have been in his local, The Cross, having a pint with his friend Doc, his usual drinking partner. Doc had signed up. Wanted to do the right thing. Cook knew the chasm between the chivalry a man thought about when he read the recruiting leaflet, and the reality of war. He thought he'd done a good enough job of letting slip enough details over the many years, and the many pints. But no man believes it until he's seen it.

Cook was mindful of something his old CO, Blakeney, had liked to say. 'There are two types of people in this world, those who wait for something to happen to them, and those who make things happen to other people.' Cook was aware of his many faults, but he also knew his strengths. Making things happen was at the top of the list.

Cook walked towards the couple at the bar. The pilot officer was gesturing with his hand, his heroic exploits shooting down a Jerry, by the look of it.

The prostitute ignored Cook as he approached them, but the pilot watched him coming, moved his body slightly to protect his privacy. Cook ignored the move, and stepped between the two. They stopped talking, embarrassed by Cook's awkwardness.

'Dowding's on his way in,' Cook said. 'Wouldn't want to have a prostitute on your arm the first time you meet him. Assuming you're even allowed to be here.'

The pilot looked at the entrance to the bar with alarm.

'Best to slip out the back,' Cook said. 'Live to fight another day and all that.'

'Thanks,' the pilot said, gulping down what remained of his pint.

'You owe me,' the young woman said to Cook, once they were alone.

'I'm over there,' Cook nodded towards his table. 'Join me for a drink.'

Cook returned to his table. The prostitute was angry with him. It was fifty-fifty what would win out – her anger, or her desire for money.

She left him waiting five minutes, no doubt proving to herself she was in control, then made her way towards him. Respectable men, having an early-evening drink with their respectable wives, pretended not to watch as she passed by.

'Three pounds, up front,' she said, even as she pulled out the chair and took a seat.

'I was told it was two,' Cook replied. He kept his voice low. It didn't seem like the sort of conversation you'd want to have overheard, not that his new companion seemed bothered.

'It's gone up,' she said. 'Or I can call the police. Tell them you propositioned me. Not something your wife would like to find out about.'

'Does that often work?' Cook asked.

She gave him a blank look, took the glass of champagne he offered and sipped it.

'What's your name?' he asked.

'Petal,' she said.

'I just want to talk,' Cook said.

The blank look persisted. Cook reluctantly took his wallet from his inside pocket, handed her a pound note. He saw the folded picture and spread it out on the table.

She took the pound note, folded it and put it in her hand-bag.

'I'm looking for this girl,' he said. 'Her name's Ruby.'

She glanced at the picture and shrugged.

'I don't know anyone called Ruby,' she said.

'What if she was using another name?'

Petal shook her head. Pushed the picture back to him.

'Don't know her,' she said.

'You heard about the girl who got blown up on the bus outside here?'

'Course I did,' Petal said, 'we all did. Stepped out of here, got on a bus, got blown up.'

It was the first time someone had connected Ruby being at the Empire, and being on the bus. It was a gap in his think-ing. A gap that had always been there, just one he'd ignored. Ruby hadn't been the one who'd taken the coat from the Lyons, then got on the bus. He'd proved that, more or less. But that didn't mean Ruby hadn't also got on the bus. Diffi-cult to prove the negative.

'Why are you asking about someone who's got blown up?'

'I don't think she was on the bus,' Cook said.

Petal shrugged.

'Was Ruby working, like you?'

'Who wants to know?' she asked.

'I know her family,' he said. 'But anything you tell me I'll keep secret. Between us.'

'What makes you think she wasn't on that bus?' she asked.

'I think someone else from the Lyons had her coat. Took it by mistake. That coat's the only reason anyone thinks she was on the bus.'

'Maybe she's better off,' Petal said. 'They reckon we're all going to get bombed at this rate. At least she's got it over with. None of this to worry about.' She looked around at the room.

'How long was she working here?' Cook asked.

'Never said she was,' Petal said.

'Look,' Cook said, 'you seem like a nice girl. And I don't want to get you into any trouble. I just thought, maybe if Ruby hadn't been on that bus, but she's still gone missing, maybe it was to do with her line of work. I thought you might know something about what had happened to her, so I could at least tell her family she was all right.'

Petal looked at Cook for a long time in silence. She was clearly trying to work out what to say.

'If,' she said, holding her finger up to stop him interrupting.

'If,' she lowered her voice to a whisper, keeping a wary eye on the bar, 'there was any such person, and that such person was working here in the same line of work as I do . . .'

She thought more.

'If everyone thought she was dead on a bus, maybe she decided to walk away. Start again. If there was any such hypothetical person . . . who *did* get the chance to walk away and start again . . . She'd be advised to stay wherever she's gone.'

'I understand,' Cook said.

'I don't think you do,' Petal said. 'Because it seems to me like you're trying to find her. And if you find her, and bring her back, she might be in a lot more trouble than if she'd never been found. She might wish she really *had* been on that bus. And it'd be your fault. So maybe we should go upstairs, you can get your three quid's worth, and then you can fuck off back to whatever hole you've crawled out of.'

She sat back in her chair, face flushed, eyes nervously scanning the bar.

Cook opened his wallet again. Took out another pound note.

He slid it across the table.

'I'm sorry I can't help you more,' he said. 'But I think I can help Ruby. I'm going to take a room. If at any time this evening you think of anything else I might want to know, anything that might help me reassure Ruby's mum that she's all right, come and tell me.'

57

Cook took a room. He had to wait behind the butler for a large family of refugees that sat, disconsolately, in the corner of the lobby. Each of them clung onto their trunk as if they were in imminent danger of robbery.

When it was his turn, he asked for the cheapest room available, braving the grimaces of the desk clerk – an ancient, wrinkled gentleman in an impeccable uniform, his starched collar so tightly buttoned around his neck, Cook marvelled that he could breathe.

'Just the one night, sir?' the clerk asked, in an accusing tone.

'Found myself in town unexpectedly,' Cook said, feeling like a boy who'd been caught scrumping apples.

'Will you need any help with your luggage, sir?' the clerk pressed.

'No luggage,' Cook admitted.

'I see,' the clerk said. He consulted a ledger, moving slowly down the list of entries, as if he was trying to decide whether to grant Cook the beneficence of a stay under the hallowed roof.

'Early meeting with General Blakeney tomorrow,' Cook added. Over-egging it, perhaps.

The clerk looked shocked, and glanced at a large poster on a cork board.

Loose Lips Sink Ships

'Quite right,' Cook said.

He gave a false name, checking in as Archie Conway. Archie was a sergeant Cook had known in India. He'd died trying to defend a stronghold overlooking the Khyber Pass. Conway had joined up to escape the poverty he'd been born into. A familiar story. But Conway was different. Unlike most of the men, he'd been on a mission to change his circumstances. Rather than going out drinking with the rest of the lads, he'd sent every penny home. He had a sweetheart, used to talk about setting up house with her. Something modest. A few children. A vegetable garden. A job that would keep a roof over their heads and food on the table. A good lad. Archie would never have allowed himself the extravagance of a night at the Empire, so Cook would do it for him.

'Ruby been in recently?' Cook asked, as the desk clerk got his key.

'Sir?' The clerk had been looking away at the moment Cook had asked, so he'd had a second to set his face. Lucky for Cook, he was a terrible actor. The name clearly meant something to him.

'Ruby Reynolds,' Cook said. 'She told me to look her up, next time I was in town. Said she'd be at the bar.'

The clerk shook his head, and turned the ledger for Cook to sign in. As he did so, another clerk leant over. The two of them conferred.

'Ruby Reynolds?' Cook's clerk asked him.

'Yes,' Cook replied.

'I think I know where she is,' the clerk said, sliding a key across the counter. 'Give me half an hour and I'll send her up. Room nine twelve.'

Cook had been right. She was here, and she was working. Not so surprising after all. Not many prospects for a girl growing up by the docks.

There was a queue for the lift. Cook was about to turn back, look for the stairs, when the lift announced itself with a bell, and the doors slid open. A lift attendant, even older than the man at the front desk, welcomed everyone in, as if he was bestowing some kind of gift on them.

The throng crowded in, and Cook found himself wedged between a tall dowager in a fur coat, diamond tiara setting off her perfectly styled hair, and a rather large man, straining at the seams of his dinner suit. As they jostled for position, Cook felt the unmistakable solidity of a gun, holstered on the man's hip. A bodyguard, Cook presumed. Not a very effective one, if he'd allowed Cook to get between him and the dowager.

Cook was the last to leave the lift, and he felt the lift attendant's eyes on his back as he walked slowly along the corridor. He was at the top of the hotel, practically up in the eaves. Infrequent windows in the corridor gave a view of the service alley.

The room was small. A single bed, a dusty chest of drawers. Didn't look like the cleaners made it this far along the corridor. The kind of room given to a man with no luggage who'd come from the bar and found a girl he wanted to spend some time with.

Half an hour, the clerk had said. Cook took his shoes off and lay on the bed. The pillow smelt of cigarette smoke. Within seconds he was asleep.

58

Margaret found a place at the bar. There was a jovial atmosphere. The city was under attack, and damn the consequences – that kind of thing. Everyone seemed to be proposing toasts, and the champagne was flowing freely. Margaret had already had a nice Bordeaux with dinner, working her way through Bunny's expense account, and then there'd been that chap from the Air Ministry who'd insisted on buying everyone whiskies. Something about a successful test flight of a new plane that didn't need a propellor.

She was being watched, by a number of people. Some she needed to be worried about, others she could use. If she played her cards right, the latter could help with the former.

In a dark corner of the dining room, two men in cheap suits were literally making a meal of it. They'd dragged out their starters and main courses, and were now sipping coffee. No alcohol. A joyless meal for two men on a government expense account. Margaret suspected they had their hands full – the dining room was full of people who needed watching. But, one thing was for certain, she was on their list. One of the men was facing her, but every time he looked her way his eyes skipped past her. He was doing a pretty good job of not looking at her, but only a pretty good job.

At the end of the bar, another two young men had her in their sights. These two were more above-board. Pilot's uniforms. Faces flushed with drink. Voices a little too loud. One of them had his back to her but the other one had caught her eye a couple of times. It was only a matter of time.

She pulled a cigarette out of her silver case, Bombay Shooting Club, first place, engraved on the cover. She looked to the barman, but before he could reach her with a light, a flame was flickering in front of her face. She lit her cigarette and nodded her thanks. The pilot who'd been watching her – ruddy face, Brylcreemed hair – winked at her as he snapped the lighter shut.

'I've been watching you,' he said.

Margaret didn't respond. There was an etiquette, of course. He'd lit her cigarette and said something half polite, half provocative. She was meant to come back with something that would make her stance clear – either way. But she was tired, and she was more than a little drunk, and she hadn't decided yet how she wanted the evening to end up. So she kept quiet. A signal in itself, she hoped.

'Do you come here often?' he asked.

'Such a lot of questions,' Margaret replied. 'Didn't your mother teach you it's rude to interrogate a lady?'

'Let me guess,' he said. 'You're one of those European imports. Left a big fat castle behind and ran from the Boche.'

'Something like that,' Margaret said.

'What are you drinking?' he asked. Margaret looked at her glass. It was, in fairness, getting empty, and she did like the idea of another drink.

'Champagne,' she said.

The pilot caught the barman's eye and ordered a bottle, as she'd known he would. He'd be expecting something in return, but he'd be disappointed. Still, she didn't mind the company in the short term, and he seemed enthusiastic enough. His friend joined them, having seen how things were progressing.

'I'm Todd,' the first man said, holding out his hand.

'Margaret,' she said, shaking his hand.

'This is Muggers,' Todd said, nodding at his mate. 'Muggers, Margaret.' Muggers raised his glass and Margaret reciprocated.

'Lady Margaret,' she said. She didn't often use the title, but sometimes it was useful. Changed the way people viewed her. Tipped the scales in her favour.

The barman delivered the new bottle and Todd did the honours. Three new glasses, spilling over the top of each. He was already drunk. Still, Margaret thought, if he'd been involved in the fighting, he deserved a night off.

'Lady Margaret!' Todd proposed. They chinked glasses. Margaret sipped hers and allowed herself a look at the table in the far corner. The men in cheap suits had ordered brandies. They'd have to lie about it on their expense form. Margaret winked as the one facing her flashed his gaze past her.

59

Three men walked along the upper corridor. A strong family resemblance between them. Three brothers, most likely. They had to walk single file in the narrow space. The first man was broad-shouldered and tall. He had a squareness about his face. A boxer perhaps, or a professional rugby player. Either would account for his nose, flattened by repeated abuse. His arms were muscular to the point that he had to hold them out from his body, his hands brushing the walls in these cramped quarters. He wore the hotel uniform – dark-blue suit with gold brocade on the shoulders. Vaguely naval.

The second man was larger. His hands didn't merely brush the walls, they knocked against them. His hotel uniform was stretched across his chest and shoulders, brass buttons struggling to keep the jacket closed.

The third man was larger still. He had to stoop to avoid hitting his head on the ceiling. The kind of man who'd have been advertised at a travelling fair – come and see the giant. He'd have been at home in the big top with both arms outspread, a pretty girl sitting on each arm. Here in the attic corridor he was like a caged animal. His hotel jacket was unbuttoned, the cuffs too short and even the shirt straining to contain him.

The three men walked quietly. Unhurried. They could have been technicians, sent to fix a faulty radiator – no sense of drama, just another day on the job.

They stopped outside Cook's room. Without a word, each shrugged off his jacket and hung it on a window crank that could have been designed for the purpose. Three men – three jackets, each one fitting over the next like a Russian doll. The men rolled up their shirtsleeves, still no sense of drama. No fear, no concern. No excitement.

The shortest man knocked at the door. There was no answer.

He knocked again, stepped back slightly, giving himself room to manoeuvre.

No answer.

It happened sometimes. The room's occupant would be busy, getting undressed perhaps. Sitting on the toilet. Having second thoughts.

The man was prepared. He had a large collection of keys on his belt. He unclipped the loop and felt for the right key, the one that opened all the doors on this floor. Then he felt in his coat pocket, a jangle of metal as he pulled something out. It took Cook a second to work out what he was seeing. Handcuffs.

Cook stood in the shadows at the far end of the corridor, around the corner. He'd allowed himself to peer around, watching the men as they stood at the door. It was dark in the shadows, but he didn't want a sudden movement to alert them to his presence.

He watched as they unlocked the door and filed in, like so many clowns squeezing into a car at a circus.

As soon as the last man was in, Cook ran lightly to the door, careful not to make any noise. He stepped in behind them.

'Can I help you?' Cook asked. The first man to enter the room, the giant, emerged from the bathroom, ducking his head to avoid the door frame. The second man, medium-sized, stood by the wardrobe – perhaps people really did hide in those things. The third, the smallest, was still near the door, within striking distance.

'We heard you was looking for a girl,' the smallest man said, with a sneer.

'I was hoping for someone a little more feminine,' Cook said.

The man looked confused.

'Who sent you?' he asked, stepping forward with what he presumably thought was a menacing grimace on his face.

Cook looked at the three men, pretended to think. In his experience, it was always a good idea to show your adversaries you were on the same page as them. In this case, he guessed these were men who took a minute or two between thoughts. So he did the same.

'Wait a minute,' he said. 'The girl's not coming, is she?'

'Quick thinking,' the medium-sized man at the wardrobe said. 'They said you was a bit clever. All that guff about meeting a general.'

'Who you working for?' the smallest man asked, now inches from his face.

Cook didn't answer. He was thinking through the chain of events. He'd asked for Ruby, and instead he'd been given these three. Clearly he'd upset someone.

The smallest man put his finger in Cook's face.

'Who . . . you . . . fucking . . . working . . . for?' he said, through gritted teeth. The middle teeth were stained black.

Cook grabbed the finger. A lightning-fast action that caught the man by surprise. Cook bent the finger back, feeling the cartilage snap. The man's face screwed up in pain, but he held his ground.

'I'm not who you think I am,' Cook said, twisting finger. The man gasped. 'I'm not a punter up from the country, wanting a bit of the other. I'm not a decent man, with a wife and kids at home. I gave a fake name downstairs and if I kill you and disappear now, they'll never find me. And I'm very willing to kill you, if you don't tell me what I want to know.'

'You're going to take on all three of us?' the giant asked.

'Two of you, really. This one's not going to be much help with his hand out of action. That, and the puking,' Cook said, driving his knee into the man's stomach. The man doubled over and went to the ground, moaning.

'My question is,' Cook asked, 'who do you *think* I work for?'

60

The manager's office was as disappointing as Cook's room had been. Clearly a 'behind-the-scenes' place, no expense wasted on any marble floors, or gold-plated fittings. A utilitarian office, the wall covered with time sheets and other paperwork. It reminded Cook of the staff room at the Lyons.

Cook stood in front of a scuffed desk, the two remaining men behind him, standing guard. The one with the broken finger had slunk back to wherever he'd come from.

Cook had let them escort him to their boss, a mutually acceptable solution to the stand-off without the need for further violence. Cook's motto, one he'd learnt from his old CO, was that you win every fight you don't have. Cook had known many men who hadn't been able to live by that, who ran towards every fight like a drunk towards a pub. Most of those men were dead, and he wasn't.

The hotel manager himself was another disappointment. Cook had expected someone as grand and imposing as the hotel itself – a personification of the marble floors and crystal chandeliers. But the man sitting behind the desk was a greyfaced pencil-pusher. He resembled the bruisers who'd been sent upstairs to teach Cook what-for. An older brother, or a cousin.

'Who do you work for?' he asked.

'Who do you think I work for?' Cook asked. 'You sent your three monkeys to beat me up. Must be someone you're pretty scared of.'

'He broke Don's fingers like it wasn't nobody's business,' the giant said.

'The Chelsea mob?' the manager asked. 'Is this a declaration of war?'

'Yes,' Cook said. 'The Chelsea mob.'

The manager shook his head.

'Wrong,' he said. 'I put in a call. Spoke to Mr Whitcomb himself, down in Chelsea. He didn't know what I was talking about. Talks a lot of shit a lot of the time, but not this time.'

Cook didn't respond.

'Are you working for the Chinese?' the manager asked.

'Yes,' Cook said. He had an intimate working knowledge of many of the triad gangs in Hong Kong. Prostitution was one of their side-rackets.

Cook felt the men behind him shift uncomfortably.

'Who? Specifically?'

'Why would I tell you?' Cook asked. 'Last time I got on the wrong side of a Chinese gang I nearly lost an ear.'

'You're assuming you could leave this room with both ears intact,' the manager said, his eyes flicking past Cook to the bodyguards.

'Correct.'

'You're overly confident,' the manager said. 'You know what they say about pride coming before a fall.'

Cook leant forwards, planting both hands on the desk.

'You've got me,' he said. 'I don't work for the Chinese. I don't work for the Chelsea mob. I'm looking for a girl. Her name's Ruby Reynolds.'

The manager stared at him. Probably thought it was unnerving. Probably saw it in a gangster flick.

'Did the old man send you?'

Cook didn't respond.

'Is this some kind of test?' the manager asked.

61

The second bottle of champagne went a lot faster than the first, and Margaret was fairly sure she'd drunk most of it. Todd and Muggers were good company, and she found herself talking, about herself, her time growing up in India. Some of it was true, most of it was a pastiche – the kind of things people liked to hear about. Tea plantations and Maharajahs. The boys listened attentively, Todd keeping her glass topped up.

Muggers didn't talk much, just gawped at her. He seemed a bit overawed, which was not at all the case for his friend Todd, he of the Brylcreemed hair.

Margaret knew what they were up to, of course. She could see their confidence growing with every glass she drank. She'd be another notch on the bedpost, perhaps a silhouette on the fuselage. It wasn't apparent whether Muggers would get to join in. Would they both make love to her at once? Margaret liked to think of herself as open-minded. She'd read about such things in racy novels, the ones that got passed around at boarding school, but she'd never considered it as an actual possibility.

When Margaret saw Todd look at the barman, about to order a third bottle, she put her hand on top of her glass and shook her head.

'That's quite enough for me,' she said.

Muggers nodded. 'Righto,' he said, looking at his watch.

'I've got a half-finished bottle in my room,' Todd said. 'Come up for one last glass, help me finish it. Waste not want not. There is a war on, after all.'

'How lovely,' Margaret said. 'I'll be right back.'

She picked up her handbag and slipped down from the stool. As she threaded her way through the tables, she knew the two pilots would be watching her, zeroing in on their target.

She paused by the men with the cheap suits.

'I'll be upstairs with those two for the night,' she said. 'I don't think either of them's a German spy, so you can count me as safely tucked up. I'll be down for breakfast at eight if you want to resume surveillance.'

She left before either man could confirm, or deny, his role as one of Bunny's watchers.

In the toilets, Margaret splashed cold water on her face, aware she was being watched by the attendant. She thought about the two men at the bar. A thrill ran through her body as she let herself think about the possibility. But it wouldn't do. The pilots were a useful distraction, an excuse for her to be seen leaving the bar without her watchers following. Once she ditched the young men, she'd have freedom of manoeuvre.

The previous night she'd come to her room to find a note under her pillow. All very cloak and dagger. The message was an invitation. Midnight, in the basement shelter. Margaret thought of the SS man, Schmidt. She'd known he'd send someone to make contact. Surprised it had taken so long.

62

Petal, if that really was her name, walked quickly through the crowds on Piccadilly, not looking back. Cook kept his distance, but she was easy to follow, a bright pink scarf covering her hair.

The conversation with the manager had been going nowhere. They were clearly paranoid that some other crime syndicate was trying to get in on their turf. None of it interested Cook.

As he was leaving the hotel, he'd spotted the prostitute – slipping quietly out the side door, pausing to light a fag then fastening the scarf over her hair. The air of someone coming off a long shift.

As she approached the bus stop, Cook turned to look in a shop window. It would be only natural for her to look back along the road, checking to see if a bus was coming. But she didn't turn, and she didn't slow down. She hurried past the bus stop, giving Cook hope that she was going somewhere within walking distance.

At Piccadilly Circus, she crossed over to the central island, past the boxed-up statue, then crossed again to Shaftesbury Avenue – even busier with foot traffic than Piccadilly, with queues of theatre-goers stretched out along the pavement. Theatres had been shut when war had been declared, but there'd been complaints. Presumably enough people high up in government enjoyed a night out to persuade the powers that be of the error of their ways. So while Londoners were being advised to avoid gathering in crowds of more than ten, sitting in a packed two-thousand-seat auditorium was given the official blessing. Cook passed under a hoarding for a Noël Coward comedy. He could think of many things in life that merited risking death in a bombing raid. Watching a Noël Coward play wasn't one of them.

Cook pushed his way through a thick knot of sightseers and realised he couldn't see Petal's scarf. If she had any sense she'd have taken it off. An effective way of losing a pursuer, Cook mused. If he was going to run a mob of criminals he'd bring it in as policy. But as he reached a side road to the left, he saw her. She was heading into the narrow streets and passages of Soho.

The crowds didn't thin out – Soho was evidently as much a draw as the theatre district, but the people changed in character. Where Shaftesbury Avenue had been respectable couples, smart officewear and light summer coats, laughing and sharing stories about the day in the office, Soho was different – crowds of servicemen, many who looked too young to be out of school, let alone wandering the streets of one of London's seediest districts, single men, furtively looking in windows, women dressed like Petal – loud fabrics and expensively curled hair. Cook passed a doorway and locked eyes with a bouncer. Cook had spent enough time in places like this to be able to recognise the difference between men who were hired merely for their physical size, and men who were actually capable of violence. The bouncer stared back, insolently, not a man Cook would choose to tangle with unless absolutely necessary.

Petal disappeared again – this time down a narrow footpath, open doorways on each side guarded by more bouncers. She stopped at one of these doorways, and the bouncer stepped aside, giving her a nod. Cook slowed, jazz music was coming from inside. He kept walking and turned the corner at the end, finding himself in Soho Square.

Cook felt in his pockets, taking inventory. He'd spent more than a year in Hong Kong, where it seemed like the whole island consisted of streets like the ones he'd just walked through. He'd developed the habit of carrying a flick knife in one pocket, and a small revolver in the other. Neither was enough if you ran out of luck, but you tended to run out of luck even quicker if you weren't armed. Those days were long behind him, but he still found himself patting his pockets out of instinct. No weapons. But what he did have, of course, was the next best thing.

Money.

The doorman stood in front of Cook, arms hanging loosely by his sides. His suit coat was a size too big, providing ease of movement if needed, and cover for a gun. He had a bandage over his left eye, and the rest of his face was pockmarked with scabs from a recent injury. He looked familiar, like a relative of the men who'd been sent to warn him off from the Empire. Another brother, perhaps. How many were there?

Cook stood a respectful distance away, and tried to look like a tourist who wanted to listen to some jazz. Since he'd never wanted to listen to jazz, he didn't quite know how to look, so he smiled.

'How much to get in?' Cook asked.

The doorman turned his head, like a bird, focusing his one good eye on Cook. He looked insulted by the question.

'Entry's free,' the doorman said, 'for the right kind of person.' He looked Cook up and down, taking his time. 'You're not the right kind of person.'

'Funny way to run a business,' Cook said. 'How do you make money if you don't let people in?'

'We get by,' the doorman said. 'But I'll pass on your concern to management.'

'How much to make me the right kind of person?'

The bouncer repeated his long examination of Cook.

'A guinea.'

'Crikey,' Cook said, leaning into his country-mouse tourist persona. 'I only want to have a drink. Don't want to buy the place.'

The bouncer shrugged.

'You want to come in, it's a guinea. You don't want to pay, don't come in. All the same to me.'

Cook produced two guineas from his pocket. A week's work for a labourer on his farm.

'For your trouble,' he said, handing over his coins. His generosity earnt him a silent nod from the bouncer, who stepped backwards to let Cook past.

'No touching the girls,' the bouncer said. 'Don't matter how much you tip, you touch the girls you're in trouble.'

'I'm just here for the music,' Cook said.

'Course you are.'

Cook climbed a steep, narrow staircase. Soft, sticky stair treads sloped to the left, as if the whole building had settled on one side. Jazz music got louder as Cook neared the top.

The jazz club was gloomy. Walls and ceiling painted black. Blacked-out windows. Tables with flickering candles providing the only light. A trio of musicians played something that featured a lot of drumming and trumpeting, as far as Cook could discern. It wasn't bad, he thought, not that he was an expert. Most of the tables were taken, and most of the patrons were facing the stage. Rather than watching the musicians, they were watching two women dancing in a state of considerable undress.

Cook stood at the bar and ordered a pint.

'I'm looking for Ruby,' Cook said to the barmaid. She looked confused.

'Usually works the Empire,' Cook explained.

But all this got him was a blank look.

A door opened at the far end of the space. Petal looked out. She caught his eye and narrowed the door. Cook left his beer on the bar and threaded his way around the tables, his eye on the door. As he approached, it closed. Not an insurmountable obstacle, all things considered, but a clear message, made even clearer by a brass plate on the door:

NO ADMITTANCE
STAFF ONLY

Cook turned the handle and opened the door. No Petal. Just a dark passage leading to more doors, the first of which showed light.

It was a dressing room for the dancing girls. Two young women sat at a make-up table.

'I'm looking for Ruby,' he said. The girls turned around.

'Staff only back here,' one of them said. She had a posh accent, like she'd gone to the right schools.

'Tell me where she's gone and I'll be on my way,' he said.

The woman sighed.

'Mister Jones!' she shouted.

She waited a second, until she heard heavy footsteps.

'Sorry,' she said to Cook.

'Her mum wants to know she's all right,' Cook said. 'Pass the message on.'

The dancer shook her head.

'If Ruby was here, she wouldn't be all right, by definition,' she said. 'But she's not here. None of the girls go by that name.'

Heavy footsteps told Cook they were about to have company.

The dancer looked nervous. 'Tell him you were looking for the toilets. Whatever you do, don't make him angry.'

'What happens to people who make him angry?' Cook asked.

'They end up in the river,' a voice said, from behind Cook. A low voice, thick with gravel.

Mr Jones was a genteel-looking man. Expensive suit, well tailored but well worn. Elderly, in his seventies if he was a day. He looked familiar. An older version of the brothers at the hotel.

'You're the father,' Cook said.

Mr Jones nodded. He seemed an agreeable sort. Someone Cook could reason with.

'I've come from the Empire. Got a complaint about the service.'

Mr Jones raised his eyebrows.

'And you are?'

'I'm nobody,' Cook said. 'Looking for a girl. Seems like you've got the trade at the hotel sewn up, so you've probably seen her.'

Cook unfolded the picture, held it up to Mr Jones, who remained impassive. Cook passed it to the girls at the make-up station.'

'I've seen her,' the dancer said. 'She's a waitress at the Lyons.'

'She's been hanging around at the Empire,' Cook said. 'Maybe you saw her there.'

'That's right,' the girl said. 'She was having a barney with this spiv. New suit. Ginger hair. I reckon he was running some kind of scam and she sussed him out. He didn't look too happy.'

Mr Jones smiled.

'Happy to help,' he said, holding out his hand to shake. 'I hope you find your friend.'

They shook hands. The old man had a surprisingly firm grip. He put his other hand on top of Cook's like some kind of blessing.

'I think it's best if you steer clear of the hotel from now on,' he said. 'Best for everyone.'

63

The phone box was dark. Ordinarily there'd be a light, so you could see what you were doing, but the bulb had been removed. Fine in daylight, but troublesome in the gloom of dusk, in a dark road surrounded by tall buildings.

The call went straight through, no operator. All very modern, compared to Cook's experience making calls in Uckfield, where you had to announce your business to Mrs Filey at the telephone exchange.

'Hello?'

The phone pipped urgently, and Cook forced his penny into the slot.

'It's Cook,' he said, recognising Gracie's voice on the other end.

'I found out where she's been spending her time,' Cook said.

'Where?'

'The Empire.'

There was silence on the other end of the line. Cook had expected some kind of surprise. The silence was surprising, almost like this wasn't new information, more like confirmation.

Silence. Then a sigh.

'Reynolds,' Gracie said.

More silence. The phone pipped again, hungry for more coins. Cook fed it, listening to the silence.

'You'd better come with me,' Gracie said. 'Stop me from killing him.'

'I'll be with you in an hour,' Cook said.

'Meet me at the Tilbury Shelter.'

'Where?'

'Number nine bus, then follow your nose.'

64

Cook sat on the bus, pressed against the window on one side and a coughing soldier on the other, a kit bag on his lap.

Somewhere along The Strand, the coughing soldier got up, and Cook felt the momentary relief of having the seat to himself. It didn't last long. The next person to sit next to him, a grimace of apology as they situated themselves, held an armful of bedding that smelt like it hadn't seen the inside of a laundry copper since the day it was turned out of the mill. Not the only passenger with a blanket. The contingent of passengers had almost entirely changed since Piccadilly, only half a mile back. There, people had been hopping on the bus to get home from work, or perhaps from an afternoon's shopping. They'd worn smart coats, carried umbrellas and briefcases, or shopping bags with store names on them. They'd sat upright, ready for their stop. Nearly home at the end of the day.

The replacements were different – dressed more casually, ties loosened. Besides bundles of bedding, they had baskets. Loaves of bread. Flasks of tea.

An elderly man climbed on, made his way back along the rows. He took a seat in front of Cook, nodding to his new neighbour, a woman with a baby wrapped in a sling.

'All right, Al,' the woman said. 'You going up Tilbury?'

Al coughed, a wet, sickly noise. It took him a while to work it through.

'All right, lass,' he replied at last. 'Thought you was trying Dickins 'n' Jones.'

'Didn't get in,' she said. 'Got there at dinner time, queued 'til they opened, but they said they was out of space.'

'You going up Tilbury too?' Al asked.

'Reckon I'll have to,' she replied.

'Heard they give out tea and cakes up West,' Al said.

The woman laughed. 'Give 'em out? You'd be lucky. Tuppence they're charging. Lovely though. Rock cakes. Got one for me and the lad the other night. Good to have something to nibble on when those bombs is coming down around you.'

The bus passed St Paul's, working its way east.

65

The lobby was quiet. The lift attendant stood aside to let Margaret in, and the two pilots followed close behind. They stood, one on each side, as the lift attendant took their instructions.

'Fifth floor,' Margaret said.

'Same,' Todd said.

The doors closed, and the lift attendant pulled a lever. The lift started to ascend.

'This has been lovely,' Margaret said. 'Two heroic pilots, all to myself. But I'm afraid this is as far as it goes. It's been a very long day and I'm going to need my beauty sleep.'

Todd didn't reply. He slipped an arm through hers. A gentlemanly enough gesture.

'I don't think so,' he said. 'We're in for two bottles of champagne, and you were fairly clear you were game. So I rather think you *will* have that drink.'

'Not tonight,' Margaret said, feeling a burst of adrenaline cutting through the fuzziness from the drink. 'I'm feeling rather woozy, and I rather fear I'll be asleep as soon as I catch sight of my room.'

'Asleep, awake, it's all the same to us,' Todd said. 'In fact, Muggers here prefers them when they're lying still. Me? I like a bit of a fight.'

'Would it help if I asked nicely?' Margaret said. She spoke politely. Demure. Ladylike. She felt it was only fair to give one opportunity for this to end peacefully, and she hadn't been lying. She really did want to lie down for a couple of hours, and if they ended up fighting, she knew where it would lead – she'd be pacing around her room, buzzing with adrenaline for hours on end until it abated, leaving her with stomach cramps. Frankly, she could do without the whole faff.

'You two chaps are obviously looking for a bit of fun. I'm sure there are plenty of ladies out there who'd like to spend the night with you, or at least as long as it takes. They charge by the hour, I'm told, so if you're quick you might only be looking at a few bob.' She looked Todd in the eye. 'And it would be quick, wouldn't it?'

'You've got a mouth on you,' Todd said, stepping away slightly, as if he was offended that the woman he'd picked as his prey talked in such a way. 'Your feller know you talk like that?'

'I don't have a feller,' Margaret said. 'Or rather, I had one, but then I had to give him up. It's complicated.' As she talked, she stared at the back of the head of the lift attendant. Would he turn around? Would he intervene? Her bet was on no. He was doing his best wise monkey impression, seeing nothing, hearing nothing, saying nothing.

'I say, is there a security detail in the hotel?' she asked, loudly, but the lift operator's only response was to lower the lever he'd been holding, slowing the lift.

'Fifth floor,' he said, averting his eyes as the doors slid open and the two men ushered Margaret out into the corridor.

'Listen,' Margaret said to Todd, putting an edge into her voice. 'We can end this right now – you go to your room and I go to mine, no harm done. Or one of you's going to spend the night in a police cell and the other's going to spend it in a hospital.'

Todd fished in his pocket for his room key with his right hand, his left arm still bent around Margaret's arm.

'I don't think so,' he said. 'We're going to have a nice time in here. Although, word to the wise, the more you run that mouth, the less nice I'll be. Got it?'

He unlocked his door and pushed Margaret inside.

Margaret stumbled into the room, putting some distance between her and the men. The door closed behind her. She was afraid, of course. Only a fool wasn't afraid at the start of a fight. But she was quietly confident.

'Last chance,' she said. 'Really. Let's say you're both good chaps who've had a few too many drinks. You've both got mothers, maybe sisters. You've signed up to do your bit to defend your country. So we can all agree it wouldn't be congruent with those thoughts for you to force yourselves on a defenceless woman in a dingy hotel room. Wouldn't exactly be your finest hour.'

Todd removed his jacket. He unbuckled his belt and pulled it out of the belt loops in one whistling motion.

'Keep talking and you'll get the buckle end,' he said. 'Muggers, help the lady undress.'

Muggers took a step towards her. He seemed unsure.

'Which one of you's the better pilot?' Margaret asked.

Muggers stopped, confused.

'Why?' he asked.

'Doesn't seem very sensible to take out two pilots,' Margaret said. 'From what I read in the papers we're running short of you lot as it is.'

'I'm the better pilot,' Todd said.

'Can you fly with a broken arm?' Margaret asked.

'If I had to.'

'Right or left?'

Todd gave a nervous look towards his friend, then took another step towards her.

Muggers lunged at her, got a handful of her dress. He pulled her towards him.

'I suppose you don't need your testicles to fly,' Margaret said, glad she'd come to an acceptable solution. She kneed him, giving it all she had, and as he crumpled, she grabbed his left arm and held it out straight, letting the weight of his falling body dislocate the arm at the shoulder, with a deep, loud snap of cartilage.

'Last chance,' she said to Todd. But he wasn't listening.

He swung at her, his fist clenched, giving it all he had. She ducked, let his amateur attempt whistle past her, then popped back up, and punched him in the throat, her fingers bent at the first joint. She tried to judge it, didn't want to kill him, but she was angry, and she couldn't be sure she'd got it right. He clutched his throat, looking at her in wide-eyed outrage as if she'd broken some kind of rule.

She used the phone, still marvelling at the modernity of it – a telephone in every bedroom – and told the man at the desk to send the police. Told him they'd need an ambulance too.

She pried Todd's hands away from his destroyed throat. He still had the room key, clutched in a claw-like fist.

She locked the door from the outside.

66

Cook stepped off the bus as it was pulling away, swaying as the momentum carried him forward. People were streaming along the pavement towards a massive warehouse. All carried bedding and baskets. Loaves of bread and flasks of tea. Some were talking cheerfully, others trudged, faces downcast. Cook slipped into the crowd.

As they neared the warehouse, Cook got a sense for how massive it was. Like filing into an ancient cathedral, the brickwork towering above them. It seemed an odd choice of a shelter. Gathering together under what would be a mountain of falling bricks if the place was hit. Perhaps there was some trick to it Cook wasn't in on. Some kind of structural integrity – maybe steel beams in the roof.

'Who set this up?' Cook asked the man next to him. 'ARP?'

'Dunno, mate,' the stranger said. 'Just heard it was where everyone was going.'

Cook nodded as if this was valuable information. He kept his place in the wave of people, all being funnelled into the great building through a loading door big enough to let a train pass through. Like livestock, walking up the ramp into the slaughterhouse.

The first thing Cook noticed was the smell. Human waste. Sweat. Fear. It was the smell of the trenches, but in this enclosed space it was worse – even more overpowering. He pushed his way to the side of the flow of people, found a spot by a brick arch where he could get his bearings.

They'd walked in on a set of train tracks, which now led away into the darkness. To each side of the track, there was a series of brick arches, each about twenty feet wide and forty feet deep, filled at ground level with crates. In the darkness, on top of the crates, where the roof curved over, Cook saw people. Some were sitting, looking out at him. Some were lying down, huddled in blankets. Shadows danced on the blackened brick arches from primus stoves.

Cook saw the man from the bus. He was being helped up onto the crates. Someone had built a staircase out of smaller cases, but it was precarious.

'All right, Al. Got you a slice.'

Al was ushered through a mass of bodies into the darkness at the back of the arch. At least Al had someone saving a place for him.

The row of arches went on as far as Cook could see. He walked along the tracks, into the darkness. Follow your nose, Gracie had said. Cook did his best to breathe through his mouth, wondering if it would be rude to put his handkerchief over his face, filter out the worst of it.

He'd been walking for two hundred yards when he got to the turntable. A cavernous open space, spiralling brick arches making a dome above a circular space, criss-crossed with train tracks. It would be set on rollers, designed to turn a train around. Leading off from the turntable, like spokes on a wheel, were seven more railway tracks, each leading into their own long tunnel of arches. On his way in, Cook had passed about ten arches on each side. Fifty people per arch. That would be about a thousand people along each spoke. Eight spokes meant eight thousand people. Cook looked up. He couldn't see anything suggesting protection from a bomb.

No steel beams. Just thousands and thousands of tons of Victorian brickwork.

A distant explosion caused a shower of brick dust. A young boy sitting in the middle of the turntable, like the king of the castle, looked at the dust, then looked at Cook. The boy shrugged. Cook felt the same. If this place was hit . . .

'Looking for a place, mate?' the boy asked.

Cook squatted down, putting himself eye to eye with the boy, who regarded him with a sombre expression.

'Looking for a person,' Cook said.

'We can help,' the boy said.

'We?'

The boy nodded behind him. Several pairs of eyes glinted in the dark.

'A penny'll get you somewhere to kip,' the boy said, 'if you're not fussy.'

He studied Cook.

'Can't work out whether you're fussy or not. Might be one of those blokes likes to look like he's going up in the world when he's not, or might be one of those blokes tries to look poor so he don't get clobbered when he's out and about.'

The boy was smart. Perhaps you had to be, to sit in the chair in the middle of the turntable.

'What's the going rate for information?' Cook asked.

'What's in it for us?' the boy asked.

'I'm looking for Reynolds, from the island,' Cook said.

The boy didn't answer. He seemed to be thinking.

'Call it a shilling,' he said, eventually.

Cook reached into his pocket and came up with half a crown. He tossed it to the boy.

The boy whistled, and one of his mates shuffled forward. They conferred.

'Ronnie's going to take you,' the boy said. 'But not all the way. Reynolds and that lot don't mess about.'

From where they stood on the turntable, some spokes were more inviting than others. Laughter, flickering light, and the smells of hundreds of dinners being prepared and eaten – all these things converged at the hub. But one spoke gave out none of these signs of human warmth. The arched entrance was a dark hole, a blankness that repelled the eye. Move on, it said, choose one of the other options. Nothing good this way. Cook didn't need a guide to tell him which spoke was the one he sought.

Cook's designated helper stood at the entrance to the tunnel and looked up at him.

'You sure about this, guv?' he asked.

'What's the worst thing could happen?' Cook asked.

'You could get killed,' the boy said, his matter-of-fact tone at odds with his age.

Cook listened to the sirens, and the distant crump of another bomb landing. Another small corner of the city turned to rubble.

'We're all going to get killed,' Cook said.

'You're a barrel of laughs, ain't you?' the boy said. He winked at Cook. 'Come on then, if you're so eager to get it over with.'

The tunnel was as dark as the entrance had promised. Cook stepped as quietly as he could on the gravel ballast beneath the tracks. The boy was silent. Cook had known highly trained soldiers with less skill and stealth. Cook kept his left hand out, alternately feeling the damp brickwork of the pillars supporting the arches, then rough crates. As they passed the crates, he felt people stirring in the darkness. He smelt the sourness of bodies and clothes unwashed for weeks. This wasn't just a wartime shelter, this felt like a place where people with no hope lived out their remaining time.

67

The lad stopped under one of the arches and nodded at Cook. His job done, he melted back into the darkness.

Cook stepped towards what looked like a wall of packing crates, looking for a foothold. In most of the bays he'd passed, people had been sprawled on top of the crates, a mezzanine level that presumably had the benefit of keeping them off the damp ground.

Some of the crates were recessed. Cook stepped into a gap left by one of the recessed crates. Three feet in, a gap opened up to his left, wide enough for him to squeeze through. When he did so, a subsequent gap opened up, leading deeper into the storage bay. Soon, he was in complete darkness, relying on the feel of the rough, wood crates hemming him in, following wherever the next gap led.

Ahead, he heard scuffling, then the low murmur of a man's voice. A complaint. Someone in pain.

Cook stepped out of the darkness into a room – a gap in the crates about twelve feet wide and twelve feet deep. There were two stacks of bunkbeds, three bunks to a stack, on the far wall. In the middle of the small room, a Formica table and four, mismatched kitchen chairs. A kettle was boiling on a primus stove, and a tilley lamp hissed softly, lighting the space with a ghostly white light.

Reynolds was standing on one side of the space, to Cook's right. He held a handkerchief to his face, a spreading bloom of blood covering the white cotton.

To Cook's left, another man was holding Gracie captive, his arms around her chest. Cook recognised the man – he'd accompanied Reynolds into the pawnbrokers when Cook had found the clock. Gracie was struggling. Cook didn't envy the man holding her. Like holding a tiger ready to take your head off the minute you let go.

'You put your own daughter on the streets,' she said, fixing Reynolds with a look conveying every ounce of the anger she was feeling.

'What's he doing here?' Reynolds asked, nodding at Cook.

Gracie stopped her struggling now reinforcements had arrived.

'Tell him,' Gracie said, to Cook.

'Ruby's been seen at the Empire,' Cook said. 'I showed her picture to some of the girls working there, the Harriers. One of them recognised her.

Reynolds pulled the hankie away from his nose, tilted his head back.

'All right,' he said, eventually. He nodded to his man holding Gracie. 'Let her go.'

'You sure?' the man replied.

Gracie wriggled out of his grasp. She took a step towards Reynolds but he held out his hand, like a police constable stopping traffic.

'Less of that,' Reynolds said. 'I let you have this one for old time's sake. Try it again and you won't be so lucky.'

'Tell us where Ruby is and we can leave you to play with the rats,' Gracie said.

'Gary, get a brew on,' Reynolds said.

*

Gracie and Reynolds sat across from each other at the table, Cook took a referee's position between the two. Reynolds's lieutenant, having made the tea, had retired to a bunk.

'When was the last time you heard from her?' Gracie asked Reynolds.

'The first day of the bombing,' Reynolds replied. 'The day Frankie came up. Which was why I assumed she'd been on the bus. She still might have been for all any of us knows.'

'She's alive,' Gracie said.

'That's hope talking,' Reynolds replied.

'No,' Gracie said. 'I got word from her. Second post.'

Gracie pulled a postcard out of her pinafore. She handed it to Reynolds. He studied it, grunted, and passed it to Cook.

Cook looked at the card – a picture of the beach. Southend. He turned it over and read the message.

'Seems like good news,' Cook said.

'No,' Gracie said. 'She's in trouble.'

68

'Why do you think she's in trouble?' Cook asked.

'She said "our Frankie". She'd never call him that.'

'Just a turn of phrase,' Cook said.

'No,' Gracie said.

'You seem very sure,' Cook said.

'Tell him,' Reynolds said.

Gracie topped up her tea, hands trembling. The adrenaline from her fight with Reynolds still flowing through her veins.

'She'd never say "our Frankie",' Gracie said. 'Because he's not. He's not ours.'

Cook felt like he was expected to make the connection. He looked to Reynolds for answers.

'He's hers,' Gracie explained. 'Her Frankie. Her baby.'

Cook thought it through. He'd been thinking of Ruby as a young woman. Too young to have an eleven-year-old boy.

'She was only a girl,' Gracie said. 'Fourteen. Got into trouble. We kept it quiet. She was a slip of a girl. Never showed 'til right towards the end. We kept her out of sight. Told everyone the baby was mine. Little runt of a thing, didn't expect it to stick around. Just a short visit. But he was stronger than we thought.'

'Does Frankie know?' Cook asked.

'No,' Gracie said. 'And he never will. I'm his mum and he's his dad.' She nodded at Reynolds. 'That's all he needs to know.'

'Who's the father?'

Gracie shook her head.

'She wouldn't say. She was a good girl. Played with the boys in the streets and all that but never got up to anything.'

'You've got your suspicious, though,' Cook said. 'You told me everyone knows everyone's business on the island.'

'If we had suspicions, there'd be one less person living and breathing on the island,' Reynolds said.

Cook looked Gracie in the eye. A mother would know, he thought.

But Gracie shook her head. 'Reynolds is right, and it wouldn't have been him doing the knife work. It'd be me, don't you worry about that. If I ever find out who did that to my little girl, God help him. He'll be going into the river in little pieces.'

'You think it's the same man, who she's with now?' Cook asked.

'I don't know,' Gracie said.

'Whoever it was, must be long gone,' Reynolds said.

'Frankie said you helped find a girl,' Gracie said. 'Another evacuee. Rescued her.'

'Tell me about the Empire,' Cook said.

Reynolds sipped his tea. Made a decision.

'All right,' he said. 'She was working with me.'

'I swear, if you've got her into trouble,' Gracie said.

'Give it a rest,' he said. 'You're angry. I don't blame you. But I haven't done anything to put her in danger. It was her idea.'

'This should be good,' Gracie said.

'She was getting bored at the tea room,' Reynolds said. 'One of the girls took her for a drink at the Empire. Show her all the toffs, how the other half live. They ended up chatting with a couple of lads. Got their drinks paid for, got a nice dinner out of it.'

Gracie folded her arms and sat back, distancing herself. Cook wouldn't have wanted to be on her bad side.

'She had this idea. Came to me, talked it through,' Reynolds said. 'A lot of the toffs were there for the night. What if she got talking to them, found out where they lived. We'd have free run of their house all night, knowing they were tucked up in the shelter there, drinking champagne and waiting for the all clear.'

'You're using her to find houses to rob?' Gracie asked.

'Her idea,' Reynolds said.

'The girl I spoke to said there was a chap Ruby was scared of,' Cook said. 'Got to know him but he turned violent. Did she mention him to you?'

Reynolds shook his head.

'If she had, I'd have gone down there and given him a new smile,' Reynolds said, his knife appearing in his hand, as if by magic.

The light from the gas lamp fluttered. Reynolds pulled it towards him, took out a metal stopper from the base and gave it three pumps, restoring the light to its former power.

'We need to find out more about this man,' Cook said. 'Well dressed. Ginger hair. If he's at the Empire, he shouldn't be hard to find.'

'I can't go in there,' Reynolds said. 'I've had a couple of run-ins. Used up most of my nine lives.'

'I'll find him,' Cook said. 'I'll have to find a way in. They've made it clear I'm not welcome back.'

'I'll go,' a voice from the bunk beds. A young woman.

Two legs swung out from the bottom bunk. Pale-blue pyjamas, slipping her feet into a dirty grey pair of slippers.

Cook recognised her. The barmaid from Gracie's pub.

'Dottie?' Gracie asked, peering into the gloom.

'If there's a bloke out there knows what's happened to Ruby,' the barmaid said. 'I'll get it out of him.'

'It's too dangerous,' Cook said.

'Dealing with a punter?' the barmaid said.

'Worth a try,' Reynolds said. 'You'll need to get your glad rags on though.'

69

Margaret took the steps down to the basement. She heard music, muffled at first, then louder. Something fun, upbeat. Something you'd want to dance to.

A doorman stood in a vestibule at the bottom of the stairs. He nodded to Margaret and stepped aside.

When she'd heard about the basement shelter beneath the Empire, Margaret had imagined rows of camp beds. Hotel guests in their pyjamas, tucked up under grey wool blankets. A nurse, perhaps, or a hotel waitress, doing the rounds offering soothing drinks, while outside the bombs crashed down and civilisation hung by a thread.

Instead, Margaret found herself in a packed bar, deafening music from a band tucked into a tiny corner marked out by red velvet curtains and a postage-stamp of a stage. The clientele was a curious mix, heavily weighted towards old money, but here, in the darkness of the basement bar, people seemed to have given themselves permission to let go. Like a weekend at a country house when all the staff had gone to bed, and the host and hostess let it be known all bets were off. No rules, no judgment, just fun.

An elderly man approached her, dressed in a stunning dress – a pre-war number Margaret recognised from a series of coming-out balls in various foreign capitals. He held a choke chain, which was loosely draped around the neck of his companion, a younger man dressed in a very close approximation of a Hitler Youth outfit – tight brown shorts and shirt, swastikas applied liberally.

'Lady Margaret?' a waiter appeared from the throng, a silver tray full of drinks held masterfully at shoulder-height. 'Your table's ready.'

Margaret followed the waiter to a small café table, squeezed between two large and loud groups – one of them the usual mix of aging Nordic aristocracy, the other an office party of civil servants – young women from the lower ranks of the upper class, and older men in sensible pullovers, earnest and dull, firsts in philosophy, snapped up by the government and installed in airless offices. None of the revellers gave her a second glance as she took her seat, deep in the shadows, back to the wall – the way she liked it.

The waiter set out two small plates and cutlery, then two brimming glasses of champagne. He winked at Margaret, then disappeared back into the crowd.

Margaret waited, scanning the crowd, trying to predict who'd be her contact. At the bar, she watched the young man she'd described to Bunny as a conman. Cheap suit. Ginger hair. Down from Manchester, had been her somewhat flippant description. He had his eyes on a rather dull young woman who, Margaret knew, was the heiress to the second-largest coal-mining family in the country.

As Margaret watched, another young woman approached the man, zeroing in. One of the prostitutes, perhaps. Pale skin. Red silk dress clinging to her curves. She was wasting her time with him, Margaret thought.

'Keep looking forward,' someone said, from her left. The party of office clerks, if she remembered correctly. It was a woman's voice. A poor attempt at an English accent – overly heightened, like a pastiche of the Queen. 'If you turn to look at me this conversation's over.' Margaret guessed the woman was American. She'd had trouble pronouncing forward without emphasising the 'r's. Made her sound like a farmer.

Margaret raised her glass of champagne. She watched the tableau play out at the bar. The girl in the red dress contrived to spill her drink on herself and the man. Shrieks of concern mixed with laughter. Stepping back. Handkerchief applied delicately. The man wasn't taking the bait. In fact, he recoiled when the girl put his hands on her chest.

'We have a mutual friend,' the American said, from behind Margaret. 'He's glad we've been able to connect. You and I are going to become pen pals. There's an address on the underside of your napkin. You'll write once a week. Nothing out of the ordinary. They're reading everything, of course, so we have to establish a pattern. We met in London, had a bit of a fling. You're nervous. Never thought of yourself that way, but you're intrigued. We'll correspond. Once we're up and running, I'll send you the code book so you can start sending more useful information. Drink your champagne if you understand.'

Margaret sipped her champagne. It was excellent.

At the bar the girl in the red dress had given up. She was pushing her way through the crowd towards the exit. The man was angry. In fairness, he looked like the kind of man who spent a lot of his time being angry. As he turned towards the coal heiress, he tried to hide it, unsuccessfully. The heiress didn't notice, or didn't care. More fool her.

'I need to give them a name,' Margaret said. 'Someone dispensable.'

'Impossible,' the woman said.

'I need to build their trust,' Margaret said.

'What if we don't think you're worth the investment?'

Margaret ignored the threat. She watched the band.

'I'll have to check,' the voice said.

'No,' Margaret said. 'Give me a name now, or this whole thing's over. You'll have to tell your boss you couldn't make it work. Maybe they'll understand.'

'You don't set the terms,' the voice said.

'If you want to work with me, I can assure you I set the terms,' Margaret said, finishing the champagne.

Margaret heard a sigh from behind her. She sat and watched the goings-on in the crowded bar.

'Here,' the woman said. A hand appeared at Margaret's elbow, holding a scrap of paper. Like passing notes at school. Margaret took the paper. A name and an address. She enjoyed the feeling of triumph, of flexing the power she was beginning to realise she possessed.

Margaret got up from the table. She didn't look back. All the cloak-and-dagger stuff was silly, she knew, but she'd learnt the people who lived by it liked it if you played along. They tended to worry if you did anything to suggest it was a game.

*

In the lobby, the girl in the red dress was placing a telephone call from one of the public phones. Margaret felt sorry for her. Not much of a life, being sent into the lion's den with the express goal of selling yourself to the worst kind of men.

'Don't waste your time with that one,' Margaret said to her, as she passed. The young woman looked around in surprise.

'He's not who you think he is,' Margaret said.

The girl flushed and moved her hand quickly behind her back, but not quick enough. Margaret caught sight of a man's wallet. She re-appraised the girl. Not such a victim after all.

70

Reynolds put the phone down and stepped out of the telephone box.

'Girl done good,' he said. 'Regent's Place.'

Cook looked at the hotel, across the road. Dark in the blackout. He could see how it had lured Ruby in. The glamour, the feeling you were in the thick of it. The problem was, that sort of place attracted the wrong sort, like wasps to a fallen apple. Cook thought of the kind of man who'd prey on a young girl. He was looking forward to having words, once Ruby was safe.

*

The sirens had been going for twenty minutes. Cook and Reynolds sat in the car, in the darkness. Reynolds had pulled up against the curved railings on the right-hand side of the road. Behind the railings, a half-moon-shaped garden. Beyond the garden, the wider expanse of Regent's Park. To their left, a handsome crescent of Regency houses – John Nash's grand design for urban living. An ancient oak hung over the road, its roots making a mess of the pavement, forcing up the tarmac in waves.

They'd watched a flurry of people scurrying out of their houses as the siren started. A nightly exodus, well honed by now.

'What do you reckon, the bombers come this far west?' Reynolds muttered. The siren had been real enough, but they hadn't heard any planes. Certainly no bombs.

'Things continue much longer like this, there won't be any East End left,' Reynolds continued. 'Then what?'

Cook had noticed a great many 'TO LET' signs in the surrounding streets. The crescent was relatively free of them. Even if the owners of these houses had left town, they wouldn't be looking to those properties to earn an income. Many of the houses here, Cook suspected, were only used for certain times of the year, when the landed gentry would come to town for 'the season'.

'Pretty smart idea,' Reynolds said. 'You've got to hand it to her.'

Cook thought about it. A crowded shelter, the frisson of excitement as the sirens wail and the bombs go off. The sort of place where a person might talk, give away valuable information, to the right sort of listener.

'Until someone makes the connection and decides to get their own back,' Cook said.

Reynolds nodded in the darkness. He leant behind the driver's seat and produced two tin hats. 'Put this on – makes you invisible.'

A standard-issue helmet, with a thin, leather chinstrap. Cook had owned any number of them during his time in the army. You got to the point you forgot you were wearing it, got the strap the way you liked it, then you'd lose it, have to get another one. This one had two major differences – it was painted black, and it had three letters stencilled across the front.

ARP

'You can go anywhere with that,' Reynolds said. 'Like having the keys to the city.'

As they walked away from the car, Cook noticed Reynolds had done the same to the car – ARP in bright white paint on the driver's door. A clever way of becoming invisible.

Reynolds pulled a key ring from his coat pocket – it held a collection of picks. He had the front door unlocked in no more time than it would take a normal person to use a key.

To their left, the sitting room had been closed up – dust-sheets covering every item of furniture, and the curtains drawn. Left in stasis, ready for its owners to return after the bombing had ended.

'Ruby?' Reynolds shouted. They stood, listening. The house was quiet.

'Check upstairs,' Cook said to Reynolds. Cook had his eye on a door under the staircase. He knew where it would lead – the cellar.

Cook trod carefully on the wooden stairs, listening to the sounds of the house. He could hear Reynolds hurrying around upstairs.

Cook had some experience of looking for a missing girl – an evacuee who'd been kidnapped and abused. Elizabeth lived with him on the farm now, but Cook had found her in the dark cellar of a country house. He realised a large part of him was expecting history to repeat itself. The logical place to put someone, if you wanted to keep them alive, and keep them undiscovered.

'Up here!' Reynolds called, his voice muffled by the distance, echoing down several flights of stairs.

*

Reynolds was in a bedroom on the third floor. A grand room, large windows that Cook guessed looked out over the park. An indoor sink, for shaving and brushing teeth. Electric light.

Reynolds was staring at the top of a chest of drawers. He turned to Cook.

'It's hers,' he said, picking up a grey box as if it were a precious artefact.

It was a gas mask box – an utterly recognisable shape and size, albeit customised to appeal to a young woman who wanted something a bit more individual than a brown cardboard box.

'Got it at the market,' Reynolds said. 'Cost her a couple of shillings. She said if she was going to have to carry it everywhere it could bloody well look nice.'

Cook opened the box. Along with the gas mask there were other bits and pieces – a lipstick. Some tissues. A few bus tickets.

'No way she would have left that,' Reynolds said.

71

Dottie had a new friend. After the success of her mission, she'd considered heading home, but the sound of the music coming from the underground bar had lured her back. The new bloke's name was Hal and he worked for the Ministry. He wouldn't say which ministry, said it was hush-hush. But he seemed frightfully excited about it. It was his first time here, he'd said. Heard all about it from friends at work.

The basement was a cacophony of sound. Dottie had to lean in close to listen to Hal, but she didn't mind.

'Do you come here often?' he asked, practically shouting in her ear, his lips brushing her skin. 'I say, that's a terrible line, isn't it! You must think me a complete bore!'

Dottie shook her head.

'I don't think you're a bore!' she shouted. But Hal couldn't hear her. She leant in closer, shouting into his ear. 'I don't think you're a bore at all!'

Hal beamed. He signalled to the barman for two more drinks.

'Be right back!' Dottie said, practically kissing him on the ear she was so close to him. She slid off the barstool, a bit unsteady on her feet. She grabbed her handbag and pushed her way through the crowd to the toilets. She was sweating from the heat, and felt a bit dizzy, now she was standing.

Someone bumped her, and she spun round to apologise, but they were gone. She felt like a pinball in one of those machines.

The toilets were empty – a minor miracle. She used the lav, then fixed her lipstick. Ruby had told her about this place, but she'd never imagined it like this. So . . . vibrant. Hard to believe this was all going on while people spent their nights in places like Tilbury, or the public shelters.

One more drink with Hal, then she'd make her excuses. What her chap back on the island didn't know about wouldn't hurt him.

The door behind her banged, but she didn't look up. If she had done, she would have seen a man with a shock of red hair, and a stain on his shirt from the wine she'd used as a decoy when she'd robbed him.

What got her attention was the click of the lock. She turned to see what was going on, but before she could see, she felt two arms around her in a bear hug. He was behind her. He wrapped one of his hands around her throat. Dottie struggled but he was stronger than she was, and her arms were immobilised.

'Where is it?' he said. His voice was calm. The calmness frightened Dottie even more than his holding her.

'Can't breathe,' she gasped.

'Give it,' he said.

His hand squeezed her throat, tighter, choking her. She felt his fingertips digging into her neck, his thumb pressed against her windpipe.

Was this what had happened to Ruby? Dottie felt a desperate urge to breathe, but she couldn't. The room was getting darker around the edges.

She stamped down on his foot, as hard as she could. Her heel dug into the leather shoe, felt between the toes. She pushed harder.

He let go of her and leapt backwards with a cry. She turned, but he hit her, hard, a backhand swipe across her

face. She felt an explosion of pain, and a gush of warm blood
– her nose broken, but at least his hands were gone from
around her neck.

She backed away into the toilet cubicle and pushed the
door closed, bolting the lock.

He had her bag, and she heard the contents clatter out, into
the sink. Everything she owned, along with his wallet. Dottie
hoped he'd be satisfied, having got what he'd come for.

The outer door banged, and then it was quiet.

*

Dottie staggered through the crowd. People were staring at
her and backing away, but she didn't care. The band music
stopped, as a door opened in front of her, the doorman giving her a quizzical look, but keeping his distance.

The phones in the lobby were all in use. She caught sight
of him, shrugging his coat on as he hurried down the steps,
heading out.

He knew.

She followed him out, torn between wanting to follow him
and needing to keep her distance.

The road was busy with evening traffic, but she couldn't
wait, so she rushed out into the first gap she saw, trusting
the driver would see her in time. She got a blare of a horn,
but made it across.

*

Margaret stood in the hotel lobby, watching through the
revolving door as the young woman staggered across the
road. She'd been undecided – wanted to get out, get some
air, but had lacked a destination. Then the man with the

red hair had pushed past her, and now came the young woman in the red dress, blood streaming down her face, following him out.

Margaret was curious. For all her confidence when she'd laid out the hypothetical story to Bunny – all that guff about stealing pearls from defenceless aristocrats, it turned out she really did want to know what the man was up to. Some kind of confidence trick, no doubt. She would have been content to let him run his game – who was she to judge? – but now she felt a certain connection with the young woman.

*

By the time Dottie got to the other side of Piccadilly, the man was gone, swallowed up by the blackout.

Both of the telephone boxes in Albemarle Street were vacant and Dottie yanked open the door to the first one. She fumbled in her handbag for her purse, but it was gone. He must have taken it.

There was one thing he hadn't got, though. She pulled his calling card from her bra. Dialled the number. It would ring, and she'd get a few words out before the pips cut her off. It would be enough to warn them he was on his way.

72

'She's not here,' Cook said.

'Maybe he did her in, dumped the body,' Reynolds said.

'She wrote that postcard,' Cook said.

'Could have got her to write it, then done her in,' Reynolds said, looking at the gas mask.

'We can wait for him. If he's at the hotel now, he'll come back at some point. Then we can have a word. Just us, and him.'

Far off in the house, the phone rang. A loud, jarring sound. Loud enough to be heard clearly in the bedroom, the sound echoing up from the console table in the front hall.

Cook and Reynolds stood in the bedroom, listening. It rang, again and again. Cook counted. Ten . . . Eleven . . . Twelve . . . yet still it rang. Cook didn't use the phone often. He didn't have a good sense for how long someone would let it ring. Ten felt right. He walked to the top of the stairs. It would stop, he thought, solving his dilemma.

But it didn't stop.

Cook jogged down the stairs, third floor to second floor. The phone kept ringing.

A warning, perhaps, either to them or to him. Only one person who would call here for them. Only one person who knew they were here.

He ran, second to first floor, grabbed the receiver.

'Hello?' he said.

Cook waited for the person at the other end to speak, but no voice came. Then the pips came and then the line cut off, and the dial tone returned.

'We're missing something,' Cook said, looking at the console table. Next to the phone was a torch – black rubber, weatherproof. Put there for emergencies. For power cuts, or times when you'd need to go into the dark.

Underneath the table, a shopping bag filled with blankets. A rudimentary emergency kit, ready for use at short notice.

The kind of bag you'd grab on your way out to the shelter.

73

The Anderson shelter was at the bottom of the garden. No logic to the location, just a thing that felt right when you had to decide where to put it. War was on the horizon, you couldn't admit the idea of the worst happening, so you signed up for your free shelter but when it arrived you felt silly parking it right up by the house, so you put it in the far corner. Out of sight, out of mind. A bad idea, in practice. When the bombs came, you'd want to get to the shelter as quickly as possible.

A path had been trodden down across the grass. Little more than a discolouration in the dew.

Cook and Reynolds exchanged glances. No words needed. Cook took the lead, walking quietly, listening for any sign someone was in the shelter.

Rifle shots cracked in the otherwise quiet evening. Cook spun around, looking for the source. Two more shots, then a roar.

Reynolds shook his head.

'Said in the paper they're shooting the animals in the zoo,' he said. 'Poor bleeders.'

Cook pictured a zoo-keeper checking his list. Reloading his rifle. Off to the next enclosure.

At the end of the garden, the door to the shelter was locked.

'Ruby?' Reynolds shouted. They listened, but there was no reply.

'Let's have a look,' Reynolds said, and Cook stood back as Reynolds set to with the lock-picks.

There was a rustle. Was it from inside the shelter?

'Quiet,' Cook hissed to Reynolds. They listened.

'Hello?' Cook called out.

'Ruby?' Reynolds shouted.

Nothing.

Reynolds fumbled the picks and Cook heard a jangle as they fell to the ground. Reynolds bellowed in frustration and kicked the door, his boot hitting the sheet-metal with everything he had, but the lock held.

'Ruby? We're going to get you out,' Reynolds shouted, as he scrabbled in the long grass for the picks.

'Don't rush,' Cook said. 'Do it once, do it right.'

Reynolds found the picks and returned to his task.

There was a click.

'There you go,' Cook said.

'Not there yet,' Reynolds said.

The click had been too loud, Cook realised. It was a click he recognised. A sound that had become a part of him. A Webley revolver being cocked, the hammer pulled back, ready to fire.

'What's going on here?' a voice said, from the darkness.

74

Thin shards of moonlight illuminated the man. He wore a black trenchcoat, and the brim of his hat kept his face in shadow. Not that it mattered, of course. The gun in his hand was all the information Cook needed.

'You're trespassing,' the man said. 'Give me one reason why I shouldn't shoot you both.'

Reynolds stepped forward, and Cook heard the snick of his knife. Cook put his hand on Reynolds's arm, holding him back. Hard enough to control a situation with an armed assailant. Harder when you've got someone else to deal with, even if he's on your side.

'ARP,' Cook said. 'Your shelter's not up to standard.'

'You're with that girl at the hotel,' the man said. Cook felt Reynolds move, and he tightened his grip on his arm. Not yet, he wanted to communicate.

Cook scanned the house in the distance. Was the man alone, or had he brought help? He'd seen a movement in the shadows.

'I'm going to call the police,' the man said.

'Please do,' Cook said. 'You can explain who you are when they arrive.'

The man was silent.

'You've got no more right to be here than we do,' Cook said. 'You're a fraud. Ruby knew it. That's why you got rid of her. You're squatting here, playing the part of the country gent in town for a few days. Trying your luck with the heiresses at the Empire.'

Cook took a step towards the gun. If he could get close enough, he could spring into action.

But the man stepped back.

'You're not ARP,' he said.

'What have you done with her?' Reynolds asked.

'Who?'

'Ruby,' Cook said. 'She saw through your cover story, so you brought her back here.'

'You've got her gas mask,' Reynolds said.

'Her gas mask?' the man asked, like he was putting two and two together. 'Her?'

Cook inched forwards. He could see the man was thinking, his attention drifting. He'd be thinking about the hotel bar. The young woman he'd been chatting up.

Cook readied himself for the lunge forwards. Grab the arm with the gun. Twist it away.

'Open the shelter,' Reynolds demanded.

The man raised the gun to Cook's head.

'I suppose you're going to make me?' he said.

'I promise you one thing,' Reynolds said. 'If you've harmed a hair on her head, you and me are going to have words. No police needed. Just the two of us, until one of us has stopped breathing.'

The man swung the gun towards Reynolds.

Cook took his chance. He hurled himself forwards, rugby-tackling the man, shoulders around the thighs, wrapping him tight, using his weight to push him over.

The man got Cook with a lucky blow to the head, hard enough to jar Cook's teeth. He felt blood in his mouth.

Cook kept his focus on the gun. He could feel it, in the man's hand. Fingers to be pried away. A fight to the death, no quarter given. Neither man fighting by the Queensberry rules. Cook took a knee to his stomach. In return he jabbed his elbow – got something soft – the neck, he thought.

Cook felt a weight on top of him. He still had the man pinned down, still struggling to get the gun. The weight shifted, the same goal – getting the gun. Another pair of hands wrapped around his, which were wrapped around the man's fingers. All trying for the same goal – to get control of the pistol.

The gunshot was deafening – inches from Cook's ear. Cook rolled away, feeling blood.

Cook stopped rolling, waiting for the pain. But it didn't come. It wasn't him.

Reynolds stepped back, the gun in his hand. He ran to the shelter, fired again, this time at the lock.

He pulled the door open and stared into the darkness.

★

Cook knelt by the dying man. He rolled him onto his side to inspect the wound. The bullet had gone into his chest, a small hole. His back was another story. Half gone. The bullet had done its job, destroying everything in its path, ripping, churning, blowing through with a building pressure-wave. Cook lay the man on his back. No sense in pretending there was going to be any recovery.

Reynolds joined him.

'Where is she?' Reynolds asked.

Cook was distracted by a sound from the house. He saw Dottie standing at the back door.

The man's breathing was ragged. A miracle he was still alive.

'Why should I tell you?' the man asked, clinging on to anger as if it would see him through.

Cook put his hand on the wound in the chest. Pushed into the inflamed flesh. The man gasped in pain.

'Tell us, and I'll stop,' Cook said.

'Blown up,' the man said, hurriedly. 'On the bus.'

'You brought her here,' Cook said. 'We found her gas mask.'

The man shook his head, gasping for air, his lungs filling with blood.

'Dead,' he said. 'Saw her leave the hotel. Then the explosion.'

'You're lying,' Reynolds said.

'Found the mask on the street. Should have left it. Sentimental.'

'Ruby was in your way,' Cook said. 'You had to get rid of her.'

'No,' the man gasped. 'We were . . . both working a scam. Got in . . . each other's way. Not her fault.'

★

Margaret hurried out of the empty house. Nobody had seen her, they'd all had their hands full with the dying man. The crescent was quiet – lots of empty houses judging by the 'TO LET' signs.

When she'd followed the young woman from the hotel, she'd imagined she'd get answers. But now all she had were questions. Of all the people she'd expected to bump into in London, Cook was at the bottom of the list. They'd spent a night in town at the beginning of their courtship. A hotel in Leicester Square, a dinner in Soho, a fight to the death with two hoodlums in the park. But Cook was no lover of the city. What was he doing here? And how was he involved with the confidence trickster?

At least she knew the girl was in safe hands.

75

The Northern Line at Warren Street was busy. Office workers kept late, now off home for a few hours' sleep between
the raids, doing their best to ignore the gallery of women
and children camped out on the platform. A line had been
painted along the length of it, halfway between the wall and
the platform edge. Two worlds. Between the painted line
and the platform edge it was business as usual – tired civil
servants in scuffed bowler hats. Women in sensible office
clothes and sensible shoes. Behind the line, blankets laid out
to claim territory, each one anxiously guarded.

The platform stank. The nearest toilet was at the top of
the escalator, in the ticket hall. Anyone who left their blanket
for that long would return to find it gone. A makeshift curtain at the end of the platform hid what Margaret assumed
was a bucket. Judging by the smell, the bucket was then
emptied onto the track, perhaps thrown optimistically into
the mouth of the tunnel. Out of sight, out of mind.

Margaret breathed a sigh of relief as a train pulled in, passing within inches of the commuters at the front of the platform. It was impossible to see in, with the blackout curtains
covering the windows and doors, installed for the sections of
the line that ran above ground.

A door stopped in front of her, and the curtains opened as
if to start a show. The train was stuffed full. Margaret shuffled
to the side to let a family out – dressed up for an evening at

the theatre. Before she could move, the gap left by the family was filled by others from the platform. Margaret forced herself into the crush, making a space where none had existed. She reached up and managed to get a strap to hang on to. Not that there was much danger of falling over, no matter how much the train might lurch. Bodies pressed against her in every direction. In any other setting it would be indecent.

Nine stops later, Margaret emerged to fresh air at Hendon Central, a pretty plaza built around a crossroads, with a large cinema on one corner, and a bank on each of the others. She checked her map and got her bearings. The Watford Road ran from left to right, up the hill – three lanes each side, like something out of a science fiction film. The northbound carriageways were all busy. Margaret wondered how many of the cars were commuters returning home, and how many were fleeing the city for the night, families heading for a cold, damp night sleeping under the stars in fields and woods outside the city. Trekkers, the papers were calling them, rather dismissively, as if taking steps to avoid being bombed was in some way a sign of moral weakness. Stay here and take your chances with the rest of us, seemed to be the underlying message.

Margaret walked up the hill, the darkness of the blackout contributing to the impression that with every step she was entering the unknown. The grand buildings along the north road thinned out quickly, and soon she was in the suburbs. As she crested the hill, she looked back. The dark city was a silhouette against the slate-grey sky. Already the first bombers had arrived, drawn to the city like wasps to a picnic.

Swynford Grove was a pretty road of detached villas, ornate brickwork and well-kept front gardens. Every house was obediently blacked out, but the half-moon was bright enough for Margaret to find her way. Even so, she was thankful for the white stripes painted on every tree trunk and kerb.

She checked the slip of paper she'd received in the hotel basement. Expensive paper, torn from a diary. Charlotte Pearson. 44 Swynford Grove. Information Margaret could use to convince Bunny she was trustworthy. Bad luck for Mrs Pearson, for whom there'd be a knock on the door late at night. Detention without trial. Disappeared, indefinitely, thanks to the Emergency War Powers Act. Fascism, when your enemy did it. Common sense, when your own government did it, for your protection.

Quite a thing to do to someone, which was why Margaret was here. Wanted to check, to look the woman in the eye, before she ruined a life.

Number forty-four was a pleasant bungalow. Two fruit trees flanked the garden path – an apple and a pear, both heavy with fruit. The grass had been freshly mown, diagonal stripes.

A woman in her fifties answered the door. She had a turban wrapped around her hair, and wore an apron over her dress. She had flour on her hands. Making a crumble, using the fruit while it was plentiful.

'Hello?' the woman said, looking past Margaret to see who else might be out there.

'Mrs Pearson?' Margaret asked, hoping it wasn't. The woman looked friendly. She'd have a husband, children. A good life, here in the suburbs, with the fruit trees.

'Yes?' the woman answered.

'I'm from Tate's Sugar,' Margaret said, with a smile. 'We're calling on women to ask how they use our products in their baking. You were chosen from a list. May I come in for five minutes?'

'Of course!' the woman answered, her shoulders rising, proud she'd been chosen. Hoping her neighbours were watching. She'd have a story to tell.

'What are you making?' Margaret asked, as Mrs Pearson led her to the kitchen – a modern room with Formica counters and brightly painted cupboards.

'Apple crumble,' Mrs Pearson replied, returning to a large mixing bowl on the counter. 'I don't love them myself,' she said, in a conspiratorial voice, 'but my husband loves them. So does Charlotte.'

'Charlotte?' Margaret asked.

'My daughter,' Mrs Pearson said, as the sound of footsteps on the stairs heralded an arrival. 'Here she is!'

A young woman stepped into the kitchen. She eyed Margaret warily.

'Charlotte's down from Cambridge,' Mrs Pearson said, full of pride. 'She loves a bit of home cooking when she can get back.'

'I can't stop,' the young woman said, giving her mum a kiss on the cheek.

'Out with Geoffrey again?' Mrs Pearson asked.

'Geoffrey's old news,' the young woman said, as she shrugged on a summer coat. 'Don't wait up!'

The front door slammed.

Mrs Pearson smiled at Margaret.

'All the young pilots from the airfield. Honestly, the life these girls lead.'

*

Margaret hurried along the pavement, past the manicured front gardens. Mrs Pearson was clearly unaware her daughter was passing along secrets to the Germans, but Charlotte's reaction had been a clear admission of guilt.

'I say,' Margaret called after Charlotte, who was doing a passable job of pretending she couldn't hear the fast footsteps behind her.

Charlotte turned, trying to master her fear, but failing.

'Charlotte?' Margaret called. 'We need to talk.'

Charlotte stopped trying to escape. Margaret could see the internal battle she was fighting – keep up the pretence, or admit it all. The girl wanted it over with. Wanted to confess – face the outcome. Anything would be better than the deception.

They walked slowly. Charlotte took them down a path between two houses, out to the fields. They walked along the top edge, the rest of the field sloping down into a gentle valley. At the bottom of the valley, a collection of low buildings, too big to be barns. A landing strip was visible in the distance, and a windsock fluttered in the evening breeze.

'I was a fresher,' Charlotte said. 'Completely alone. Out of my element. Every hour I wasn't in lectures I spent in my room. It was horrible. Not that I'm making excuses, I just want you to understand.'

'Of course,' Margaret said.

'One night I forced myself to leave the room. Went to a pub. Sat alone in the lounge bar, making up a story of what I'd tell mother. A succession of parties and friends. Everything she wanted for me. But then a professor bought me a drink. He'd come from dinner, still wearing his robes. Ludicrous really. We talked. He bought me another drink. I wasn't really used to it. He took me back to his rooms. Said he'd had his eye on me. Said I was to be his wild oat. It was flattering.'

Charlotte stopped walking and leant on a gate, watching as a Spitfire came in to land in the valley. Margaret stood beside her. Not too close to spook her. Close enough for moral support.

'I fell pregnant. He said he knew someone. Paid for it all. Nobody needed to know. But then, afterwards, he said he needed something in return. As if he hadn't already had what he wanted.' Her face flushed.

Margaret put her hand on Charlotte's.

'You'd told him you lived near the airfield,' Margaret suggested. 'Did he ask about that the first time you met?'

Charlotte nodded.

'He studies aerodynamics,' she said. 'Wing shapes. Lift. He can talk your ear off on the subject. Sounds funny, now, but I liked being the one he wanted to talk to. He said I helped him, said I was his muse.'

'He said I should write to him,' Charlotte continued. 'Over the summer hols. Asked me to keep an eye on the airfield. Wanted to know what types of planes they had. How many. That sort of thing. It didn't seem strange at first. We'd write most days. Not just about the war. Other things, like a couple would. But he wanted more and more. Wanted me to get to know the pilot officers. Report back. Where they'd been. What they were training for. By then I knew I was in shtook. All those posters. Keep mum, and all that.'

'You weren't to know,' Margaret said.

'It's all right,' Charlotte said. 'I know why you're here. I've been expecting someone. I won't blame you.'

She held out her hands, wrists together, as if she expected Margaret to produce a pair of handcuffs.

'I want you to keep writing your letters,' Margaret said, 'but I want you to send them to me first. I'll pass them on, after I've made some changes.'

Charlotte brightened. A light at the end of the tunnel. But the light disappeared as she had a thought.

'Will I still be working for Hitler?' Charlotte asked.

Margaret smiled.

'No dear, you'll be working for me.'

76

Cook let the evening crowds swirl around him. He was at an impasse. No route forward. No information. No job to be done.

Reynolds had taken Dottie back to the shelter. He'd be briefing Gracie by now.

Cook had made a mess of things. He'd got nowhere, and now a man was dead. He should go back to the farm. A short enough walk down to Victoria, catch a late train back to Uckfield.

But something held him here. Leaving now would be like walking out of a show halfway through.

'Is it that dreadful in there?'

Cook recognised the voice without needing to turn around. The American woman. The journalist.

'I was having the same thought,' she said. 'Sometimes you want to sit in a regular bar and have a regular drink, without all the hysteria.'

They were across the road from the Empire. Cook had walked here without thinking. The place the trail had gone cold.

'You look like you'd like to buy a girl a pint,' she said.

They found a pub on a side street a couple of hundred yards from the hotel. A narrow frontage, one bow window, blacked out. A heavy, narrow door set back in an alcove.

Cook bought two pints of best. Eleanor had been very insistent – whatever he was drinking. He carried them through the fog of cigarette smoke to the window seat – a broad bench set in the curving bay. The pub was busy. She'd done well to find a space. Looking at the expanse of glass at her back, Cook realised why. Thin strips of tape, criss-crossed across the windows, peeling off in curls, defeated by the humidity generated by the crowd. If a bomb landed in the street, the window would be death for anyone near it.

Eleanor sat in the window seat, nodded to him as she took her drink. They clinked glasses as he took his place next to her. Awkward, sitting side by side, facing the interior of the pub.

'Cheers!' she said.

'Cheers,' he reciprocated. He was somewhat unsure why he was here. Like being ordered by your sergeant major. You didn't stop to think, you just did. In the absence of a way forward, it wasn't the worst detour.

The beer was excellent. He savoured it.

'I gather you've become persona non grata at the hotel,' she said.

He must have looked surprised, because she smiled, like she'd admitted to knowing a secret.

'I keep my eyes open,' she said. 'Hard not to pick up on what's going on if you watch for long enough.'

'What *is* going on?' he asked.

'The usual, for a big hotel,' she said. 'Prostitution, of course. Extortion. Several long-running scams working their way through the process.'

'Seems like it's a family business,' Cook said. 'All those brothers.'

She nodded.

'A fascinating twist,' she said. 'When I arrived it was all Italians. Then Mussolini declared war on Britain and suddenly the Italians had to be rounded up, sent to concentration camps.'

'Internment,' Cook said.

She made a face. 'You say tomahto, I say tomayto.'

'Then what?'

'It was chaos. Half the staff gone. You couldn't get a decent drink for love nor money. And then the next morning, nine o'clock sharp, a whole new crew. Doorman. Front desk. Maître d'. Bartender. The lot. All of them related, if you ask me. New girls, too. A complete regime change, overnight. Very impressive.'

Cook thought of Mr Jones in his jazz club, seeing an opportunity, sending his boys in.

'Now, you've pumped me for information, time for me to ask some questions,' she said.

Cook sipped his beer.

'What are *you* doing here?' she asked. She took a notepad from her inside pocket. Pulled a pencil from the same pocket.

'Remember I'm a journalist,' she added. 'So you've been warned.'

She put pencil to paper.

'What do you do?' she asked.

'I'm a farmer.'

'Not many farms around here,' she said. 'What brings you to the big, bad city?'

'It's a long story,' he said.

She put her pencil down. Took a long draught of her pint.

'That's all right,' she said. 'We've got all night.'

★

The hotel was quiet. The dining room was dark, and a skeleton staff remained in the lobby.

'Guests are sheltering in the basement,' the man behind the desk said, as he handed Eleanor her key.

'No, thank you,' Eleanor replied. 'The people of New York want to know what's going on as the bombs fall. Can't do much reporting from a basement.'

The desk clerk glared at Cook.

'He's not welcome here,' he said to Eleanor.

'I'm paying for a room,' Eleanor replied. 'I'm allowed to have any guests I want.'

'Not him,' the clerk replied.

'Perhaps I should do a story about the prostitution racket you're running out of the bar,' she said, taking out her notebook. 'My readers love that kind of thing. What's your name?'

She leant forward, theatrically, peering at the clerk's name badge. She wrote it in her notebook.

'Or maybe we should both mind our own business. What do you think?'

*

Eleanor's room was a world apart from the box room Cook had been given. A luxurious four-poster bed faced a floor-to-ceiling window. Eleanor pulled a cord by the window, and the curtains parted.

It was like watching the war on a cinema screen. Searchlights panned across the clouds, catching the highest buildings as they traversed the sky. Cook didn't know the city well, but St Paul's was unmistakable, its dome higher than any of the surrounding buildings. Beyond, he could see the steel skeletons of cranes, watching over the docks.

The clouds themselves were alight, pulsing with explosions. The order had come from Churchill himself – every available anti-aircraft gun in the country had been sent to defend the capital. Every gun was to be firing non-stop.

Cook didn't know how effective they'd be, but he had to admit it felt comforting.

The eastern sky was orange as once again the docks burnt.

Eleanor poured two glasses of whisky, handed one to Cook.

'Cheers,' she said.

They drank. Cook checked his watch, calculated the walk to catch the last train. He'd have to be going, if he was going.

Eleanor finished her drink with a second gulp and hurried into the bathroom, leaving the door open behind her.

'You said you're here to describe it,' Cook said. 'But which side are your readers on? You must have just as many immigrants from Germany as from England.'

'We're still deciding,' Eleanor shouted out of the bathroom. 'Churchill's doing everything he can to lure us in, but there are still lots of people in power who think this whole thing has nothing to do with us.'

Cook stood at the window, like having a balcony seat for London's final act. It was obscene, of course, but no more obscene than anything else in war. Certainly a lot more comfortable than sheltering in a trench as the bombs flew, or cowering in a cave overlooking a mountain pass.

'What do *you* think?' Cook asked.

There was a creak from the bed behind him. Cook looked at the reflection in the window. Eleanor had returned from the toilet and kicked off her shoes, and now she lay on the bed, on her front. Watching him, watching the war.

'I think we should put this bed through its paces,' Eleanor said.

'Are all you Americans this forward?' he asked.

'I can't speak for the entire population,' she said.

'I thought you wanted to hear my story,' he said. 'Why I'm in London, and not on my farm.'

'Sounds like more of a breakfast conversation,' she said.

'There's a girl,' he said. 'She's in trouble.'

Eleanor raised an eyebrow.

'There's a chance she's dead,' Cook continued, 'but it's not a certainty.'

Eleanor got up and stood in front of Cook. She unbuttoned his shirt. Cook let her.

'It must seem like a very small thing,' he said, 'compared to thousands being killed by the bombs.'

'Is it thousands?' she asked.

'You're the journalist,' he said. 'Just a guess, from what I've seen in the docks.'

'What's it like down there?'

Cook thought of the shelter. The child's hand, covered in dust, the rest of the body under tons of concrete.

'Not pretty,' he said.

'You think the people are with Churchill?' she asked, undoing his belt.

'No,' he said, realising it was the truth as he said it. 'There's no support. No food. No housing. There's looting. Not a good situation. Not like all this . . .'. He looked around the luxurious hotel room, the sheer opulence of ice cubes clinking in his glass.

'That's what I'm here to report,' she said. 'But they've got people watching me. Making sure I don't see too much.'

'People?'

'My chaperones,' she said. 'Keeping me safe. Making sure I see what they want me to see. Working-class neighbourhoods with Union Jacks in every window, cheering Churchill when he gets out of his armoured car for ten seconds.'

'Where are they now?'

'I gave them the slip,' she said. 'They think I'm in the basement bar, listening to jazz.'

'You should come to the island, see what's happening.'

'Would you take me?'

'It's a free country,' Cook said. You can come with me or you can get on the tube and see for yourself.'

'I've never taken public transport,' she said, 'sounds like quite the adventure.'

She kissed him.

'What about the countryside?' she asked. 'What's the sentiment down there?'

Cook opened his mouth to answer, but something stopped him. He thought of the posters behind the check-in desk:

Keep Mum, She's Not So Dumb
Careless Talk Costs Lives

Simplistic messages, unnecessary and over the top. Heavy-handed propaganda designed to keep people in a state of panic. But now he found himself talking freely with a woman he'd only recently met. Suddenly the posters didn't seem so unnecessary.

'Come down sometime and I'll give you the tour,' he said.

She peeled off his shirt, threw it towards a chair. It slid down the polished leather and crumpled on the floor. Cook felt a flash of irritation – fought the urge to hurry over and pick it up. He distracted himself by looking at the cityscape. A bomber went down, trailing fire. A series of explosions erupted where it had gone down, its own bombs triggered by the impact. Somewhere beyond St Paul's.

'I'm going to need you to get your head in the game,' Eleanor said, as she stepped out of her dress. She let her slip fall to the floor. Naked, she looked suddenly vulnerable. Exposed. Cook put his arms around her, feeling goosebumps on her skin.

'You've got my full attention,' he said.

He reached for the curtain pull.

'Leave them open,' she said. 'We can watch.'

She crawled into bed, held the covers open, ready for him.

'I trust I'm not going to end up on the front page,' Cook said.

77

A clatter of metal woke Ruby. It sounded like someone had thrown a handful of gravel at the roof of the shelter.

Ruby huddled under the thin blanket. She opened one eye, fearing the worst. Some kind of new torture he'd devised for her.

There was a pinprick of light in the curved ceiling. A star. Ruby moved her head and the star disappeared. She moved back and saw it again.

She smelt burning wool, like when she was ironing and she left the iron on a piece of cloth a moment too long. It was coming from her blanket. She kicked out with her legs and heard a small thump as something landed on the floor.

Ruby got out of bed and felt on the carpet. She found it almost immediately – a lump of metal, hot but cooling. It felt like a button mushroom. It must have fallen out of the sky, made the hole in the metal roof.

Ruby got back into bed and pulled the blanket back over her. It was the first night she'd felt cold. Winter was on its way.

What would happen to her? The row of graves answered that question. Girls who'd been taken. Presumably they'd all slept in this bed. Lain awake in fear. Fought back when they could, and suffered when they could not.

Next time he came, she'd fight back. Keep fighting until the end. Him or her.

78

Cook lay in bed, the American journalist asleep beside him. He'd made a mistake. He didn't know what it was, but he felt the fact of it. It wasn't the sex. He wasn't a puritan, and if a beautiful woman wanted him to spend the night in her luxury hotel room he felt it was perfectly reasonable of him to take her up on the offer. But the feeling was there, whether it was logical or not.

Something felt wrong.

He thought back through the day. Taking the bus through the city, retracing the route the girl from the Lyons would have taken. Perhaps that was it – getting into the head of a girl who was almost definitely dead. Showing up at her home, sharing his thoughts with her parents as if he had any right to intrude on their lives. Shattering their dreams that perhaps their daughter had walked a different way home, taken a different bus. Met a chap, perhaps. Walked into a recruiting office and signed up for a war job that had meant she'd been spirited away to the country there and then, hush-hush and all that. Fantasies her parents would have been spinning, rather than face the truth.

Meanwhile, he'd been spinning the same story about Ruby – making up an elaborate work-around, designing a world in which she hadn't been killed by a German bomb.

Some kind of desire to be the hero, Cook suspected. A life of solving problems when they came along, a pattern of expectation teaching him he had the power to over-write what the world had planned, whether it was him walking out of the trenches alive, when so many had fallen, or turning the farm around, when so many were failing. Get lucky a few times, and you start to think it's you who makes the luck. Who'd said that? Was it Blakeney, his old CO?

Of course, there was the postcard. But that could have been written by someone else, despite Gracie's faith in it being a coded message.

But who knew enough to know they needed to send it? For all everyone knew, Ruby was dead.

Perhaps it was Gracie who was reading too much into things. The simplest answer was that Ruby really was at the coast with a boyfriend. The odds were she'd walk into the pub in a few days' time.

Cook slipped out of bed and dressed quietly. He needed to think, and he thought best when he was walking.

*

He breathed more easily as soon as he left the hotel. He took a left into the park. Suddenly it felt important to have the grass under his feet, to be amongst the trees. Instinctively, he headed for the deepest reaches of what could pass as a small wood, where a gentle slope gave the impression of the countryside, and the trees blocked out most of the city.

In the darkness, amongst the trees, he realised others had sought the same escape. Bodies rustled in the autumn leaves, some sleeping, some coupling. He walked on, to the far end of the park, crossed the road.

Hyde Park was larger. Wilder. All he could see was grass and trees. His kind of country.

Cook walked for five minutes, through grass that grew less manicured. As he walked, he became aware of someone following him. He slowed his pace, and his follower slowed. They were good, whoever they were, silent as they walked through the long grass, hardly more than a whisper of leaf on stalk.

He was completely cut off from the city. Cook wouldn't have believed it, but here he was, in the heart of London, and all he could see on every horizon was the dark silhouette of grassland and trees. He could have been out in his own fields.

Time to deal with his shadow. He made for a thicket of trees – a wall of darkness against the glowing sky. Even before he reached it, he'd be invisible to anyone behind him. He dropped to the ground and crawled sideways, through the long grass. If his pursuer followed in his footsteps, he'd see them against the sky.

Cook lay in the grass. He could smell damp earth and dry leaves. The smell of England, in autumn. A faint hint of coal-smoke from the invisible city, and fainter still, an acrid smell, from the burning docks. Or perhaps that was his imagination, filling gaps, telling stories.

He couldn't hear the other man. It had been a minute since he'd last heard the crunch of a leaf or even the whisper of grass. Perhaps he'd been wrong. Imagining enemies. It wouldn't be the first time.

Give it another minute. Worst case, you're lying in the grass, the stars overhead, a chance to forget you're in the big city.

A snap of a twig. He tensed. Listened. An animal. A fox, probably. On its own night manoeuvres.

Cook rolled, fast. Instinct had alerted him, and then launched his body into action while his conscious mind was still wondering about the bloody fox. Instinct, and then training.

It was training that stopped the roll, countering the movement to launch back, towards the attacker. Never do what
your opponent expects. Take control, set the tempo. He was
onto the man in an instant, using momentum to throw him.

The man was lighter than he'd expected. He'd thought it
would be one of the brothers from the hotel. Big, bigger or giant.
This assailant was half the weight of the smallest of those men.

'Cook!' she yelled, as she hit the ground with a thud. He
was on top of her before he had a chance to think, pinning
both arms down, his weight on her legs.

It took him a second to realise.

It was Margaret.

Impossible of course. The last time he'd seen her she'd
pointed a gun at him, ordered him out of the rowing boat
they'd both taken, then disappeared into the darkness, to
rendezvous with a German U-boat out in the Channel, her
pockets stuffed with details of a secret radio installation.

'Whose side are you on?' he'd shouted back then as she'd
disappeared into the dark, heading out to sea, but she hadn't
answered. Her silence had been enough.

Now, she lay underneath him, writhing to get out from
his grip.

'What the hell are you playing at?' he asked, his blood
still up.

'Good to see you too,' she said.

She grinned. It annoyed him. This was no laughing matter. She'd crept up on him in the dark and attacked him.
Cook could think of several men who'd tried that same trick
who wouldn't be trying it again.

'What the bloody hell,' he said.

'Don't be ticked off,' she said. 'Just a bit of fun.'

He kept her pinned down, in the darkness. He felt her
pushing her body up, testing his weight, trying to escape.

Cook had a lot of questions. A lot of things he'd imagined saying since the night she'd left him. All led back to the big question – was she on his side, or theirs? He hadn't known then, and in the intervening time he hadn't come to any conclusions.

He still didn't know.

She craned her head forward and kissed him. A surprise attack. He pulled back, better to look at her. He tried to think. To weigh the logic. But rational thought eluded him.

He kissed her back, keeping his hands on hers, either side of her head, pushed into the grass.

She pushed her body against his, a memory of the weeks they'd spent together, living as man and wife. She rolled, and he let her, reversing their positions, her above, looking down, her hair a curtain around her face.

'Why the hell would I trust you a second time?' Cook asked.

Margaret kissed him again. She let go of his hands, and he ran them down her back, finding bare skin under her dress, then back up, under the fabric.

He rolled her again, the grass whispering against her dress. She arched her back as he drew the dress up, over her shoulders.

'You missed me,' she said.

Cook kissed her. It seemed to be the best way to keep her quiet.

*

Cook sat with his back against a chestnut tree, Margaret leaning against him, his arms wrapped around her. He told her about Ruby, and Frankie, and everything that had happened.

'There's a lot going on at that hotel,' Margaret said. 'A lot of people with a lot of secrets. What are the odds she got caught up in something?'

Cook thought about Ruby, and the man she'd crossed, now lying dead in a back garden near Regent's Park.

'The hotel's a distraction,' he said.

'Maybe. Maybe not.'

They sat in silence, watching searchlights paint the underside of the clouds with light.

'So there's a woman out there who needs help, and you're the man for the job. Or, alternatively, she's dead and you're chasing ghosts around the city.'

'It's not quite that simple,' Cook replied.

'Sounds pretty clear to me,' she said. 'Fifty per cent chance there's a job to be done only you can do, with a young woman out there desperately counting on you doing it, even though she doesn't know it. Fifty per cent chance you're wasting your time. But what else would you be doing?'

An owl screeched. Cook listened to the sounds of the woods in the night.

Margaret was right. She had a way of putting things that cut through the noise.

They walked back through the park, past a humming generator powering a bank of searchlights. Past a winch and crew of balloon operators.

'What's it like out there?' she asked.

'Out where?'

'The docks.'

'Same as all wars,' Cook said. 'The rich play at strategy while the poor die by the thousand. I don't see any reason why this one will be any different.' He thought of the island, more than half the warehouses destroyed. The shelters, badly built, not fit for purpose. A world away from the West End, even if it caught the occasional raid.

'Bunny's trying to sell the idea of the blitz spirit,' Margaret said.

'He might be selling it,' Cook said, 'but the people I've seen aren't buying it. Bunny should keep his fingers crossed the Luftwaffe try to bomb Buckingham Palace or Number Ten – might show the people we're all in it together. If Hitler keeps targeting the working class, he'll turn us all into communists. And we've seen how that story ends up.'

Outside the Empire, a crowd of onlookers watched. An ambulance and a police car were parked in the street. Two ambulance-men carried out a stretcher, a man lying on it, covered with a bloodied sheet.

'I can't tell you what happened over there,' Margaret said, as they both watched a second man being escorted out by the police. A pilot, judging by his uniform.

Margaret felt for Cook's hand. She took his little finger and squeezed it, hoping to convey everything she couldn't say out loud.

Cook didn't answer. He wanted to tell Margaret it would be all right. That they could take up where they'd left off. Her, and him, and the evacuees, and the farm. A life they'd both had the barest glimpse of.

But that would be a lie. The life they'd left off was gone.

79

No one was coming to help. Ruby looked into the darkness and told herself the truth. She wasn't a child any more. This wasn't one of those fairy stories where the knight in shining armour was hacking his way through an overgrown forest. If there had been anyone outside the hotel who'd seen her get into the car, they'd had ample time to report their suspicions.

No. The truth was far more simple. She was going to die here, and then he'd bury her, next to the other girls.

Ruby found a certain comfort in her new-found clarity. It helped with decision-making.

She had an idea. A bad idea. Almost definitely bound to fail. But, it turned out, almost definitely bound to fail started to look a lot better when you compared it to the alternative of definitely going to be killed.

The Anderson shelter was designed to be put up quickly. Anyone with a garden could erect one themselves. They'd been giving them away free to anyone who wanted one.

The shelter wasn't meant for anyone to live in long-term. If you were building a house, you'd want some kind of concrete floor. Something to keep out the vermin and the damp. The Anderson shelter, on the other hand, didn't need any such foundation. Just put it in the ground and Bob's your uncle, as they said.

He'd put down a scrap of old carpet. A man's attempt at making a hole in the ground into a home.

Ruby peeled back the edge of the carpet. As she'd thought, underneath was bare soil.

Soil underfoot. Soil outside. The metal sides of the Anderson shelter would have been stuck into the soil to keep the whole thing stable, but not very deep. Ruby hadn't seen one going up, but she guessed about a foot. A foot of corrugated metal in the mud, between her and freedom. All she needed was some way of digging. She could use her hands, but it would be too slow, and while she was prepared to take a risk, she wasn't stupid. The faster she could dig, the better chance she had of doing it in one go, between visits.

He'd left her a plate. He'd brought her a slice – a common meal on the island. One slice of day-old bread, fried in whatever fat was left over from the last meal. To Ruby, half starved, it had been one of the most delicious meals she'd ever had, the bacon grease coating her lips and fingers. She could still smell it. She'd licked the plate clean once she'd finished, and then, again, an hour later. Just in case.

Now, the plate would serve another purpose. A spade, of sorts.

Ruby pushed the plate into the soil, and scooped back a handful. She looked around. She slung the soil under the bed. It wasn't perfect, but if her plan was going to work, she'd be gone before he saw the inside of the shelter. The same logic suggested she could simply pile up the soil where she knelt, but that felt too brazen. So under the bed it was.

She dug right at the edge, where the corrugated iron wall disappeared into the ground. As she dug down, the metal wall continued. She got a foot down, and stuck her fingers in the hole, trying to feel the bottom edge. But the metal wall continued down.

It took another hour to get two feet down. This had been a bad idea. She looked at the soil under the bed. She couldn't believe how much there was – it seemed so much more than the size of the hole she'd dug.

It wasn't too late to put it back. Lay the carpet over it. Pretend it had never happened.

She stuck her fingers into the soil. It was damp at the bottom of the hole. A worm wriggled against her hand. Just a worm, she told herself.

Then she felt it. The bottom edge of the wall. Sharp metal. She was right. The plan was going to work. She'd need another foot down to give her space to wiggle underneath, then she could come up the other side.

*

Ruby was practically upside down, lying on her back, leaning backwards into the hole. She had her head and one arm under the wall, all her narrow tunnel allowed, and was digging upward. Every movement of the plate, a shower of soil landed in her face. She'd worked out a system. She kept her eyes and mouth shut, let it fall, then wriggled out of the hole, turned over, and scooped out the loose soil.

It wasn't very efficient. Her back was killing her. Her hands were bleeding from all the times she caught them on the underside of the metal wall, and her eyes, nose, and mouth were full of soil. But she was making progress. At least, she had been, until she'd hit a snag.

There was a big stone in the soil. It was a problem. Ruby was underneath it, looking up. Her plate scraped across the stone and she shuddered, like when the teacher scratched her nails on the blackboard, back at St John's. Ruby reached up and felt the stone. It was the size of a football. She loosened the soil around the edge, then stopped, realising the dilemma. If she loosened the stone enough, it would fall downwards, onto her face.

She loosened a bit more soil to the side of the stone. It shifted. Keeping the plate in her hand, she felt the stone to see if she could judge its weight. But it was still supported by the soil. Would she have time to wriggle backwards once it fell?

Ruby reminded herself of her decision rule. Was the chance of getting a rock in the face better or worse than the certainty of being killed?

She kept digging, wincing with every shower of soil, anticipating the weight of the stone on her face.

The rock gave way gently, almost elegantly. It slid down into Ruby's hand, and she wriggled backwards, letting it fall. Then it was a simple matter of reaching back into the tunnel, pulling it out, like delivering a baby.

Without the obstruction, the digging was easier. Soon she was digging through roots. She punched the plate up, and with a final shower, she saw stars.

*

Ruby took one last look around the shelter. There was nothing she could take. Nothing useful. She left the plate, and wriggled into the hole. Under the sharp edge of the wall, then up, into the moonlight, climbing out onto the grass. She must have looked a sight. A mole-child, being given up by the soil.

She lay on the grass, feeling the breeze.

Time to go.

There was a house in the distance. His house. He'd be gone, back to the island. Back to his duties.

Her stomach growled. The house would have food. It might have a telephone. But most of all, food.

She'd be in and out quickly, then she'd be on her way.

The back door was unlocked. It let her into a kitchen. Linoleum floor. Paraffin cooker. A dresser holding plates and cups. Two of each. Not a family's home, or a place to welcome visitors.

There was a cold-cupboard, the door opening onto a metal box clamped onto the outside of the house. Ruby's stomach groaned as she opened it, praying there'd be food. Her prayers were answered. A bottle of milk and a block of cheese, wrapped in cloth. She found a loaf of bread on the side, ripped it apart and ate, alternating between mouthfuls of bread, cheese, and milk.

She didn't hear the footsteps behind her. Didn't see the other woman, even as the marble rolling-pin swung towards her head.

Ruby felt a sharp pain above her ear, then nothing.

It wasn't like being asleep. She had no sensation of time passing. It was instantaneous. One second the rolling-pin was coming towards her, the next second she was opening her eye, one side of her face pressed against the lino floor, her head pounding with the worst headache she'd ever known.

A pair of flowery slippers appeared, eighteen inches in front of her face.

Something poked her in the shoulder. A broom, held backwards, the handle wavering above Ruby's face. It poked her again. She opened her other eye. An elderly woman was sitting on a kitchen chair, watching her.

She held the rolling-pin in her right hand, using the left to wield the broom like a knight at a jousting tournament.

'You been playing the tease?' she asked. 'Father tells me all about you girls, prancing around the West End with your tits and your arse on display to the world, as if there weren't a lick of decency left in people. You were lucky it were Father what brought you in. Could have ended up much worse.'

The woman studied Ruby as if she were a butterfly pinned to a collector's board.

'You'll be wanting to play the good girl. Let him put a baby in your belly. That'll be the easiest way out of it.'

Ruby didn't respond. She kept an eye on the rolling-pin. Another knock and she might never wake up.

'Not like it's the first time, is it?' the woman said. 'Baby-snatcher we call you, Father and I.'

Ruby didn't respond. Not that it seemed to matter to the woman.

'Course I knew,' the woman said. 'My idea. All you girls sent here, rude not to take advantage. You always seemed like a strong lass. Good bones. I was right, weren't I? How's the lad turned out?'

Ruby kept quiet. Frankie was her secret. What felt like a lifetime of keeping it quiet certainly wasn't going to stop now.

The woman smiled.

'Father tells me all about him. Got him evacuated for me. Got him away from you and yours. Give it a year and he'll have forgotten you all.'

'Stay away from him,' Ruby said.

'Or what?' This was accompanied by another poke from the broom. Ruby grabbed the end of the pole and pulled it away. It clattered on the ground.

'Always knew you was a strong 'un. Picked you out myself.'

The woman got up from the chair and walked, warily, towards Ruby. She held the rolling-pin ready.

'Going to put you back in your hole now. You be good and I'll send you down a bit of fish, keep your bones strong. Make another baby.'

The rolling-pin swung and Ruby heard a crack. The pain was ten times worse this time, but she welcomed the blackness.

80

Cook nodded to the bouncer and tossed him another half a crown. The bouncer stepped out of the way and let Cook through, up the sagging stairs, towards the music.

Cook had a plan, in as much as going back to the last person who'd seemed willing to give information was a plan. In Cook's experience, when someone grudgingly gave up information, they often held something back, parcelling it out just enough at a time to keep the questioner at bay. It was certainly a technique that had worked for Cook, when he'd found himself in the uncomfortable position of being under suspicion. It gave him a certain sympathy for the woman who'd told him about Ruby and the red-headed conman.

Cook sat, and drank, and tried to let the music wash over him, although music was a stretch for what Cook was hearing. Noises, certainly. Cook guessed they kept the better acts for the peak hours. Bad news for him. Not so easy to think when you were being confronted by the full range of squawks a trumpet could be forced to produce.

Margaret had put it simply. Either there was a girl out there who needed his help, or there wasn't. Fifty-fifty. If there wasn't, he was wasting his time. But Cook's time had no particular value. If he was hit by a bomb, there'd be a few people who'd mourn his death, but life would go on for all concerned. Bill Taylor, his farm manager, would keep things ticking over, providing an income for Mum and Uncle Nob, at least for the duration of the war – as long as the government provided a guaranteed market for every bushel of grain his farm could produce. Frankie would go back to his own people, and Mum would take care of Elizabeth.

The staff door opened a crack, then closed. It had been open for just long enough for Cook to recognise the girl, the one who'd given him the information.

Time to make something happen.

'Mr Cook,' a gravelly voice from behind him.

Cook turned. The man was standing. Not the optimal situation. So Cook stood. It was Mr Jones – tailored suit and immaculate tie.

'You're becoming a nuisance,' Mr Jones said. 'I'm going to have to ask you to leave.'

Cook wasn't worried about Mr Jones. He was an elderly man, his days of being a physical threat long behind him.

Mr Jones stepped aside, and another man stepped out of the shadows. The giant from the hotel.

Cook looked up at the giant. It was a novel experience. Cook was a tall man, not often he found himself looking up. He didn't like it.

This was the point where an adversary would provide a clue as to his intentions. A man who knew what he was about, who knew how to use violence and the effect it produced on others, would proceed straight to action. A head-butt, perhaps, or a blow to the stomach, doubling over the adversary to be followed up with a knee to the face. A less serious man, one who played to the theatre of the role but didn't follow through, would talk. Threatening words would be exchanged, like two dogs barking at each other, both safe in the knowledge their owners wouldn't let them fight.

The last time they'd met, the giant had seemed open to talking, which Cook saw as promising. Nevertheless, while hoping for the best, he prepared for the worst. He set his legs, one slightly forward, thigh muscle tensed, so he could spring back if it was a head-butt. He kept his eyes on the giant's arms, waiting for a swing – a fist, or a knife.

The blow came from the giant's right hand, a fast movement, a jab to Cook's solar plexus. Cook tensed his stomach muscles. Ten years of swinging bales of hay and sacks of grain, if he'd tried to design a better regimen for this exact moment, he'd have struggled to improve on his life on the farm. But even so, the blow was as powerful as Cook had ever felt. Like a horse had kicked him. If he hadn't been tensing his stomach muscles, it would have crippled him temporarily, doubled him over. Perhaps even left him with fatal injuries. Internal bleeding. The kind they said finished off Houdini. As it was, Cook reeled, stepping backwards, but didn't go down.

The giant looked down, ready for Cook to double over, ready to put his knee into Cook's face. So Cook reached up, grabbed the back of the giant's head and forced it down, bringing his own knee up into the man's face.

The giant staggered back, his nose disintegrated, hardly any cartilage there to start with. Blood sheeted down his shirt front. The immaculate suit ruined. Cook stepped forward with a quick rabbit-punch to the man's throat, turning slightly with the punch, giving it the weight of his whole body. The giant gasped, fell back against the far wall of the corridor, clutching his throat.

'Bloody hell,' the girl said, stepping out from behind the staff door. 'You've done him in.'

Cook turned back to her.

'Tell me something else about Ruby,' he said.

'Whoever she was working for,' she said, 'I think she was trying to get out of it, but they wouldn't let her. I heard her on the phone once.'

'Anything else?'

'No. Honest.'

Cook believed her. There were plenty of reasons for her to lie to him, but he believed her nonetheless. A weakness, perhaps.

'You should stay for a dance,' she said, winking at him.

'Another time,' Cook said, turning back to check on his assailant, who'd gone quiet.

But there was nobody there.

From the corner of his eye, Cook saw the weapon. A crowbar, perhaps. Large, black, incoming.

*

Cook could see the musicians playing, but the angle was wrong. They were far away, and yet looming over him. The music sounded like it was coming at him from underwater. A blessing, at least. He was looking up at the dancer. She was shouting. She was angry. But he couldn't hear her. Then someone must have turned the lights off because everything went dark.

81

Ruby hadn't thought she would sleep – every time she turned her head on the thin pillow she felt a wave of pain that made her want to scream. But eventually sleep had come. Until the crows had started their cawing. Even then, Ruby had fallen back to sleep. But then another sound cut through her dreams. A sliding sound, followed by a thump. It had taken the longest time to work it out – someone was digging a hole.

Every time the spade slid into the earth, Ruby pictured it. From the sound of it, the ground was full of stones, scraping against the steel blade, frustrating the digger.

Ruby opened her eyes and squinted at the door. A tiny gap around the metal frame showed her it was daylight outside. Her stomach growled.

A clang of steel on rock resulted in a scream of anger from outside. A woman's scream.

'Brought you a cuppa,' he said. Ruby could just make out the words, through the corrugated iron walls. The digging stopped. Ruby pictured the two of them, standing in the garden, sipping tea, eyeing the grave-in-progress.

'Give it time,' he said. 'It doesn't always happen right away.'

'What do you know about it?' she snapped back. 'The look of that girl, she's ready for a baby. You do your job, put one in her tummy.'

'They're looking for her,' he said.

'Good luck finding her when she's six feet under.'

'It needs more time,' he said.

'And I'm telling you. I'm sick of waiting. If her tummy doesn't start growing, she's going in the ground with the rest of them.'

82

Frankie sat at the kitchen table looking at the postcard. He'd never got post before, but here it was, delivered by Mr Smith, on his bicycle.

Cook's mum was watching him. She'd been tip-toeing around him since the funeral, but Frankie didn't mind. She was a nice lady. Uncle Nob was in his armchair, same as ever. It had taken Frankie a long time to get used to the old man, with his shaking hands. He'd thought the not talking was a trick, some kind of test, but in the end he'd got used to it. Nob was nice too. Even Cook was, in the end.

'It's from Ruby,' Frankie said. His head was spinning. One minute he'd been thinking about Ruby being blown up, the next minute all that was changed.

'She's met a fella,' he said. 'Gone to the seaside.'

He knew Cook's mum must have read the card too, but she'd let him find out for himself. She was good like that.

There wasn't much else on the card, but Frankie pored over it. The postmark was blurry, but he could see the date. Two days ago. Would have got here yesterday, Cook's mum had said, but they hadn't got the address perfect. It had been made out to Frankie Reynolds, Mr Cook's farm, Uckfield, Sussex. Other than that there was the message, and a picture she'd drawn. A little joke. A couple of birds and a tree. Frankie had sent a card to Ruby once, and he'd drawn the same picture. The only other time he'd been outside London, before all of this. All the children had been driven out to the countryside, stayed in an old barn. They'd played games in the long grass and got sunburnt, and all of them were given a postcard to write and send home, even though they'd be home themselves before the cards arrived.

Frankie hadn't liked the place. It was all sky and trees and those awful squawking birds. He'd missed the gloomy canyon of the high street, and the smell of the river. When he'd written his card, he'd written it to Ruby. 'Come and get me,' he'd written, and drawn the picture, hoping it would help her find the place. He'd only been small, of course, so the picture wasn't much good. Now he was a year older. Now he'd draw a map, or at least a better picture.

83

The world was spinning and rocking at the same time. Cook had never felt so dizzy. He held his eyes tightly shut, the only thing in his power, but it didn't do any good. His internal sense of equilibrium told him he was in some kind of spinning top.

His hands were tied behind his back. Rough rope, digging into his wrists.

The left side of his face was numb. It was pressed against something cold. Metal but liquid. He smelt petrol, and something rotting.

He was going to be sick. He felt it coming, and reared his head up, opening his eyes.

'Watch out, mate,' someone said. 'He's doing it again.'

'Not on my fucking shoes he's not,' another voice.

Cook felt someone manhandling him, tilting him over an edge that dug into his ribs. He felt the spray of water on his face, and his stomach heaved.

'We should drop him in now,' the first voice said. 'No one'll be any the wiser.'

'Til the tide brings him back up,' this from the second voice, 'and the old man finds out. The old man wants a trip to the outflow, he gets a trip to the outflow. You fuck around with the old man you'll be the next in the river.'

'He got it on my shoe.'

'Shoes can be cleaned. You fuck about with the old man you'll wish you only had to worry about a dirty shoe.'

Cook opened his eyes as he was pulled back over the edge. He was in a small motorboat. The giant sat behind him, wads of toilet paper stuffed in his broken nose, one hand on the tiller, an outboard motor throbbing and sending up a thin whisp of exhaust. The other voice was the medium-sized brother from the hotel. Keeping it in the family, Cook thought.

He'd let himself get distracted by the dancer. Stupid. A pretty woman, looking at him with her big eyes. Smiling at him, making a connection. But she'd said something important. He tried to remember. Something about Ruby trying to get out of her situation. Getting in trouble with the person who was running her.

Reynolds.

Would Reynolds hurt his own daughter? Cook didn't know very much about the man. He knew Gracie had thrown him out. He knew Frankie was scared of him.

Cook moved his legs. They were tied at the ankles, but he could use them to push himself up into a sitting position. He was on the floor, in an inch of water, rainbow patterns from oil or petrol on top.

They were passing the island. Cook could see the spire of the church behind the river frontage of warehouses. The damage from the bombs didn't look as bad from this side.

'What if we get bombed?' the giant, at the tiller, asked.

'Why would they bomb us?' his brother replied, looking up.

Cook looked up and saw the source of the buzzing noise. Apparently it wasn't just in his head. The sky was full of planes. Hundreds of silvery fish, up in the clouds.

The giant reached his foot out and wiped it on Cook's leg.

'See if you can keep the rest inside you,' he said.

Cook glared at him. He didn't engage. Not much point, hands tied behind his back, feet tied. Outnumbered, on a one-way trip to a point where presumably they'd put a bullet in his head then tip him over the edge.

Why hadn't they killed him already? They seemed to know what they were doing. From the sound of it, he assumed this was something they'd done before. They didn't seem overawed by the task. Their banter and their relaxed attitude spoke of men doing something regularly. Another day on the job. Maybe they'd tried it both ways round. Kill the man early on, you have to carry him, move his corpse. Hard to get him overboard. Keep him alive, you can point a gun at him and get him to do the work for you. Maybe get him to jump out of the boat at the final moment – let the river do the rest. Preferable in case the body washed ashore. More believable as a suicide without a bullet wound.

'Don't you want to beg?' the giant asked. He seemed genuinely curious, like Cook was disrupting a pattern.

Cook ignored him. He'd never been this far down the river. It was curving to the right, massive docks ahead. The royals, Reynolds had called them.

'We're open to offers in terms of letting you go,' the brother said. 'Just putting it out there. Course, we haven't had an offer yet that was attractive enough to overcome our fear of what the old man would do to us if he found out. But we're open to discussion.'

'Helps pass the time, if nothing else,' the giant said.

'What happened to Ruby?' Cook asked.

'He don't fucking give up,' the giant said.

'I'll tell you the truth,' the brother said. 'Since we're about to tip you into the river. None of us have got the faintest idea who you're talking about.'

'There isn't a Ruby,' the giant said. 'God's honest truth. We've got a Petal, a Jewel, a Flossie, a . . . who's that one never smiles?'

'Missie,' the brother said.

'Missie?' the giant said. 'Haven't heard about fucking Missie for ages. She's been out of the game for years. Who's the new one? Sour face?' He answered himself. Clicked his fingers and pointed at his brother. 'Suzie.'

'She has got a sour fucking face,' the giant continued. 'Mind you, I'd have a sour fucking face if I had to do what they do for a living.'

Cook was going to die. But all men die. If he'd wanted a long life he wouldn't have signed on for more years in the army after the armistice. Wouldn't have raised his hand when volunteers were needed to scout enemy positions above the Khyber Pass. Wouldn't have walked alone, unarmed, into a jazz bar in Soho on the off-chance of learning about the last movements of a girl he didn't really know.

But if he was going to die, the least he could do was rid the world of the two men who were accompanying him.

One would be easy. He could do it right now. Launch himself, head first, crack his head into theirs, pushing him and the other man out of the boat. They'd both hit the water unconscious. The brown waters of the Thames would welcome them.

So, one was a given. Easy. Not worth giving extra thought. But two. Two was the challenge. Particularly with them separated, one at the front and one at the back. Perhaps that was why they sat like that. Some kind of low cunning. Criminal intuition.

He could try to tip the boat over. Take his chances the men couldn't swim. But the boat felt stable.

Better to bide his time. If he saw an opportunity, he'd take it. His life, for these two. A worthy trade. One last job.

'You know what really done you in,' the giant said, giving Cook a wink. 'Wasn't coming round asking after no Ruby, who, like we said, nobody's ever heard of or likely ever gave a fuck about.'

Cook stared back at the man. He'd decided. If he was only going to be able to take one with him, it would be this one. He improved his plan. His hands were tied but he'd still be able to get his arms over the other man's head. Then it would simply be a matter of holding on tight, while they both sank to the bottom.

'You was making a nuisance of yourself at the hotel. That was what done you in. Can't have the likes of you or me upsetting the clientele. No, what we gets up to has to stay hidden, in the alleys, and the clubs.'

'Was this girl hanging about the hotel too?' the brother asked. Cook didn't respond. 'Stands to reason if that's why you were there.'

The man seemed interested. He'd been sent to drop off a body, but he was getting involved in the story. Wanted to solve it.

'What about that girl kept hanging around the bar?' he asked the giant. 'She wasn't one of ours, was she?'

The giant shook his head, thinking. Then he remembered.

'Fucking hell,' he said. 'Was that her?'

The other man nodded. They both looked at Cook, proud of themselves.

84

The SS *Addington Lass* had sailed from Baltimore six days earlier, carrying three thousand tons of ammonium nitrate pellets to be used as fertiliser on Britain's fields. Captain James Steingard was anxious to get the ship into dock. It had been a quiet crossing, a mercifully short six days with no sightings of U-boats. As the men stood on deck, waiting for the signal they'd been given permission to enter the Albert Dock, he checked his watch. If everything went according to plan, he could be handing the ship over to the pilot for unloading in less than an hour. If the trains played ball, he could be at home in Suffolk with his wife before nightfall, a glass of last year's elderberry wine in his hand, and his dogs at his feet.

The wave of bombers had given Steingard a fright. Not what he'd been expecting once he'd made the safety of the Thames. His cargo was designed to be spread on fields depleted of nutrients by two years of intensive farming. But he'd been given the full briefing on accepting the job. The Yank who'd signed over the cargo couldn't wait to get off the ship. Said it felt like standing on top of a bomb the size of a city block. Ammonium nitrate was an excellent fertiliser, but an even better explosive.

'Sir . . .'

One of the German fighters above was trailing smoke, high up in the cloud. A Stuka. One of the RAF boys must have clipped it.

'Get the gun up,' Steingard ordered. Almost definitely overkill, but better safe than sorry. The Admiralty had given him a large-calibre, high-angle machine-gun, along with two crew members seconded from the Royal Navy. Much better than their old Vickers, which had always felt like a pea shooter against the fighters coming at them out at sea.

Was he being over-cautious? The men looked to him to set the tone. If he showed his nerves now, they'd all go to pieces. But why not? They'd lugged the gun and its crew across the Atlantic and back. Might as well put it through its paces.

The trail of smoke from the Stuka described a graceful arc, a curving trajectory as it slowly fell out of formation. Slowly, at first, then faster. Now it was falling towards them with its distinctive scream, the horn designed purely to inflict terror on those who heard it.

Men ran to their stations, the navy gunners to the bow where the gun had been bolted to the deck. Everyone watched, eager to see the big gun firing. Steingard was glad he'd given the order. It gave the men something to rally around, and a sense they were defending themselves.

The Stuka was getting lower, and Steingard could see smoke pouring from its engines. If the pilot was still alive, he'd be blinded by the smoke. At least he wouldn't be able to aim at the ship.

Steingard lit his cigarette and tossed the match overboard. It was a long way down to the brown water, which was rushing past as the tide ran out. There was a small craft down there, and for a second he thought it was pulling alongside. Perhaps the pilot coming aboard. But the boat made its way along the shadow cast by the *Addington Lass*. Three men. A large man at the stern looked up, and he nodded accordingly.

A splash of wet hit Steingard, and he wiped his face. His hand came away red, as his mate, standing next to him, suddenly sunk to the deck, like his legs had been taken out from under him. The next thing he knew, the world had slowed down. Loud metallic pings sounded out, as sparks flew from a line across the deck. Bullets, he realised, fired from the plane still bearing down on them. His mate had caught an unlucky rico-chet and blood was pumping from a hole in his neck. Steingard dropped to his knees and held his handkerchief to the wound. He didn't know much about doctoring, but he knew enough about stemming leaks, and this was a bad one.

The *Addington Lass* was a sitting duck. Out on the high seas it was a nimble craft, under Steingard's expert touch. Give him a fair fight, and a good crew, and he'd take his chances. But here, idling at the river's edge, waiting for the illusion of safety being in dock would provide . . . this was hell on earth. The anti-aircraft gun was firing lower and lower as the Stuka plummeted. If they weren't careful, those navy boys were going to end up firing straight across the length of the cargo hold, into the bridge. The fighter was impossibly big now, filling the sky, then gone, as it disap-peared below him. He returned his attention to his mate, who was clutching his arm. Steingard forced an easy smile onto his face.

'Hold on there, Mick, we'll have you on land before you know it.'

Mick opened his mouth to reply but, instead, a bubble of thick blood burst out, splattering Steingard's face. So Steing-ard missed what happened to the German plane, not that he worried. It had evidently missed his ship, and that was all he needed to know.

There was an explosion from close by, sounded like the river bank. The plane must have hit the concrete road along-side the quay. A fireball rose up with a woof as the plane's fuel tanks went. Steingard winced, the heat singeing his face.

Burning debris fluttered down, out of the sky, some of it landing on the thick planks covering the cargo hold.

One of his men stepped across the planks and kicked a piece of flaming debris. Some kind of fabric. It caught on the crewman's foot, prompting good-natured laughter from the other men.

The crewman was shouting, his trousers catching fire. Something sticky and flammable on the burning debris, perhaps. The crewman panicked, jumped backwards, trying to escape the flames from his own leg. He tripped on a timber and went down, into the hold.

Steingard listened for a shout from down in the hold. Some kind of sign the crewman was all right. There wouldn't have been too much of a fall – the cargo was piled high.

85

Cook watched as the Stuka came out of the sky. He prayed a bullet would hit one of his captors, evening the odds, but no such luck.

The plane missed the freighter, hitting the ground at hundreds of miles an hour on the far side of the ship. There was an explosion from the wreckage of the plane.

Soon after the explosion Cook heard shouting, and laughing. The sounds of men who work together, blowing off steam.

The small boat was dwarfed by the freighter. At the tiller, the giant had taken them in close to shelter from the fighter, a tactic that had almost backfired. Cook could sense both men getting ready. They were nearing the point where they'd been told to dump him, he could see it on their faces, the way they looked out at the water, avoiding him.

Cook thought of one of Blakeney's favourite aphorisms. God helps those who help themselves. He didn't think God had much of an opinion about whether he lived or died, but he felt the principle was sound. Take control. Make things happen.

Cook kicked out, towards the giant. The man leant backwards, but Cook was aiming at his hand, holding the tiller handle. Cook gave the kick everything he had and he felt the man's fingers crunch between the sole of his boot and the oak handle.

The giant pulled his hand, but Cook kept his boot pressed against it, pinning him in place.

'Nice try,' the other man said, pulling his gun out of his belt. He cocked the hammer and levelled the revolver at Cook, before realising the problem. If he fired from where he stood, he'd be shooting through the base of the ship.

Above them, the freighter was experiencing its own troubles. A porthole exploded, showering the men in the small boat with glass. The man with the gun looked up as a jet of flame burst out of the hole, then disappeared almost instantly, the flame sucked back in as the ship gasped in oxygen, through the broken window. There was a roar, then a moan of bending metal. Sounded like the whole ship was trying to fold in on itself.

Cook pulled his legs back and pressed them against the side of the boat. He leant forwards, like he was doing a sit-up, legs bent, muscles taut. Coiled, like a spring. He could see up to the main deck of the freighter. There was a sailor standing there. The sailor raised his hand. Looked like he was going to say something.

The flash of light was brighter than the sky. Brighter than anything. It was as if the sun itself had exploded, and everything was light.

Cook pushed his feet against the side of the boat and thrust himself backwards.

He went into the giant, his momentum carrying the two of them past the point of no return. Mission accomplished, Cook had time to think, as the giant went backwards over the side of the boat, Cook following him in. No control. Two bodies tangled, both panicking, Cook and the man falling into the brown water as above them the whole world turned into a ball of fire. The blast from the explosion swept across the surface of the water, and the keel of the boat disappeared. The boat they'd been in only a second before suddenly didn't exist.

Cook went under, his legs and hands tied, and the giant's arms wrapped around his chest, scrabbling to push him down, to use him as some kind of ladder back to the surface, back to a chance of life.

Cook gasped, straining every muscle in his neck as he pushed his face to the surface. As a reward for his effort, he got a brief taste of oil and burning air, and a large gulp of water. He choked, but stopped himself. One more big gulp and his lungs would fill, and that would be it.

Cook was under no illusions. He was going to die. But at least he could take the other man with him. A man who trafficked in women, a murderer. Cook felt the man behind him and swung his elbow back, feeling it connect. The man backed away, and Cook turned around, grabbing him, looping his tied wrists over the man's head, embracing him.

They were sinking. The light from the fire above was fading. Cook felt the pressure increase as the water pressed on him from every side. The giant was struggling with everything he had. He came at Cook with a head-butt, but the water slowed his action, dulled the effect.

Now it was simply a battle of wills. Cook's will to die, taking the man with him, and the giant's will to live. Cook had gravity on his side, and the weight of the water in their sodden clothes, pulling them ever downward. But most of all he had his will, which had never failed him, and would see him through this one last test.

The other man knew it. He gave his all to one last struggle, writhing like an eel. Cook brought a knee up, into his groin. The giant opened his mouth, a reflex action, a gasp. A stream of bubbles rose up, large, then small, then the bubbles stopped.

Cook tried to unwrap himself from the corpse, but his strength was gone, and his lungs were burning, and the desire to breathe in was everything.

It was the end.

Cook felt a searing pain in his scalp, his hair was being torn out at the roots. It cut through the numbing caused by the cold water, even cut through the desperate desire to open his mouth and gasp for air, even though he knew there was no air to be had.

But then he felt an arm under his shoulder. The tillerman, he assumed. The boat must have survived the blast.

'He's gone,' he heard a voice say as he was dragged out of the water. More hands grabbed him and pulled him over the side.

It was a different boat. Similar smells of foul water and petrol, but a proper wooden deck. Cook rolled onto his stomach, and vomited what felt like ten pints of river water, again and again, until he was heaving with no result.

'He's tied up,' someone said.

'Untie him.' Another voice. A voice of authority.

'Looks like an execution.'

Cook felt his hands and feet being cut free and he rolled onto his back. Three fishermen looked down at him.

'Were you on that boat just went up?' one of them asked.

Cook tried to respond, but he couldn't speak. He tried to get up, but his legs failed him. Instead, he lay on the wooden deck, looking up at the burning wreckage of the *Addington Lass*. A column of filthy black smoke poured into the sky. Two fireships already circled it, arcing jets of water into the flames.

Frankie didn't have money for the train fare, but he reckoned he'd worked out how to avoid the conductor. Last time, with Cook, he'd watched the conductor doing his rounds – starting at the front of the train, then slowly walking through each carriage, punching tickets. Every stop, he had to leave off the ticket-punching and lean out the door, making sure everyone was all aboard before he blew his whistle to let the driver know it was safe to go.

So Frankie was in the middle carriage, towards the back of it. He'd kept an eye on the conductor, working his way along the corridor, popping into each compartment, the click of his ticket-puncher keeping everyone informed of his whereabouts.

When they'd come into Cowden, halfway through the journey, Frankie had hurried along the corridor, past the conductor who'd been leaning out of the window, waiting to blow his whistle.

With any luck he'd be safe for the rest of the journey. But he'd have to keep his eyes peeled, just in case.

Frankie took the postcard out of his blazer pocket, and looked at it again. He had a feeling about it. He wanted to show the postcard to his mum. At the very least, he wanted her to see it to know Ruby was all right.

He had a feeling Ruby was trying to send him a message.

If he was right, she was telling him to come and get her.

Of course, he didn't know where she was, but maybe his mum would know. And if Cook was there, he'd work it out. Cook was good at things like that. He didn't give up. Cook kept on going and going, until the job was done.

88

The Times had stopped reporting the bombings. Didn't want to give too much away to the Germans. A strange thing, Margaret thought, to be in a city under attack, reading the news, unable to learn what was happening outside your own door. Instead, she had to put up with a lengthy and gushing article about a new musician at the Café Royal, of all things.

The hotel lobby was busy. Across from Margaret, on another settee, a woman was writing in a spiral-bound note-book. The woman was dressed as if she was ready for a safari.

From where she sat, Margaret didn't have a view of the revolving front door. Judging by the reaction of the man behind the front desk, she had to wonder if Hitler himself had walked in. Who on earth could inspire such a reaction?

It was Cook. Of course it was Cook, sopping wet, dripping on the pristine marble floor, bleeding from a nasty wound on his head. Even from across the lobby, Margaret could smell him. Sewage, definitely. Oil, perhaps. Something else, a memory from the farm. Was it fertiliser?

'Darling, what on earth happened?' It was the safari-clad woman, putting down her notebook and rising to meet Cook. For the briefest second he looked past her, and met Margaret's gaze. She gave him the briefest flicker of a cold smile, then returned to her paper. *Gone with the Wind* was playing at the Odeon, in technicolour no less. She'd never seen a film in colour – heard it was quite the thing. She checked the show-times carefully. Nothing worse than arriving halfway through a performance.

When Cook and the American had departed, Margaret judged it was safe to look up from her newspaper. A voice piped up from a nearby armchair – an ancient dowager who Margaret had assumed was either asleep, or dead.

'Old flame, dear?'

Margaret hadn't realised she'd been quite so obvious.

'It's complicated,' she said.

'The best ones usually are, dear,' the dowager replied.

Margaret folded the paper neatly and rose to go.

'Worth fighting for, I'd imagine,' the dowager said, a glint in her eye.

'Yes,' Margaret said. 'Worth fighting for.'

*

Cook lay in the bath, coming to the end of the bar of soap. He'd washed, drained the bath, refilled it, and repeated the cycle three times. The boat crew had told him what happened to people who went in the Thames, especially if they swallowed the water. From the sound of it, he was on borrowed time.

A door closed, and Eleanor joined him. She sat on the toilet, the seat down, and patted his forehead with the flannel. It was still coming away bloody, but the worst of the filth was gone.

'I'll pay you back for the clothes,' he said, 'once my wallet dries out.'

She'd phoned down to the front desk, put in an order from a tailor on Jermyn Street. His old clothes were already on their way to the incinerator.

'Nonsense,' she said. 'It's all very exciting. I've never met a victim of an honest-to-God mob hit before.'

'Just some people who didn't like the questions I was asking,' Cook said.

'Seems like you struck a nerve.'

'What do you do when you get to a dead end?' he asked. 'When you're reporting a story.'

She thought about it. One professional to another.

'I retrace my steps,' she said. 'Go back to everyone I've spoken with. There's always someone who didn't tell you everything the first time.'

'Where do you start?' he asked.

'At the beginning,' she replied.

89

Margaret almost left it too late. Too busy gossiping with the dowager in the lobby, when she should have leapt on the opportunity as soon as it presented itself.

She waited impatiently in the lift while the attendant took them up. She'd asked for the second floor. But as soon as the doors opened she could see it wasn't what she was looking for, so she made her apologies and asked for the third.

Margaret had spent a lot of time and energy trying to work out how to locate the room number of her go-between, the woman who'd sat behind her in the basement bar. She'd known she was American from her accent. Luckily for Margaret, it seemed there was only one American woman staying in the hotel. But how could she track her to her room?

Cook had unwittingly provided the answer, walking into the lobby and dripping water on the marble floor. River water, unless Margaret was very much mistaken.

The trail of wet footsteps had led to the lift. It would be a relatively simple matter to follow them to the room. As long as they hadn't dried out.

It took until the eighth floor, the lift attendant getting increasingly annoyed. Margaret wasn't about to lose any sleep over the happiness of a man who, only a day earlier, had been content to let two young men attack her.

Margaret followed the trail of damp footprints along the eighth-floor corridor. The pattern in the carpet made it hard to see every footstep, but each time she thought she'd lost it, she saw another one further ahead.

The damp footsteps ran out at Room 814. Margaret walked further on, just to make sure, but 814 it was. She put her head to the door and listened. She could just make out the woman's voice, muffled as if it was in an interior room. The bathroom, most likely. If ever there was a man in need of a bath . . .

90

The Lyons was quiet. The dinner service was ending, and the waitresses were ready for the end of the shift.

Cook ignored the protests of the waitress on the door and took a seat. Another young waitress approached him, but he pointed behind her, at the girl he'd talked with the first time. The time he'd come looking for Ruby.

She took her time about it, finished what she was doing at the till, then eventually joined him. She stood over him, her notepad out, ready for his order.

'There's something you didn't tell me,' Cook said.

'No law against that,' the waitress replied.

'I wasn't the only one who was asking about Ruby,' Cook said.

'Never said you was,' the waitress replied.

'You didn't mention it,' Cook said.

'You didn't ask.'

'It was a young man. A soldier,' Cook said.

'See? You didn't need me to tell you.'

'I'll buy you a cup of tea,' Cook said.

The waitress looked around to see if she was about to get in trouble. Evidently, she didn't see anything alarming, because she pulled out a chair and sat opposite Cook. She took a packet of cigarettes from a pocket in her apron and lit up.

'When did he come in?' Cook asked.

'Came in a few days in a row, couple of weeks ago,' she said. 'Watching, he was. Watching out for her.'

'But she was already gone,' Cook said.

The waitress pointed her cigarette at him.

'There you go again. Asking me a question but you know the answer. You'd better buy me that cuppa before you realise you don't need me sitting here.' She waved to her counterpart, at the counter.

'Tea for two over here if you don't mind. And a slice of lemon cake. He's buying.'

'What did he say?' Cook asked.

'Had a nasty cut on his face.' She drew a line down her cheek. 'Reckon he was back from Dunkirk. Didn't want to let on. Which meant he'd deserted, if you ask me.'

'Her boyfriend,' Cook said. 'Gone into the army. Gone to France to give Hitler what for.'

The waitress poured tea for two and started in on the cake.

'He's spending his nights in the shelter at Dickins and Jones,' Cook said, remembering where the young man's father had been heading. A loose end he'd let go. As he said it, he knew it was the missing piece of the puzzle. A burst of adrenaline as he saw the end in sight.

'Wrong,' the waitress replied, shaking her head. 'They wouldn't let him in. They've got their standards, see. They get so many people lining up they can be picky.'

She nodded at Cook.

'Unlike us,' she said.

Cook thought she was mistaken. Either way, it was something he could test. He gulped down his tea. Dickins & Jones was only a ten-minute walk.

'He's in the same place he always is,' she said. 'Since I told him where Ruby was working.'

Cook must have looked blank, which pleased the waitress. She knew something he didn't.

'You come from Piccadilly Circus?' she asked.

He nodded. The truth was more complicated, but he didn't want to slow down her narrative.

She smiled, pleased she'd got it right.

'You walked past him just now,' she said. 'Opposite the hotel. I think he's keeping an eye out for her. Maybe you should have done that if you were so keen to find her.'

91

The tramp was in his usual place, in the doorway. Invisible.
Part of the wallpaper. Perfectly placed to keep an eye on the
comings and goings at the Empire.

Cook dropped half a crown in the upturned hat. The
tramp looked up at him with a nod of thanks.

'Arthur Burton?' Cook said.

Panic flashed across the man's face. The scar on his cheek
a livid red.

Cook held out his hand, palm forward, like trying to calm
a skittish animal.

'I'm a friend of Ruby's,' Cook said.

*

Cook carried over two pints from the bar, having rescued
enough coins from his sodden wallet. The pub across the
road, the same one he'd taken the American to. Burton nodded his thanks.

'What happened?' Burton asked. Cook felt his forehead
and his hand came away with fresh blood.

'I've been looking for Ruby,' Cook said. 'Some men took
exception to that. Tried to dissuade me.'

'Looks like they succeeded,' Burton said.

'You've been watching the hotel,' Cook said. 'Why didn't
you go to her place?'

'I'm AWOL,' Burton said. 'They'll be keeping an eye out for me. Thought I'd talk to Ruby and we could slip away. Get married.'

'Then what?'

'Wasn't thinking that far ahead,' Burton said.

'Where is she?' Cook asked.

'I haven't seen her since the bus went up,' he said. 'If I had, I wouldn't be sitting out there, day in, day out.'

'What did you see that evening?' Cook asked.

'She wasn't on the bus,' Burton said, 'I know that much.'

Cook drank, and thought about what Burton had said. It was the first time someone had said it out loud, the thing that had been keeping him awake, the thing he'd started to doubt. She wasn't on the bus.

'She was crossing the road, then she got waylaid. Some woman. Looked like they were having a barney. Ruby could be like that. Didn't like to back down.'

'What about the other girl? From the Lyons?' Cook asked. Not essential to nail down that part of the story but it was a niggle.

Burton nodded.

'She was there. Ran right past me, kicked my hat. I had to grab it. The bus was pulling away but the conductor must have seen her. Took pity on her, I suppose.'

He took a long gulp.

'Poor girl.'

'Her parents think there's still hope,' Cook said. 'You could talk to them. Tell them what you saw.'

Burton nodded. He seemed like a good lad.

'What happened to Ruby?' Cook asked.

Burton shook his head.

'The bus blew up, and all hell broke loose. It was worse than anything I saw in France. People with limbs blown off. They didn't even know. There was an old gent, came towards me, asking where he could get a cup of tea. Had a piece of metal right through his stomach.'

Burton closed his eyes.

'He died in front of me. Sat down on the pavement and curled up, like a little boy going to sleep. Old gent he was. He didn't have a chance. By the time I looked for Ruby, she was gone.'

'Perhaps she was killed?' Cook asked.

'No,' Burton said, firmly. 'I spent an hour looking for her, or for . . . parts of her. There wasn't anything.'

'So that's it?' Cook asked. It didn't seem right. He'd tracked down this lad, gone through all kinds of hell. Felt like he deserved to know how the story ended.

Burton finished his pint.

'There was someone else, who would have seen,' he said. 'I've been waiting for him to come back.'

'Why would he come back?' Cook asked.

'It's his job,' Burton said. 'He was the doorman. He caught a bit of the shrapnel. When I was looking for Ruby he was sitting on the steps of the hotel, blood all over his face. I think it got him in the eye. But he was watching. I reckon he would have seen where she went to.'

'Was he one of the brothers?' Cook asked.

'Yes.' Burton nodded, obviously glad to be finally talking to someone on the same wavelength. 'Normal size, though, not like the big one.'

'And you think he knows what happened to Ruby,' Cook said.

Burton nodded.

'He'll be back, sooner or later. Then I'll have a word.'

'I know where he is,' Cook said.

92

'We need to talk,' Cook said, as the doorman stepped back into the doorway. He looked like he'd seen a ghost.

'Tell the old man they were doing a good job of it – didn't just dump me straight away,' Cook continued.

'He's upstairs,' the doorman said.

'I'm not here for him,' Cook said.

'What's he doing here?' the doorman asked, looking suspiciously at Burton.

Cook realised they knew each other, after a fashion. Two adversaries who'd faced off across the busy road, hour after hour, day after day.

'Same as me,' Cook said. 'Looking for Ruby.'

'You saw her,' Burton said, 'after the bus was hit.'

The doorman looked up, into the stairwell. The powers that be.

'Tell me,' Cook said, 'and that'll be an end to it.'

'She was running across the road,' the doorman said, his shoulders slumping, his decision made. 'Got into a shouting match with another guest. Nasty woman, always looking for a fight.'

'She wasn't on the bus?' Cook asked.

The doorman shook his head.

'She was back over my side of the road. Must have got hit. She was bleeding. I didn't see much else.' He pointed to the bandage over his eye.

'Where did she go? Burton asked. 'You must have seen something.'

The doorman shook his head.

'I thought she was all right,' he said. 'I remember thinking she was taken care of.'

'An ambulance?' Burton guessed.

The doorman started to nod, then stopped.

'A car,' he said. 'Had something written on it. Like where it would say police. I saw it drive off.'

'Someone took her?' Burton asked.

'He didn't take her,' the doorman said. 'He helped her.'

'We need more,' Burton said. 'For God's sake.'

The doorman shut his eye. Thought. Shook his head.

'I'm sorry,' he said.

The man had been half blinded. He would have been going into shock.

'You remember anything, her mum's the landlady at the King's Stairs, on the island,' Cook said. 'Let her know.'

'We can't just give up,' Burton said, as they left the doorman, took a side street back towards Shaftesbury Avenue, turned the corner.

A siren started up. Cook looked at the sky. Heavy clouds. Impossible for a bomber to aim.

Burton followed his gaze.

'I don't think they're aiming any more,' he said, reading Cook's mind. 'Just follow the river if they can see it then drop their bombs anywhere on the city.'

An ARP warden hurried past them, blowing a whistle.

'Everyone to the shelter,' he shouted. Shoppers turned to each other, unsure whether to carry on or obey. Nobody wanted to be the first to give in to the fear.

The ARP warden turned the corner and Cook heard his whistle again. He doubted the doorman would be persuaded to abandon his post. Probably considered himself immune, now he'd already been bombed.

'Now what?' Burton asked.

'Back to the island,' Cook said. 'See if Gracie's heard anything.'

'I can't go back there,' Burton said. 'The military police have been sniffing round.'

'Keep an eye on the hotel, then,' Cook said. 'I'll go to the island, let them know what we found out.'

Cook heard heavy footsteps. Somebody running. Others heard it. Soon everyone on the street was hurrying one way or another, ducking into buildings, following painted signs on brickwork, finding the nearest shelter.

The doorman rounded the corner. He slowed when he saw Cook.

'I remembered,' he said. 'The word on the car. It wasn't a word. It was letters.'

'What was it?' Burton asked.

'ARP,' the doorman said.

93

Margaret was back outside Room 814. She'd waited in the lobby for the American woman to leave. She'd heard her ask the doorman for a taxi to Maida Vale, so Margaret knew she had time for what she had in mind.

The hotel had been built in the 1890s. When they built the place they couldn't have known how important it would become to international espionage – how many dignitaries and spies would make the place their temporary home. If they had, they might have sprung for better locks. As it was, the lock on Room 814 surrendered to Margaret's somewhat ham-fisted technique in about twenty seconds. She made sure she hadn't been observed, and slipped into the room.

The smell of the river was stronger in here, overlaid with the smell of soap. The last time they'd talked, Cook had mentioned a girl he was looking for. Hopefully the river trip was some version of Cook homing in on his prey.

Other than the large bed, there was an oak wardrobe and a chest of drawers. The same layout as Margaret's room. The bed was flanked by two bedside tables, each with an electric lamp. No desk. No obvious place to put paperwork.

The wardrobe was full. More clothes than Margaret had owned in her lifetime. Too full for a suitcase. Margaret leafed through the outfits quickly, out of curiosity. There was a definite big-game hunter theme. Margaret blamed Hemingway – he'd set the tone for a whole generation of American writers. She'd met him once in Paris. A long and tiresome evening fending off his advances.

She pulled out the drawers in the bedside tables. One of them was empty apart from the obligatory bible. The other had a collection of tissues, receipts, scribbled notes. Margaret read the notes. *Aides-mémoire* – 'ask T about fishing quotas', 'Kennedy speech!', 'candy bars for C and L'. Not exactly the work of a disciplined spymaster, unless there was some kind of elaborate code.

Margaret stood in the room and looked around for inspiration. For a woman who was collecting intelligence and somehow feeding it to the Germans, there was precious little paperwork in the room. Perhaps Margaret had underestimated her. Not like she'd have left a neat file in her hotel room, all laid out ready to be discovered.

A quick check in the bathroom told her nothing useful.

A bust, then.

Margaret was on her way out, but paused. Better safe than sorry.

She checked the bedside table again. The empty one. Took out the bible. Held it upside down and shook. A leaf of thin paper fell out. Neat handwriting. Ten names and addresses. One of them had been crossed out.

Charlotte Pearson. 44 Swynford Grove.

That left nine names. Nine people who'd thrown their lot in with the Germans, no doubt feeding the American with bits and pieces of intelligence.

'I've got a name for you,' Margaret said, waiting for Bunny to catch up. They'd taken a stroll around the block but Bunny had stopped to buy a newspaper. They both ignored the siren, buffeted by people running to shelter.

He scanned the front page and grimaced, folded the paper and stuffed it in his suit pocket.

'Go on then,' he snapped, 'or do I have to drag it out of you?'

She passed him a folded note, The Empire on the letterhead, watched him closely as he read the name.

'Don't tell me you're surprised,' she said.

'Of course, I'm not surprised. Of course, I know she's a bloody spy. But I can't go around arresting Americans left, right, and centre. We're playing a very dangerous game as it is. If we don't win them over we'll be speaking German in a few months, those of us who aren't dangling from a rope.'

'So she gets a free pass?' Margaret asked.

'This won't do,' Bunny said. 'It won't do at all. I didn't put you in there so you could bring me problems. You're better than that. Bring me solutions. Use your imagination, for Christ's sake.'

The key in the lock brought her out of her dream. She'd been stuck in a hole, earth falling on her. Buried alive.

The door opened.

'Ruby?'

She almost fainted when she moved her head.

The shelter was a mess – soil everywhere. The woman hadn't paid attention, had thrown Ruby in like an escaped chicken returned to the coop.

But he would see.

Ruby was out of ideas. The only thing left was to fight. Fight for her life.

It was blindingly bright as the door opened. A sunny day outside. He'd be stepping into the darkness, eyes adjusting. An advantage to her. A slim advantage, but something was better than nothing.

'Ruby?' he said, as he stepped into the shelter. She heard him shuffle through a pile of loose soil. 'What's this?'

The plate was where she'd left it, on the ground, by the entrance to her tunnel. She brought it down, hard, across the bedstead. It cracked in two. She felt the broken edge and winced – it cut her finger – a wickedly sharp porcelain blade. She was angry with herself. She should have thought of this from the beginning. He'd been using the same plate day in, day out. Left it for her more than once.

'Ruby, are you all right?' he asked. He sounded absurdly concerned for her. As if he hadn't been keeping her prisoner and taking advantage of her.

'I'm here, Father,' she said.

He took a cautious step forward, into the darkness. She saw his silhouette against the bright daylight from the door.

He reached out for her, or where he thought she'd be.

Ruby took a quick step to the side, felt for his head with her left hand. She got a handful of his hair, slick with tonic. It was enough. He tried to jerk backwards, but she held his head steady, and quickly drew her makeshift blade across his throat. She barely felt it, the edge of the plate was so sharp.

He cried out, but the cry turned to a gargle as his throat flooded with blood. She felt it against her, gushing from his neck, pumped straight from his heart. It splattered against the corrugated metal wall, splattered against the ceiling. She stumbled backwards, trying to get out of the way, but he fell towards her, grabbing her as he went down.

His lips moved. 'Ruby.' But no sound. No air from his lungs, the connection severed. In the darkness, she saw his eyes, pleading with her. But there was nothing she could do.

She stepped over him, the open door within reach. The freedom she hadn't dared hope for. She needed to get away, to breathe fresh air. To run as far as she could from this place.

The sun was blinding. She closed her eyes and it was still too bright. She stumbled up the steps and felt grass beneath her bare feet. She opened her right eye a crack, enough to orient herself. The house was far off, straight ahead. The horrid graves were at her feet, to the right. She shuddered at the fresh grave, waiting for her.

Where was the woman?

The garden was quiet. Empty. The crazy woman must be in the house. She spun around. The garden was hedged in on all sides. But a hedge would have gaps, even if she had to push herself through.

She ran for the closest hedge. She got two steps, clearing the Anderson shelter, not noticing the woman standing there, watching her.

The rolling-pin hit her at full force, across the temple. The sound echoed back off the distant trees. The last thing she heard was crows taking flight, cawing angrily.

96

It was two miles back to the island. Cook walked quickly.

Cook had sat in that car, with ARP written on the side. He'd gone into the house by Regent's Park, side by side with Reynolds. But Reynolds hadn't been looking for Ruby.

Had he taken the gas mask in, planted it upstairs? He could have gone back to the car and fetched it, while Cook was in the basement.

Did Dottie know? He didn't think she did. She'd risked life and limb to get the address from the red-headed man. A lot for her to volunteer for if she'd known it was all for show.

Cook was angry with himself. He'd known Reynolds was dangerous from the first time he'd set eyes on him. In Cook's experience, first impressions were seldom wrong. He'd let Reynolds help him with the bomb, and that had thrown him off the scent. Gracie hadn't been fooled. She knew the man. She'd thrown him out and clearly had no time for him, keeping a bare veneer of civility for Frankie's sake.

Several roads were blocked off due to bomb damage, and the two miles turned into three. Even at Cook's pace, it took him an hour.

'Where is he?' Cook demanded as he burst into the pub at the far end of the high street – the World's End. Reynolds's usual table was empty, even though the rest of the pub was full.

'He's not here,' the barman said.

'Where is he?' Cook repeated.

The barman looked impassively at Cook.

The door opened behind Cook and the man from the pawnbroker's shop stepped in, his tommygun at his waist. He kept his distance so Cook couldn't repeat his disarming trick.

'Don't be a bloody idiot,' Cook said. 'You pull that trigger now and you'll kill fifty people. Is that what you want?'

The pawnbroker stepped back, suspecting a trick. But there was no trick. Cook simply strode towards him and grabbed the gun, pulled it out of his hands.

Cook removed the magazine, set the selector to fire, held the trigger, and pulled the receiver away from the body. With the guts of the mechanism exposed, he stripped out the firing pin and put it in his pocket. Then he threw the remains of the gun at the pawnbroker.

'If I see you with this again, I'll use it like a club and beat you with it,' Cook said.

*

Half a mile back along the high street, past buildings still smouldering from the previous night's bombing, rats already claiming territory in the piles of filth. Gracie's pub was boarded up, but open for business.

'It's Reynolds,' Cook said, before Gracie had a chance to ask. She didn't seem surprised. She opened a drawer behind the bar and took out a flick knife.

'He's not the only one knows how to use one of these,' Gracie said.

'He's not at his local. I haven't tried Tilbury yet,' Cook said.

'He's got a warehouse,' Gracie said. 'He thinks it's a secret.'

97

Halfway back along the high street, towering warehouses on both sides. A metal gantry four storeys up, like a footbridge crossing a canyon.

'He's on the river side,' Gracie said. 'We can get in this way.' She opened a metal gate on the left side of the street, the inland side. Cook followed her up a concrete staircase that smelt of piss and something rotting. At the top, it opened out onto the metal gantry – thin metal grate for a floor, iron railings on each side.

'He keeps it locked,' Gracie said.

The door was on the other side of the street, five yards across the gantry. It looked solid. A wooden door, two different locks judging by the keyholes. Solid surround.

Cook backed up into the stairwell, focusing his attention on the door. Another test of will. His will to take the door down, versus the craftsmanship of whoever had installed it.

Only one way to find out.

Cook sprinted across the gantry. Only five yards, but enough to get some speed up. He turned his shoulder to the door and imagined himself going through it – the idea that it would stop him not even a possibility.

His shoulder went into the door with all the force he could muster, pushing through to an imaginary point several feet beyond. The door splintered, and sprung open, and he stumbled through, Gracie only steps behind him.

'What've you done with her?' Gracie yelled, flying at Reynolds, her knife blade flashing in the light of a gas lamp.

Reynolds, up on his feet the second the door crashed open, skipped backwards, out of Gracie's range. He left behind a workbench covered with treasures, Ruby's gas mask pride of place, its contents spread out across the benchtop, amongst strings of pearls, gold rings, and knick-knacks.

'Where is she?' Cook asked. 'Is she alive, or did you kill her?'

Reynolds kept his eyes on Gracie's knife.

'I don't know what you're talking about,' he said. 'But get this crazy bitch out of my face before I take offence and fight back.'

'Try me,' Gracie spat, thrusting forward.

Reynolds stepped into the thrust, grabbing Gracie's arm and twisting. Her knife clattered to the floor.

'What've you done with Ruby!' she screamed.

Reynolds stepped away, his hands in the air. He looked at Cook for confirmation.

'You think I hurt our girl?'

'Where is she?' Cook asked.

Reynolds was incredulous, looking back and forth, Cook, then Gracie, then back again.

'You think it's me?' he asked.

'Tell me it wasn't,' Gracie said. 'And if you're lying, I swear to God.'

Reynolds kicked Gracie's knife back to her.

'If you think it was me, you'd better do me in,' he said. 'If that's what you think of me.'

'You were seen picking her up outside the Empire,' Cook said.

'I was on the island all night. I was in the hole with that bomb for half of it. With you.'

'Before then,' Cook said. 'Before you showed up at Frankie's party.'

'Who said they saw me?' Reynolds asked.

'They saw the car,' Cook said. 'Markings on the side. ARP.'

Reynolds sighed. Shook his head.

'I'm not the only one with an ARP car,' he said.

98

Beaumont's lacquered front door gave way to Reynolds's boot on the first attempt. The fury of a father whose daughter had been taken from him. No need for messing around with disguises or lock-picks. This time they had righteousness on their side.

Cook followed Reynolds into the house.

'Ruby?' Reynolds bellowed.

But the house was silent. A stillness in the air. None of the smells that come from habitation.

Reynolds ran up the stairs, full of hope. Gracie felt it too, he could see. Putting together the answer, hurrying through the streets. The satisfaction of kicking in the door. All of it led to an expectation, like turning the page and starting the final chapter.

'It's my fault,' Gracie said.

'No,' Cook said. 'Evil men do evil things. It's in their blood. You couldn't have stopped this any more than you could stop the tide.'

Cook saw the console table – a lamp and a telephone. A carbon copy of the house on Regent's Place.

'The shelter,' Cook said.

99

Halfway down the garden was a potting shed – walls of thin wooden slats. The door was unlocked – nothing of value inside, a tower of terracotta pots, stacked inside each other, a garden fork, a spade, a rake. Cook grabbed the spade, feeling its heft. Not the perfect tool for the job, but it would do. Sheffield steel, designed and manufactured for punishing work, day in, day out.

The Anderson shelter was undisturbed, still locked. The neat gravel path leading down three steps.

The padlock would be stronger than the spade. It was looped through a metal hoop on the door, overlaying a piece of flat metal screwed into a wooden doorframe – the weakest part of the security arrangement. Cook wedged the edge of the spade between the metal plate and the door frame. The spade was four feet long. A lot of leverage.

He tested the spade's strength. He wasn't worried about the steel. It was the handle that would give – ash wood, dried and cracked. Beaumont was evidently not a man who took care of his tools.

The handle creaked, but held. Cook gave it more, and the metal plate popped off the door frame. Cook pulled the door open.

The shelter had been locked for days. Possibly weeks. He was prepared for what he might find. Or so he thought.

A cloud of flies filled the air, disturbed by the opening door. Cook put his hand over his mouth against the stench, but he had to turn back.

Gracie pushed past him.

She turned away and rushed from the shelter, vomiting into the grass.

★

Inside the shelter, a large mass moved in the darkness. As his eyes adjusted, Cook saw more clearly. Maggots. Thousands of them. Tens of thousands. Underneath them, a corpse.

It was a shape and size any farmer would know instantly. An adult pig. Against the rules to keep one for your own use. Difficult to get rid of, if you wanted to suddenly leave. Not like you could load it up in the car.

'When was the last time you saw him?' Cook asked.

'Couple of nights ago,' Gracie said. 'Doing his rounds.'

'So if he hasn't been staying here,' Cook asked, 'where's he been hiding?'

100

Margaret walked cautiously up the sagging stairs, the sound of an experimental jazz quartet coming from a room at the top.

She enquired at the bar. Said she had a message for the proprietor. Well, not so much a message as an offer. Something that might allow him continued and unfettered access to the various financial opportunities a long-term situation at the Empire might represent.

She drank over-priced champagne as she waited for the message to work its way to the right man. At one point a staff door opened and several young women looked out, curious to see the well-dressed and well-spoken woman who'd arrived unannounced with such a strange message.

Mr Jones found her pouring a second glass. He sat next to her and they both watched the band.

'There seems to be a misunderstanding,' he said, eventually.

'I don't think so,' Margaret said. 'You got my message, and you wanted to talk to me. My understanding seems to be spot on.'

'Who are you?' he asked.

'We've been getting complaints,' she said. 'Through various channels. Untoward goings-on at the hotel.'

'Your message referred to a path forward,' Mr Jones said. 'I believe you mentioned continued and unfettered access. Which leads me to wonder what you'd want in return.'

'Oh, I'm just here to listen to the music,' Margaret said.

She passed a slip of paper across the table. He unfolded it, read it, and passed it back.

'You're with the farmer,' he said.

'Not really.'

'I don't want to see him again.'

'He has that effect on people.'

'What's going on?' Gracie asked as she stepped through the door, into the pub.

Cook and Reynolds followed close behind, wrapped up in their failure.

'What's he doing here?' Reynolds asked, as he saw what Gracie had seen – Frankie sat at the corner table, by the front window, half a cheese sandwich on a plate and a mug of tea in front of him. Annie at his side.

'He's got a postcard from Ruby,' Dottie said, from behind the bar.

Cook realised Frankie didn't know. He'd left the boy in the dark, thinking his sister was still dead.

Gracie took Frankie's face in her hands.

'You're a good lad,' she said, kissing him on the forehead. 'Let's see it.'

Frankie showed her the postcard, and Gracie pulled her own one from her pocket.

'Let's hope she's all right,' Gracie said.

Dottie pulled two pints and passed them across the bar to Cook and Reynolds.

'Now what?' Reynolds asked.

Cook sipped his pint.

'Wait for Beaumont to make an appearance,' he said.

'What if he doesn't?' Reynolds said. 'What if he knows we're on to him?'

Frankie ran past them, and Cook heard his footsteps on the wooden stairs. He'd never thought about where the family lived, presumably in rooms above the bar. He could hear Frankie clattering around up there, then the footsteps on the stairs again, coming back down.

'Look,' Frankie said. He had another postcard in his hand. A plain one, a simple rectangle of card, space on the front for the stamp and the address, and on the back for the message.

Frankie put this new card on the bar, next to the one he'd got from Ruby.

'Whose is that chicken-scratch?' Reynolds asked.

'That's mine,' Frankie said. 'When I was young.'

'Last year,' added Gracie.

'I sent it home when we went on the holiday. Look!'

Frankie pointed to the picture he'd drawn. Two birds, simple v shapes, above a child's drawing of a tree – a fat trunk and bushy canopy of leaves.

'And look!' he showed them Ruby's cards, the one to him and the one to Gracie. Both of them had the same picture, but smaller. A little doodle. A whimsical afterthought.

Cook read Frankie's note, written a year ago when he'd been taken away from his home and shown the countryside.

Come and get me.

He winced. The boy had had the same feeling when he'd been evacuated. And Cook had done precious little to help him settle in, too focused on his own troubles to see how scared the lad had been.

'Where did they take you?' Cook asked.

'Dunno,' Frankie said. 'Hours away, in the middle of nowhere.'

Annie smiled.

'The church does it every year,' she said. 'They take a different group of children, give them a taste of the country. I went with Ruby that time, about ten years ago it must have been.'

'Beaumont's been scarpering to the country,' Cook said.

'So would you lot if you knew what was good for you.' A voice from the doorway.

Beaumont let the door close behind him.

'This place is finished,' he said. 'You can stay here if you want, but I'm leaving for good.'

'Not *his* place,' Annie said. 'The church place. Father Ryan's people own it. Up Essex way.'

'I didn't like it,' Frankie said.

'That's the problem,' Annie said. 'All these young girls go off to the countryside for their health, come back with secrets.' She winked at Frankie, who seemed nonplussed by the odd statement.

'This place,' Reynolds asked Annie. 'You know where it is?

'Course,' she said. 'Went up there with the nippers every summer.'

102

Ruby was stuck in a nightmare, the same scenes repeating. She had a headache, worse than she'd ever experienced. She was digging, soil in her eyes and mouth, her hands scrabbling. It had been bright for a while, but now it was dark – one small mercy. The brightness had hurt her head, even through closed eyes.

Her mouth was full of soil. She spat, but as soon as she opened her mouth again there was more soil.

Not a dream, she realised.

Ruby tried to bring her hands to her mouth, to scrape away the soil. But her hands were stuck, held down by a weight. She squinted, opening her eyes the barest crack, the piercing pain in her head unbearable.

It was dark. Ruby couldn't move. Soil everywhere.

She heard a distant noise. Familiar. A spade, slicing through loose soil, then a thud. She felt the thud, as if at a distance.

She was being buried.

She tried to get up, but the weight of the soil on top of her was too much.

'Let me out!' she screamed, through a mouthful of soil.

The noise from above stopped. She pictured the woman. She'd hear Ruby screaming. She'd realise her mistake.

Thud.

Another load of soil. Another tremor. Then the sound of spade in soil again.

Ruby screamed. It didn't slow the thuds of soil, but she had no choice. She screamed without hope of being heard, because not to scream was to give in, and Ruby wasn't ready for that. Not yet.

103

Reynolds pulled into an overgrown farmyard – weeds coming up through cracks in the concrete, and the remains of a rose bush in a long-dry water trough.

Reynolds was out of the car in an instant, hammering on the front door with his fist. Cook stood back, looking up at the house. Dark, dirty windows. The white render on the house was stained green with moss. More moss hung from the eaves. This was what his farm would have looked like if it had been left to rot.

'Ruby?' Reynolds shouted. He kicked the door but it didn't give. Flakes of green paint fell from where his boot made impact, only to get caught in a mess of cobwebs. This wasn't a door that was used often, Cook thought.

'Round the back,' Cook said. There was a side gate, sagging on its hinges. A rut in the ground where it had dragged, until the day when it stopped dragging and sat open.

Frankie stepped out of the car. He'd insisted on coming.

'Stay in the car,' Cook said to the boy. ''Til we know what's going on.'

Frankie looked pale. He nodded quickly and retreated. Cook didn't envy him. If they didn't find Ruby, she was likely gone forever. And if they did find her . . .

The garden was half an acre, secluded, hemmed in by a thick beech hedge. A private place. Further in the distance, beyond the hedge, crows squawked at the invaders, lifting off from a line of trees and circling in the sky.

Cook saw it straight away. They both did. The same as the house in Regent's Place. The same as Beaumont's place. The shelter, at the end of the garden.

Cook ran, his boots heavy on the grass, his breathing ragged. Reynolds passed him.

'Wait,' Cook shouted. Something was different about this shelter. A slight thing, but he felt a warning in his subconscious. Something was wrong. The door was open.

Reynolds didn't slow. He reached the door while Cook was twenty yards back. Cook watched as he peered in, then turned back, shaking his head.

Cook reached the shelter, his eyes on the open door. No good was inside, he thought to himself. A premonition perhaps.

The shelter was pitch-black. Cook stood in the doorway, letting his eyes adjust. Reynolds was kneeling. Cook followed him in. The ground was soft, and Cook felt the familiar sensation of standing on freshly dug soil.

'It's not her,' Reynolds said, his hope gone.

'I tried to stop him.' A woman's voice from the darkness. Weak. Elderly.

'Let's get her up. Get her into the light,' Cook said.

They carried her out and laid her on the grass. She was covered in blood. Cook looked frantically for the injury, but he couldn't see it. She was old. Frail.

'He's in there,' she said, her distress evident. She clutched a shard of porcelain. A smashed plate. 'He's a monster,' she said. 'Please. Don't let him hurt me.'

Cook left Reynolds tending to the woman and returned to the shelter. Less hurry now. He stood in the dark and let his eyes adjust.

The place looked like a slaughterhouse. Blood dripped from the ceiling. Blood had been sprayed on the walls like some kind of abstract painting. It was a pattern Cook recognised. A severed artery.

Father Ryan was dead, his skin blanched white from loss of blood, his throat severed from ear to ear, a grinning mess of meat and gristle. A stark contrast with the dog collar below the ruined throat.

It was a relief to step back into the light.

'Where's Ruby?' Reynolds asked, shaking the woman by the shoulders.

'Give her air,' Cook said.

'Damn the air, tell me where Ruby is,' Reynolds shouted.

Cook put his hand on Reynolds's shoulder.

'Christ only knows what this woman's been through,' Cook said. He knelt in the grass.

'Mrs Ryan?'

The woman looked at him. She was terrified. She nodded. Looked at the shelter.

'He's gone,' Cook said.

The woman relaxed. Still scared, but the panic subsided. Cook had seen it before, in men back from a raid across no-man's-land. Gradually accepting that the worst was behind them.

'Was Ruby here?' Cook asked her.

She looked him in the eye. Nodded.

'Where is she?' Reynolds asked. Cook put his arm out to keep Reynolds back.

'What happened?' Cook asked.

The woman's eyes flicked past Cook, past Reynolds. She thought the priest was coming for her. Couldn't quite believe it was over.

'He can't hurt you any more,' Cook said.

Cook stood up, looked around. The garden. The orchard. The distant trees, crows circling in the grey sky. Then he saw it.

'We're too late,' Cook said.

'Where is she?' Reynolds yelled.

'She's here,' Cook said.

Reynolds pushed himself to his feet and turned to see for himself. The two men stood in silence, looking at the patch of ground on the edge of the orchard.

A row of graves. Five covered with grass, just humps in the ground. The sixth looked different. A line of disturbed earth. Six foot long. A recently dug grave.

104

'When?' Reynolds asked.

'Yesterday,' she said. 'Poor mite. He'd been having his way with her, but she wasn't having any of it. I kept telling her to play along, but she was a fighter.'

Cook looked towards the carnage in the Anderson shelter.

'What happened in there?' he asked.

'I put an end to it,' she said. 'Disgusting business. All those girls.'

Cook felt empty. They'd failed. Worse, they'd come close. A day too late. He thought of the time he'd wasted, watching prostitutes, messing around with gangsters. Spending the night with the American woman. All distractions.

'She came here when she was younger,' Cook said.

The woman nodded.

'Just before Frankie was born,' he continued. He wanted to see how the woman reacted. She looked down.

'You knew,' he said.

'He was a terrible one for the girls,' she said. 'But what could I do?'

⋆

Cook picked an apple from one of the trees. A reflex action. He took a bite. It was sour. A cooking apple. A wasp buzzed angrily, emerging from a hole in the apple. Cook threw it into the hedge.

Six graves. Six young women. Buried in plain sight.

'You knew about all this,' Cook said.

'And I'd be in one of those if I'd spoken up,' she said.

Cook knelt by the freshest grave. The soil smelt different here than on his farm. Darker. More clay, less chalk. He picked up a handful and brought it to his nose.

The soil was damp.

Cook looked at the woman. She was watching him closely.

He put his hand on the top of the grave. The disturbed soil was all damp. It had been a dry night and a dry day.

Cook didn't know much about digging graves, but he knew plenty about soil. Half of his life had been devoted to digging and planting. Many of his best days were those spent leading a team of horses, the ploughshare turning over a fresh row of earth. The smell of it. Coming to it the next day, after it had dried, tilling the large lumps of soil, breaking them up, ready for planting.

This soil hadn't dried out. It hadn't been a day. It hadn't been an hour.

He pushed his hand into the loose soil.

Too late, he thought. But still, he pushed his hand in further.

'What are you doing?' Reynolds asked.

Cook shook his head. Didn't want to give false hope.

But then he saw it.

The ground rose. A slight movement. Ever so slight. An optical illusion. Seeing what he wanted to see.

Cook scooped a handful of soil out of the grave, keeping his eye on the woman. She didn't like it. She didn't like it one bit.

Another movement. A slight mound forming, then falling back.

Someone was pushing up, from underneath.

'Help me,' Cook said. Without waiting, he scooped out soil with his hands. More. Whole arms full, like he was trying to swim, pushing the soil behind him.

Reynolds ran to him, dropped to the ground, joined in.

'Shovel,' Reynolds said.

'No,' Cook said. 'Too dangerous.'

Cook and Reynolds pulled earth out of the hole. The more progress they made, the more movement they saw. A knee, trying to push up.

'Ruby!' Reynolds yelled.

Cook pushed his hand down, a new tactic. No need to excavate a perfect hole, he just needed to get his hand on the girl. Pull her out.

His fingertips brushed skin and wool. Suddenly a hand gripped his. He pulled.

105

Cook pulled Ruby's hand. The earth didn't want to give her up, so he pulled harder, and got movement. Then more. Then all of a sudden she was moving, and the earth parted, and he pulled her up, out of the grave, like pulling a drowning man onto a boat.

She retched, soil and mucus and blood. Again and again, gasping for air. She wasn't out of the woods, but she was alive.

'Ruby!'

It was Frankie – out of the car and running across the grass.

Cook saw the boy coming, and he saw the woman, but it was too late. She had a stick in her hands, something she'd picked up from beside the shelter. But it wasn't a stick, and she raised it to her shoulder, aiming at Frankie.

'Frankie!' Reynolds yelled, as he hurled himself between the woman and the boy.

The shotgun boomed, and shredded leaves fell from the apple trees. Reynolds ran to his son, enveloping him in a bear hug.

A second shot rang out, and Reynolds and Frankie went to the ground.

Cook ran to them. Reynolds had Frankie completely covered. Reynolds was still, his back a torn mass of blood and flesh. Frankie pushed his way out, flecks of blood on his face.

There was a click from the gun. The woman trying to fire again. But she was out of options. Two barrels. Two shots.

Cook launched himself at her. She was surprisingly strong, and she fought with everything she had. She ripped at his eyes with her hands, dragging deep gouges across his face. He craned his neck, head-butted her. Her nose exploded, but she didn't stop fighting. She rolled, getting on top. She raised the gun like a club and jabbed it at his throat – a killing blow.

The spade hit her head with a thud, and she fell sideways.

Ruby stood over her, the spade in her hand. The blow to the head had stunned the old woman, but she was opening her eyes.

'Ruby,' Cook said. She looked at him, trying to work something out, held the spade over the woman's neck, her arms trembling.

The crows returned to their roost on the distant line of trees with a succession of angry squawks.

'Don't,' Cook said. Didn't want her to live with it.

Ruby brought the spade down, through the woman's throat. It was a fine tool, kept sharp by its owner. Good enough to get the job done.

*

Ruby knelt by her father, his eyes flickering open.

'We got you back,' he said, his voice a whisper.

She held his hand, hugged Frankie, keeping him safe. Her boy.

106

The funeral procession started at the World's End, at the east end of the high street, and made its way west, towards the church, past the bombed-out shells of warehouses and tenements. *London can take it!* was the message from Churchill and the press, but from what Cook had seen, it was places like the island that were taking it. And there wasn't much of it left.

The American had her notebook out. Cook had told her to come. See what was really happening. Tell the people back home how close to defeat the great city was.

Ruby walked ahead, holding Frankie's hand like she'd never let go.

*

They held the wake at Gracie's pub. One of the few buildings still standing.

'It's not too late,' Cook said, to Beaumont.

'For what?' the ARP man replied.

'To find your courage,' Cook said. 'Make a difference.'

Beaumont didn't seem convinced.

'Do you think there'll be an end to it?' he asked Cook.

'One day there will, and you'll remember how you got through. Good and bad. It'll be a part of you for the rest of your life.'

Frankie interrupted them.

'Ruby's going to come and see the farm,' he said, his eyes full of the excitement of it, despite the sombre occasion.

'Just a visit,' Ruby said. 'Mum's going to need me up here, keep this place on its feet.'

'You should come,' Cook said to the American. 'See what the rest of the country's like.'

107

Eleanor rode the escalator down to the underground platform at Green Park, her weekend bag over her shoulder and her notebook in her inside pocket. The smell as she descended got steadily worse. Her first time on the tube, and probably her last. The things she did for her readers.

She hadn't known what to expect when she'd first arrived in London. So close to the war, and yet at the same time so removed from it. It had been hard to imagine anything she'd see or write could be of use, far less be worth the rather generous sum she was being paid.

Did it bother her, writing articles that were sent, first to New York, then forwarded to the German intelligence services? Why should it? The United States wasn't at war with Germany, any more than it was at war with Britain. If a US citizen wanted to visit either one of those countries and write home with her observations, she was free to do so. Besides, it was only a game. And whoever won, America would be safe, with its oceans protecting it.

Eleanor followed the signs for the Victoria line. One stop, the ticket attendant had said, southbound, to Victoria station, where she'd meet the farmer. She was rather looking forward to seeing him again. He was a brute, of course, but sometimes a brute was exactly what a girl needed.

She'd seen the way he'd looked at Margaret in the lobby. Something going on there, no doubt. But Eleanor could hold her own against any of these English roses. The British didn't understand. Americans had a scrappiness that people from the Old World underestimated. Besides, Margaret was a pawn, working for Eleanor. A precarious existence, only ever one false move away from a knock on the door by the police, and a dark cell, or worse.

The platform was full. One half of it, behind a painted line, given over to a mass of unwashed humanity that seemed to have camped out, avoiding the bombs. Eleanor tried not to breathe through her nose. The stench was indescribable. All details for the story though, the terror in the eyes of the poor. Wanting it over with. Only a matter of time before they rose up and got rid of Churchill.

A warm breeze blew through the station, and Eleanor heard the train approaching. She felt a tingle of anticipation. Her first trip on the tube.

The train roared into the station, and the crowd on the platform surged in anticipation. Eleanor didn't feel the hand on her back until it was too late.

Mr Jones took the escalator back up. No point waiting on the platform. The train wasn't going anywhere. They had a procedure for when someone jumped. Paperwork to be completed. The body to be recovered. A thousand commuters would be late home, but they were used to it. Seemed like every day now there was some kind of delay.

108

Cook waited on the platform at Victoria, the train ready to go. The American was late.

She could follow them down. He'd wait for her at the station. Walk her across the fields. Show her what they were fighting for – the real England.

'All aboard!' the guard shouted. Cook was holding up the train.

The distant crowd parted and he saw her. Running towards him across the concourse. A bag slung over her shoulder, low heels clacking.

It was Margaret.

She saw him, holding the train, and reduced her run to a hurried walk.

The train whistled.

'Shut that door will you, we haven't got all day!' the guard yelled, following up with a blast of his whistle. Cook felt the prickle of impropriety, but he waited until Margaret reached him, stepping out of the way to let her on the train, then following her inside. The train moved instantly, and he slammed the door. Huge, angry clouds of smoke rose up through the forest of ironwork holding the vast roof aloft.

'She asked me to send her apologies,' Margaret said. 'Something came up.'

109

Tea was sausages, boiled potatoes, and baked beans. Frankie's favourite. They ate at the kitchen table, a full house. Mum stood at the stove, Uncle Nob kept to his armchair by the fire, watching silently.

'Will you stay long?' Mum asked Ruby. She'd been desperate to ask, for her own sake as much as for Frankie. Visions of a young woman to brighten the house, help keep Frankie out of trouble. Someone Elizabeth, their other evacuee, could look up to.

'I'll go back tomorrow,' Ruby said, between mouthfuls of food. Mum put another couple of sausages into the pan. The girl wanted feeding.

'Can't let Hitler drive us all away,' Ruby continued. 'Those boys'll be working the docks day and night, working up a thirst. Me and Mum'll be there to give them a pint.'

'Cook said you've got a chap,' Mum said.

Ruby nodded. 'He took the amnesty. Gone back in. Up north for training but he reckons he'll get leave soon.'

The army had a new policy. A blind eye to the thousands of men who'd given themselves unofficial leave after Dunkirk. An act of expediency – they needed the men. Besides, it would have been a bad look to prosecute, and execute if the letter of the law was followed, so many of Britain's returning heroes.

The music programme on the wireless finished, and they heard Big Ben chiming six.

'This is the BBC,' the newsreader announced sombrely. 'In the early hours of this morning, Buckingham Palace was hit by two bombs. The King and Queen are safe, and in good spirits. A palace spokesman observed that nobody is safe from the terror raids sent by Hitler. Today, the King and Queen visited other parts of London hit by German bombs. *We're all in it together* was the message from the cheering crowds.'

Cook looked at Margaret, a question on the tip of his tongue. She smiled.

There was just enough light in the sky for a walk across the fields, the nights drawing in, Frankie keen to show Ruby everything. The rabbit warren at the far end of Dadswell's Flat, the glade in the woods, the cricket pitch he'd marked out behind the barn.

Cook took Margaret's hand.

'How long can you stay?' he asked.

'How long will you have me?'

Cook didn't answer. Easier to walk in silence.

A swarm of bombers appeared on the horizon, over the Downs. Specks in the dark sky.

'Looks like London's in for it again,' she said.

'Margaret,' Cook said. 'I need to ask you a question.'

She kissed him, and he slipped his arms around her. She looked up at him, vulnerable. Someone he could protect. Someone he could keep safe from all that was coming. To live in peace, to work the land, until the day came that peace was no longer an option.

'It's complicated,' she said, kissing him as the bombers rumbled overhead, and a distant siren wailed into life.

She looked him in the eye, her hand on his as it cupped her face.

'But then, the things worth fighting for usually are.'

110

All of Hendon was tucked up for the evening, blackout curtains drawn, milk bottles out, cats brought in. The first chilly evening, a reassuring feeling – the last remnant of the Indian summer now just a memory, and winter not far ahead. In Swynford Grove, only Mr Forshaw was still out, the rattle of his push mower a rhythmic sound, his rightly admired lawn getting one last cut before the first frost. He liked to mow in the evening. Said it got a better cut. He'd leave the clippings on the grass as a mulch.

The two fruit trees at number forty-four had been picked. Those apples that hadn't gone immediately into a pie or crumble had been individually wrapped in sheets of newspaper, and laid carefully in wooden trays, no apple touching another. Some would emerge from their wrappings with a spot of mould, but most would last throughout the winter.

Mrs Pearson stirred custard powder into a half-and-half mixture of water and milk. It wasn't the same as real, but everyone was doing their bit, and powdered was a lot better than nothing. Her daughter Charlotte sat at the table, waiting. Father would be home late again, the Ministry keeping him longer and longer as things got worse. Mrs Pearson reflected on how quickly things had, indeed, got worse.

'It's time I did my bit,' Charlotte said, pouring tea for them both from the heavy earthenware pot in its knitted cosy. 'I'm thinking of signing up as a Land Girl.'

Mrs Pearson snorted. Her daughter on her way to a double first from Cambridge – mucking out pigs? Really, the things the young people came out with nowadays.

'I suppose you could give it a try,' she said, thinking of early mornings, heavy work, filth everywhere. She'd give it a week then she'd be back.

'Sussex sounds nice,' Charlotte said.

Which explained the farming.

'Isn't that where *she*'s from?'

Charlotte did the honours, pouring milk into the tea.

'I think so,' she said, trying and failing to be off-hand about it.

'Quite a charisma, I thought,' Mrs Pearson said. 'I hope you're not going to get tangled up in anything.' She didn't look at her daughter but she could practically feel her blushing. Charlotte had always been susceptible to a strong character. Perhaps it was growing up as an only child, missing out on an older brother or sister.

The custard was ready. Mrs Pearson poured it over two bowls of crumble and brought them to the table. Her daughter blew on hers, in a hurry to eat it before a skin set. Always in a hurry.

'I suppose they'll want you to kill her at some point,' Mrs Pearson said, taking a delicate bite. The apple was sour. Not enough sugar to balance it. She wondered how much longer they'd have to put up with it all, before Hitler arrived and set everything back to normal. It couldn't go on for much longer. The rationing. The blackouts. Girls being sent out to work. Made you wonder what you were fighting for if this was all they had to look forward to.

'I suppose so,' Charlotte said. 'But in the meantime, I think we're going to be the best of friends.'

Author's Note

This is a work of fiction, and of course my primary responsibility as a fiction author is to create a story that keeps the reader turning the pages. The joy of writing historical fiction is that it provides such a rich setting, but there is a tension between my desire to 'get the facts right' – indeed to be respectful to all the people who lived through the War – and on the other hand the need to tell the story. While I hope I got many of the details, and the feel of the period, right, there are no doubt many things I got wrong, either because I made a mistake, or didn't know, or sometimes deliberately because I needed to prioritise the story.

Nevertheless, there is a lot in this story that did come from history. If you enjoyed reading the book, you may enjoy delving deeper.

The opening scene on the darkest day of the Battle of Britain comes almost directly from Volume II of Winston Churchill's *The Second World War*, published in 1949. Churchill's writing is some of the most dramatic and the most readable in all of the history books I read on the subject, albeit no doubt skewed towards presenting him in the best light. The actual location is still intact as a fantastic museum – the Battle of Britain Bunker Museum in Hillingdon, not far from Heathrow airport. If you visit, make sure to book in advance for a guided tour of the bunker, which is set out exactly for the scene that opens this book. Huge thanks to the incredibly knowledgeable guide who put up with all my questions!

The Blitz is a very well-researched and well-documented part of British history. In particular, I enjoyed *The First Day of the Blitz*, by Peter Stansky, *The Battle of London 1939–45* by Jerry White, and *The Blitz* by Constantine FitzGibbon. For a child's perspective, I found *Growing Up in the Second World War* by Nance Lui Fyson invaluable. As mentioned in this book, the Blitz was well reported by American journalists. In particular, I highly recommend *Bomber's Moon: London in the Blitzkrieg*, by Negley Farson.

This is the first time in the John Cook books we significantly leave behind the setting of Sussex, and Cook's farm, largely because I wanted to explore the effects of the Blitz on London. While all of London was targeted, it's clear that the docks 'got it worse'. I chose to focus on Wapping, referred to by its residents as 'the island'. There are a number of excellent histories of Wapping from first-hand accounts, of which I'd recommend *Between High Walls*, *Four Meals for Fourpence*, and *My Part of the River*, all by Grace Foakes. It's fascinating to visit 'the island' today, although almost all of the docks are entirely gone now. The high street is still there, with a number of excellent pubs, but most of the basins that ships would have come into have been filled in. Shadwell Basin remains, along with the metal drawbridge. If you spend a few hours exploring Wapping you will find many places that inspired my writing, but none of them are exactly as described in the book, so don't expect to find the exact pub, or the exact church.

The experience of being an ARP warden, of hearing bombs come down with a swoosh, witnessing the damage that they did, is taken largely from a first-hand account published in 1941 – *Post D* – *Some Experiences of an Air Raid Warden*, by John Strachey. Although I featured in this story an ARP warden who did not find his courage when the time came, I hope this doesn't offend readers who may have cherished family memories of ARP service. The story of how London got through the Blitz is very much a story of volunteers – ARP, Volunteer Fire Department, and many many others who gave their time, and in many cases their lives, to help their fellow citizens get through the worst.

London's great hotels played a key role in the war, and as described in the book were places that attracted many of the incoming refugees (particularly the wealthy ones), as well as many elements of the underworld. *The West End Front*, by Matthew Sweet, is a great read absolutely chock-full of shenanigans and memorable characters.

The idea of public shelters being built to a shoddy standard is one that I was keen to work into the book. Having gone through the pandemic, where we saw so much government money being given out so quickly, it's easy to imagine similar things happening in 1939 and 1940. There was indeed an issue with many public shelters being built without enough cement in the mortar mix. Eventually the government put out a memo claiming that the original instructions had been 'misleading', admitting that the mortar mix should include cement. I don't think you need to be a crime-writer to imagine that there is more to this story than meets the eye.

The Tilbury Shelter was, indeed, a vast, unofficial shelter that thousands of people flocked to, despite it being very unsuited for the purpose. People took comfort in being together, in a place that 'somebody' had presumably decided was safe. In fact, it took local and central government quite a while to catch up with where people wanted to shelter. Eventually the local government stepped in and provided sanitary arrangements, but we can only imagine what such a place was like beforehand. There are vivid descriptions provided in *Living Through the Blitz*, by Tom Harrisson – a collection of first-hand accounts from the Mass Observation organisation.

Perhaps my favourite book that my research introduced me to is a collection of letters from a young woman in London to her boyfriend in the army. They are stunningly well written, full of detail about life throughout the war, alongside all of the poignancy of a growing romance. I highly recommend *Love in the Blitz* by Eileen Alexander. Unlike many of the books I refer to, this one is still in print, and well worth a read.

Margaret's sojourn in France was inspired by a visit to Chenonceau – a beautiful château in the Loire Valley that is well worth a visit. As described in the book, it spans the river that separated occupied France and Vichy France, so as you walk the long gallery you can certainly imagine that it might have been used as a conduit between the two territories.

The idea that Churchill deliberately provoked Hitler into bombing London (thus sacrificing the city in return for delaying the invasion and ultimately saving the country) is not one that I had seen before I began my research for this book, but it is put forward quite persuasively by Peter Fleming (brother of James Bond creator Ian Fleming) in his excellent book *Invasion 1940*, published in 1957.

As usual, for all things related to the farming calendar, my guide is A.G. Street, a farmer and writer from the time. *Country Calendar*, published in 1940, is a lovely book that walks the reader month by month through the year.

I hope you enjoyed the story, and spending time with John Cook and Lady Margaret. If you did, please consider leaving an online review or recommending the book to your friends. And look out for book four – John Cook and Lady Margaret will return!

Acknowledgements

I would like to thank everyone who has helped make this book, and the John Cook series, such a success.

Cara Chimirri is my fabulous editor. All of her ideas make the books better, and she is a joy to work with. In addition, I'd like to thank all of the team at Hodder & Stoughton – it is a pleasure working with you. Thanks in particular to The Brewster Project, for my beautiful covers.

Thanks to my agent, Hattie Grunewald, and the team at The Blair Partnership.

Thanks always to Jordan and Morgan, for being the first to believe in John Cook.

Thanks to the many writers I've encountered along the way who have given encouragement. One of the greatest joys of becoming an author is finding that the community of fellow authors is so welcoming. In particular, thanks to Patrick, Naomi, and Diane.

The biggest thanks, though, go to you, the reader. Whether you have quietly read and enjoyed, or told a friend about John Cook and Lady Margaret, or written a review, or blogged, Instagrammed, or shared on TikTok – you are very much appreciated.

Until next time . . .

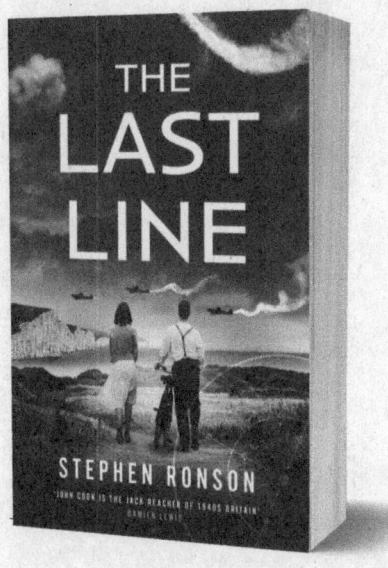

RAISING READERS
Books Build Bright Futures

Dear Reader,

We'd love your attention for one more page to tell you about the crisis in children's reading, and what we can all do.

Studies have shown that reading for fun is the **single biggest predictor of a child's future life chances** – more than family circumstance, parents' educational background or income. It improves academic results, mental health, wealth, communication skills, ambition and happiness.[1]

The number of children reading for fun is in rapid decline. Young people have a lot of competition for their time. In 2024, 1 in 10 children and young people in the UK aged 5 to 18 did not own a single book at home.[2]

Hachette works extensively with schools, libraries and literacy charities, but here are some ways we can all raise more readers:

- Reading to children for just 10 minutes a day makes a difference
- Don't give up if children aren't regular readers – there will be books for them!
- Visit bookshops and libraries to get recommendations
- Encourage them to listen to audiobooks
- Support school libraries
- Give books as gifts

There's a lot more information about how to encourage children to read on our website: **www.RaisingReaders.co.uk**

Thank you for reading.

[1] OECD, '21st-Century Readers: Developing Literacy Skills in a Digital World', 2021, https://www.oecd.org/en/publications/21st-century-readers_a83d84cb-en.html

[2] National Literacy Trust, 'Book Ownership in 2024', November 2024, https://literacytrust.org.uk/research-services/research-reports/book-ownership-in-2024